CAKEWALK

Cakewalk

CLAIRE HASTINGS

HeartEyes
Press

This book was inspired by the True North Series written by Sarina Bowen. It is an original work that is published by Heart Eyes Press LLC.

In loving memory of Nate…

AUTHOR'S NOTE

Content notice: This story explores themes of domestic violence.

1

GIGI

"Where in the H-E-Double-Hockey-Sticks am I?" Gigi Hawthorne muttered out loud, as if there were someone else in the car. All this time alone was starting to get to her.

Three days.

That's how long she'd been driving. That was how long it had been since she'd left her husband at the altar back in Atlanta. At least, she assumed he had made it to the altar. If there was one thing Bradley was a stickler for it was tradition. There was no way he would have tried to seek her out before the ceremony, even if it was a vow renewal rather than their actual wedding. Not that these vows would have been any less of a sham than their first set.

Gigi sighed heavily, trying to come to terms with the fact that she had no idea where she was or how she got so lost. Actually, that wasn't true—she knew how she got lost. She'd taken a wrong turn somewhere around Philadelphia and then another just outside of New York City. Potentially one or two in Massachusetts. Which is what led her into Vermont. At least she was pretty sure that's how she got here.

Jesus, now would be a really *good time to take the wheel…*

Figuring out where she was going had never been much of a problem, but then again, that fancy navigation system built into her BMW had been much easier to use than an app on her phone. Her BMW was also a lot more comfortable than the fifteen-year-old Jeep she'd bought from some random independent car lot on the outskirts of Atlanta. Gigi had said a silent prayer when she purchased it that it wasn't stolen. The car salesman had been all too eager to accept her paying him in actual cash for her to not worry about such a thing. But she'd needed a car that couldn't be traced back to her—and preferably one that would blend in with the surroundings—for her fresh start in the great white north.

The two-lane highway she was on was starting to seem like it would wind and stretch on forever though. Did Vermont not believe in road signs? How was a girl supposed to know where she was? The navigation app had alerted her that there was a big accident on the interstate and that the best route was to get off the highway and follow this road. Although now the GPS seemed to have cut out completely.

"You can do this. You can do this," she repeated, again out loud, giving herself a little pep talk. *You've got this. You're a new woman. A strong, independent woman.*

"You've never done anything on your own, ever, Georgia. What makes you think you can start now?" Her husband's voice rang out in her mind, in his usual condescending tone.

Late husband. Bradley is your late *husband,* she reminded herself, rehearsing those words again. His opinion didn't matter anymore. Bradley was the past.

Glancing back at the phone to check the GPS, Gigi was more than a little frustrated to find nothing but a large gray rectangle. The little blue dot was drifting all over the screen, almost like it was possessed. She sighed again, trying not to let the frustration get to her. The last thing she needed was to get all worked up on top of being lost. A quick look around her revealed nothing but more wooded area, same as it had been since she'd gotten off the interstate, other than a break for a few homes or farms. At least she thought it was farms that she passed. What do farms look like in New England? Do they look the same as they do in Georgia? Gigi gripped the steering wheel harder, trying to channel her frustration. There had to be a road sign somewhere, right? She figured it'd be asking way too much for some kind of sign pointing her back to the highway, but maybe, just maybe, there would be a gas station up ahead where she could get directions.

Suddenly, the steering wheel jerked underneath her hands, and the Jeep's back end started to fishtail. *Oh shiitake, do I turn in or out of the skid? Why don't I remember this?* Slamming on the brakes, jerking the wheel to the right, Gigi prayed she was doing the right thing. The front end seemed to have a mind of its own now, as it stopped on a dime, but her back end was still in motion, sending her into a spin. Gigi could only see the blur of trees and overcast skies surrounding her as if she were in some kind of vortex. She could feel her heart pounding so hard that it felt like it could burst through her chest as she slammed her eyes shut and let out a little shriek.

A moment later—one that had simultaneously felt like forever and an instant all at once—the Jeep stopped moving. Gigi placed her hand over her heart, feeling its rapid movement under her breastplate as she tried to catch her breath. A quick glance over at the passenger seat revealed that the contents of her purse were now in a pile on the floor, but that seemed to be the only harm done. At least inside the vehicle. Once her heart had calmed a bit, she glanced outside to see if there was any oncoming traffic before opening the door and hopping out. Sliding her eyes along the vehicle, she quickly found the culprit.

Her rear tire was flat.

"Okay, Gigi, time to learn how to change a tire!" she said, looking up and down the road again. She hadn't seen another car for miles, but a girl could hope in a moment like this. *Just one question...where was the spare tire?*

Grabbing her phone from the car, Gigi closed the navigation app. Stupid thing wasn't doing anything but eating battery at this point anyway. Typing into Google, "where is a spare tire on a Jeep?", her heart sank when the screen immediately flipped to a message telling her that there wasn't service and it would save her search for when there was.

Oh for heaven's sake! What good is that going to do? What would Scarlett O'Hara do? she thought, taking in a long, deep breath. *She wouldn't have been stupid enough to get herself into this kind of mess…*

Feeling the sting of tears start to prick at the corner of her eyes, Gigi surveyed the scene some more. She couldn't let herself cry. She hadn't cried once since leaving Bradley, and she wasn't going to let something as stupid as a flat tire be what got to her. She was a strong, independent woman. Not that that reminder meant a whole lot right now as she stood on the side of the road, stranded in the middle of nowhere Vermont. If anything, all it was doing was increasing the volume of the little voice in the back of her mind telling her that she was as useless as Bradley used to say.

"Georgia," his deep southern accent would drawl. *"You're a pretty face and a great hostess. You can organize a luncheon like none other. But when it comes to practical things, maybe it's best you left that to others more capable."*

"I am perfectly capable of figuring things out!" she'd retorted more times than she could count. But it didn't matter—he wasn't listening. He'd made up his mind long ago that she wasn't good at any number of things, and his mind was not about to be changed. So what if she wasn't a natural at cooking or cleaning or any of those things normal people did. She'd gone from her parents' house—that had a staff taking care of all of that—to her husband's house. The fact that he was more than happy to hire a staff rather than give her a chance to prove herself was not something she could really control. He'd kept such a tight grip on everything that even if she had tried, all she would have been met with was his fist.

Bradley was dead though. At least dead to her. Without him, she was finally going to figure out who GeorgiaGrace Elyse Hawthorne, née Shaw, really was. Maybe not the fun college coed version she had been when they'd first got together, but a more mature, grown-up version. She was going to be the sweet, southern widow getting back on her feet after the sudden loss of her husband. While part of her was going to miss being a "lady who lunched," a bigger part was looking forward to this new adventure. She knew it wasn't going to be easy, but that didn't matter. She had something to prove, even if it was just to herself.

The sound of gravel crunching and the hue of flashing blue lights brought Gigi's thoughts back to the present and the still very flat tire in front of her. Swiping away the tears that seemed to have escaped, she turned to see a police cruiser pulling up behind her Jeep. A tall, well-built officer stepped out from the car and made his way over, surveying the flat tire.

"Ma'am," he said, a slightly southern accent poking through. His accent had been diluted, probably from years living up here, but it was there. A little wave of relief rushed through her at the sound.

"Officer," she returned.

"Looks like you got yourself a flat tire, Miss..." he replied, drawing out the end of his sentence, looking for an answer on how to finish it.

"Hawthorne. Gigi Hawthorne," she said, letting her own drawl shine through.

"Pleased to meet you, Miss Hawthorne. I'm Officer Nelligan. Would you like some help?"

"I...um...well. This isn't my usual vehicle, and I'm just a tad unsure where the spare is exactly," she admitted, hoping he wouldn't ask any more questions.

Officer Nelligan let out a little chuckle, seeming to understand. "On these vehicles they are usually part of the undercarriage," he answered, flicking his finger in an upward motion to indicate where he meant.

"Oh." *How in the world was I supposed to find that?*

Squatting down, he leaned over and peered underneath the

Jeep. He placed a hand on the ground to balance himself, before shaking his head and popping back up to his full height.

"Well, Miss Hawthorne, it seems you are missing a spare tire."

"Missing?"

"It's not uncommon. They climb under the car and cut the cable, and make off with your spare."

"Oh for heaven's sake." She'd known the salesman was shady, but no part of her had thought to ask to make sure a spare tire was included.

"Not to worry. We're only a couple of miles from town. We'll get you towed to the gas station and have the guys there take a look and see if they can't patch your tire. You can hang out in the Busy Bean while you wait."

"Thank you so much."

"Sure thing, Miss Hawthorne. Now, you wait in your car so you don't catch a chill, and I'll radio in for the tow."

Gigi simply nodded in response, for the first time noticing the slight chill to the air. It had still been in the mid-seventies in Georgia, which was their usual fall weather. She'd known it would be colder the farther north she got, but she hadn't been expecting quite the drop in temperature she seemed to be experiencing. Climbing into the car, she pulled out a cardigan that she'd packed in the overnight bag that was in the backseat, hoping it would be enough.

Half an hour later, Gigi found herself sitting in the Busy Bean café, sipping on a cup of coffee. The café was a decent-sized, lodge looking building with large windows that looked out over the river and purposefully mismatched furniture, upholstered in dark, rich colors and funky animal prints, that oddly complemented each other. A plush peach-colored couch sat off to one side, and Gigi thought about how that seemed like a nice spot to curl up and read. The floor was beautiful wide-plank hard wood, the walls were a warm brick color, and the ceiling beams looked like chalk boards. There were fun, snarky sayings written on them, and Gigi couldn't help but laugh as she read the one right above her—"If I'm silent, I might be furious or maybe I'm just chillin'. May the odds be ever in your favor." It was the kind of place she would have loved in college, but she and her friends would probably never find their way into now.

She was finally back in cell phone range, but since Officer Nelligan had helped get her car towed to the gas station, it didn't really matter much. The new prepaid phone looked almost identical to her old one, just a cheaper version. The kid at the store had helped her transfer all her contacts and pictures over, but there wasn't really anyone to call. Nor could she hop onto social media. That was the part about running away that she knew would be the hardest. Not having any contact with her old life. But if it meant not spending another moment living in fear of her husband, then it was just the burden she'd have to bear.

Gigi picked at the pretzel she'd ordered. It was the first thing she'd eaten since breakfast that day, and she should probably be hungrier than she was, but the events of this afternoon had drained her. There would be more food options when she found her way back to the interstate, and she told herself she would grab a real meal then. She had no idea how long her car would take, and the clock on her phone was telling her it was already four in the afternoon. Doing the math in her head, she figured if her tire was fixed in the next couple of hours, then she could still make Montreal tonight. A quick search had told her she was a good bit off course from the interstate, but that once she was back on the highway, it should only be a few more hours until she was there. It would be late by the time she arrived, but at least the journey would be over.

"You know what I'm dying to add to the menu?" Gigi overheard a woman from the next table over. "More sweets. Now that Crumbs is closed, there isn't really anywhere selling cakes, and the diner wants no part of it."

"Are you going to do those in all that spare time you have?" another woman asked with a laugh. "Just add 'Cake Boss' on top of running this place, cider, the farm, oh…and being wife and mom."

"As much as I would like to, it's not feasible for me to do it, and Roderick has made it clear—he doesn't decorate cakes. Not that I would want to put one more thing on his plate, so we'd have to find someone. Besides, they'd have to be pretty, and I don't have the special touch it takes to *really* decorate a cake."

"Oh, it's not that hard," Gigi said, turning toward the two women. She had no idea where her sudden brazenness came from or why she was inviting herself into their conversation.

Both women looked at her, a little taken aback. Gigi couldn't tell if she'd overstepped by interrupting or if it was what she had said.

"Sorry, I didn't mean to interrupt. It just…well, I took a class," Gigi said, feeling the need to explain herself. "And this master baker taught us all about how to do all the fancy stuff with the fondant and icing. It was easier than I thought! And if I can do it, anyone can!"

"I didn't even realize such a class existed outside culinary school," the shorter of the two women said. She was blonde and pretty, with a smile that seemed to light up the whole café. The other woman was tall and slender, with long dark hair that gave her a bit of an edgy look.

"I won it at a charity auction," she answered. "I think it was a special, one-time thing that this chef did. But it was so much fun! Here, I can show you pictures." Reaching for her phone, Gigi pulled up some of the photos on her phone and leaned over to show the women. The first photos she pulled up were of a small round cake with white icing. Around the bottom of the cake were bright, multi-colored sprinkles embedded into the icing to look like confetti, while the top played host to light pink colored roses made from buttercream.

"This is so pretty! You did this?" the tall brunette asked.

"I did," Gigi answered proudly. "Here, this one's better!"

Scrolling a bit in her phone, she found the one she was most proud of.

Handing the phone back to them, she watched as their eyes widened taking in the cake. This one was a little bigger than the last, but still round, and covered in chocolate buttercream. The outside edge of the cake was lined with KitKats, while on top of the cake three little pink fondant pigs were strategically placed to look as if they were bathing in the "mud" of the chocolate buttercream. One pig was sitting in an inner tube, complete with book in hand, while another sat holding a parasol. All that was seen of the third was his rear end poking up out of the frosting.

"That's adorable!" the brunette said. "Hi, I'm Zara Rossi, and this is Audrey Shipley. We own the Busy Bean."

"Nice to meet you. I'm GeorgiaGrace, but you can just call me Gigi."

"Need a job?" Audrey asked, looking back at the pig cake.

"Oh," Gigi said, startled by the question. She hadn't meant to volunteer anything. "I'm just passing through. I'm on my way to Montreal."

"From that accent it sounds like you're a long way from home. Vacation?"

"No, I was recently widowed," she said, reciting her practiced response. "There wasn't much left for me with my husband gone, so I decided to start over somewhere new."

"What's in Montreal?" The blonde's smile was bright and cheerful, and she seemed genuinely curious. Gigi didn't know why, but she liked these women, even though they'd barely had a conversation.

"Nothing specific. I've just always wanted to go."

"Then why not stay here? We need a cake person, and obviously you were just dropped in our laps for a reason."

Gigi was taken aback by the suggestion. Stay here? In Vermont?

"I don't have anywhere to stay," she told them, not sure if it was an excuse or a plea.

"We'll help you get settled!" Audrey said. "Just say yes—I want these pretty cakes for the Busy Bean."

Gigi's head was spinning. Could she really just stay right here? She didn't even know the name of the town, and it seemed awfully small. But maybe that was just what she needed. A small town in the middle of nowhere Vermont where she could be anything she wanted. The people here knew nothing about her or her history, so they wouldn't question her story about being a widow. These women were offering her a job and to help her find a place to live, so she was already off to a better start than she would be in Montreal.

"Okay, deal."

"Wonderful! You can bake and decorate out of our kitchen here to start since you don't have a place of your own yet. If you want, you can start tomorrow. Kirk is our morning barista and Roderick runs the kitchen, so we can have them train you on how the whole place works. We should have most of the basics you need to bake, but if there is anything special you need, just let us know and we'll get it ordered for you!"

"Great! Thank you so much!"

Gigi couldn't believe that had just happened. Was it really that easy? The more she thought about it, the happier she was. She had a plan. There was just one problem.

She didn't actually know how to bake…

2

HOLDEN

Holden St. James tapped the screen of his phone currently strapped to his arm, skipping the song that had just started playing as he pushed into mile three of his daily run. He wasn't in the mood for classical today. He needed something that was going to inspire him. *Today I'm actually going to write,* he told himself.

Of course, he'd said that every day for the last six years, and yet his manuscript still sat there, barely touched. He had some basic notes and ideas, even a half-decent start on chapter one. But nothing that one could actually call a book. He'd spent hours just staring at the blank page and that stupid blinking cursor, trying to find the words to write, but they never came. They were gone. Gone and had never come back.

Just like Hannah.

He shook his head and sucked in a deep breath of crisp, cool morning air, trying to center his thoughts again. It was the perfect fall morning—bright and clear, crisp but not bone-chilling cold yet, and the leaves were still their fantastical fall colors. He knew this wouldn't last for long—soon enough all those glorious leaves would fall, they'd see less and less of the sun, and the cold would settle in for the long haul. These were the kinds of mornings that were perfect for running. That led to the kind of run that almost made him miss playing professional soccer.

It'd been six years since he stepped away from the pitch...and the world. Six years since the most important thing in the world had been ripped away from him. Since he'd walked into his London apartment after celebrating winning the championship with his team to find the front door wide open, house ransacked, and his wife and unborn child murdered. He'd loved the game, but he'd loved his wife more, and losing her and their daughter, especially like that, was more than he could handle. Walking away from it all after her death was the easy part—it was the picking up the pieces that he was still struggling with. He knew that he couldn't keep letting himself think of Hannah and the baby girl they planned to name Hermione after Hannah's favorite Harry Potter character, yet he just couldn't stop. His brain's default setting was always right there with his girls, reminding him that he hadn't been there when they'd needed him. That they were dead because of that.

It's not that he hadn't tried. He'd gone to therapy. Twice. Both of the therapists he'd seen had told him that he needed to find his passion again, to find something to pour himself into. Which is why he'd finally tried to start that novel he'd always talked about writing. Professional sports had never been his plan, but when he was recruited out of college, it was an opportunity he couldn't say no to. But as the son of a literature professor and a special education teacher who'd majored in creative writing, sports were always just going to be a means to an end. Maybe even inspire a few characters or stories. A year later when Chelsea FC came calling, he knew his novel would just have to wait a few more years, so he and Hannah packed up and moved to London.

"It'll be an adventure!" Hannah had said when his agent called with the offer. "Think about it. The home of Dickens and Jack the Ripper! Paddington Bear!"

"You did not just lump Jack the Ripper and Paddington Bear in the same category," Holden laughed.

"You know what I mean!" she responded with a playful smack. "We can do weekends in Paris when you're not playing, and explore all sorts of new things. Maybe you'll even find the object that you'll base your best-selling book series off of. Who knows what could happen!"

If he'd only known what would happen, he would have stuck to his original plan and just become a teacher.

Come on, slow poke, pick up the pace. Coffee awaits us, he thought as he pushed himself up a slight hill.

Up until moving to Vermont, he'd never been a morning runner. He'd always preferred the evenings, watching the sunset and the day wind down. However, five years ago, after more than a year of him almost never leaving the house, his housekeeper, Mrs. Welch, told him that he wasn't allowed to be home anymore while she cleaned his house. Well, not his house, exactly. It technically belonged to his godfather, but Holden had been living there since he'd walked away from his professional soccer career in London six years ago, and his godfather had moved to Florida to be closer to Holden's parents. Mrs. Welch had been taking care of the 1850s Victorian home for as long as Holden could remember, and so when she informed him he was to get out, he did as he was told.

Rounding the corner into town, he passed Speakeasy, the new taproom that was exactly the kind of place that Holden and his buddies would have hit up. Now, however, there wasn't anyone in his life to do that with. Not that his old teammates from Chelsea or even the US Men's National Team wouldn't come visit if he asked, but he didn't plan on asking. He enjoyed his life of solitude. The quiet and privacy of the big old house allowed him to wallow in his own self-pity. And it wasn't like he was a recluse —he did get out. He ran the five miles into town every day to get his coffee at the Busy Bean and catch up on the news. So what if he didn't actually talk to anyone? You didn't need to actually speak to people in order for it to be socializing. Slowing down, he ducked off the side of the road and into the parking lot of the taproom. He slowed to a walk by the time he'd hit the wooded area in between the two buildings, allowing him to take it all in.

A lady carrying a to-go carrier of coffee about knocked Holden over as he opened the door to the Busy Bean. She was in so much of a rush she barely paused long enough to throw him a dirty look, as if her not watching was his fault. He responded with a forced smile, knowing that if he stopped to engage, all it would do is delay him getting his own coffee. She was lucky she hadn't spilled on him though. Then he probably wouldn't have been quite as understanding.

"Oh, for heaven's sake!" he heard a sweet, southern-sounding voice say. It was light and melodic and, for some strange reason, kind of reminded him of home. Looking around, he couldn't quite tell where the voice had come from until his eyes caught sight of the strawberry-blonde beauty behind the counter.

She was pretty, but in an understated way, yet Holden's eyes were immediately drawn to her. There was something about those lush curves on her petite frame that he just could not ignore. She couldn't have stood more than five feet two, but every inch of her seemed to call to him. He felt his pulse pick up slightly as he watched her move behind the counter, her hips swaying as she tried to maneuver around the small space. He hadn't felt like this about a woman since he'd first seen Hannah across the quad their sophomore year in college, and it was throwing him off more than just a little. Who was she, and where did she come from?

Obviously new and trying very hard to figure out how it all worked behind the counter, she seemed a bit overwhelmed by everything. Kirk—current Busy Bean barista and the kid who until recently had been renting the apartment above his garage—was trying to show her how the steam wand worked, even though it was very evident by the mess on the counter and how wet their aprons were that she was not taking to the machine. Kirk towered over her, but at six feet two, he tended to do that to a lot of people, Holden included. But their height differential was seeming to make her even more nervous, and Holden felt his heart give a little tug.

What was that, dude? he asked himself. He didn't understand what it was about her, but there *was* something.

Maybe he was just worried that yet another new person behind the counter would mean his standing order would end up getting messed up. He'd seen staff come and go from this place, some better than others, but Kirk had actually taken to the job rather well. The kid had lived over his garage for almost two years, working odd jobs around the area. When Mrs. Welch had asked Holden as a favor if her nephew could move into the studio apartment, he'd reluctantly agreed. However, a month ago Kirk moved in with a friend to save money before they moved to a "a permaculture, eco-village" in Costa Rica sometime after the first of the year. Kirk was a nice enough kid, although his dry personality sometimes reminded Holden of a robot and made for rather awkward interactions. Holden couldn't say he'd been sad to see the kid go. He liked being alone, and even though they weren't sharing a roof, even having him on the same property was sometimes just a little too close.

"Morning, Kirk," Holden said, walking up to the pair.

"Holden," Kirk responded, his dry tone and expressionless face greeting Holden. "Usual?"

"Yup. Regular coffee, two sugars, and a muffin."

"Right. What kind of muffin?"

"Surprise me."

Kirk heaved a sigh before turning to the blonde. "Think you can pick out a muffin?"

She smiled sweetly in return, even though her gray eyes seemed sad, and Holden could see the southern manners shining through, though she hadn't even said anything. His mother was the same way, just not southern, and he could feel the corner of his mouth lift into a smile just thinking about it. Who was she?

"I can pick out a muffin just fine, thanks," she drawled.

Heading over to the display case, she grabbed one and put it on a plate, which she slid over toward Holden. "And you said a regular coffee?"

"Yes, ma'am," Holden nodded.

She grabbed a cup from the stack on the counter and turned around to fill it from the large, industrial carafe behind her. He could see her body tense as Kirk stood over her and watched her pour the hot liquid. It was a little overbearing of him, but if she was as awkward with everything else as she had been with the steam wand just now, then maybe he could see where the kid was coming from. Holden continued to take in her curves as she faced away from him. When they turned back around with his drink, he had to tell himself to stop staring.

"Oh, Gigi, this is Holden, the guy I was telling you about," Kirk said as she put a lid on the cup and slid it toward him.

"Me?" Holden questioned.

"Gigi is new in town and needs a place to live. She's a widow. I was telling her that I just moved out of your garage apartment."

A widow? His ears perked up at the word.

"You're kinda young to be a widow, aren't you?" he asked. *Way to be an asshole, dude. She's not that much younger than you and you're a widower.*

"Heart attacks don't discriminate," she answered, sounding a tad skittish. *Of course she did—you just called her out about her husband dying, moron.*

"And because of that you need an apartment?" Holden asked, making sure he was tracking this. He wasn't sure how he fit into this picture exactly.

"Yeah," she said, blushing. A small, hopeful look filled her eyes as she continued. "It's a bit of a strange situation. I was passing through yesterday after getting lost and having a flat tire, but then I met Zara and Audrey and they said they were looking for help with cakes and one thing led to another and here I am."

"Yesterday? Where are you staying now?"

"Yeah, like I said, it all happened kinda fast. I spent last night at the motor lodge. Although, I'm not entirely sure that the little old lady running the place isn't there now going through my things. She seemed really suspicious of me. But, I just lost my husband and I'm starting over so I don't have a lot, and I need a place I can pay cash until some insurance stuff gets sorted out. Kirk here mentioned that he's been paying you in cash, so maybe you might consider letting me do the same?"

Fuck. Thanks, Kirk, Holden thought. Sure, the space was empty, but Holden didn't have any intention of filling it. Kirk had been an exception. He didn't need the money. He had plenty from being a professional athlete, and it's not like he was paying a mortgage. He liked being alone, and he didn't want the company. He wanted solitude, not another renter. Why did this have to be the one time Kirk tried to be helpful?

"I hadn't really planned on renting that space again," he said, trying to be careful how he worded things. He didn't want to come off as "that guy," but he wasn't looking to be anyone's landlord again either.

"Oh, okay," she said, that polite smile still plastered on her face. Holden could see that hopeful look in her eyes disappear.

Holden felt his insides squeeze. He had no idea why he was about to say this, but against his better judgment, he told her, "It's not much. Really, just a bedroom with a little kitchenette. But if you really have no other place to go, I guess you could rent it for a few months until you figure something else out. At least it gets you out of the motor lodge."

"Really?" she shrieked, causing Kirk to grimace and step away from her.

"Sure. Kirk can give you the address, and you can move in whenever," he said. He really had no idea why he was agreeing to this, but here he was.

"Thank you!" she said.

"Sure," he replied, taking his order and finding a seat at the counter by the window, trying to avoid whatever-her-name-was that always sat on the peach-colored couch. Her conversations sometimes got a little loud, and this morning he just needed to eat his muffin and finish his coffee so he could get out of here. Forget catching up on the news, he could do that at home. And forget trying to be creative and writing today. He was too worked up by what just happened. Why the fuck did he say yes?

The run home did little to soothe his agitation. More than anything, he couldn't stop thinking about that sad look in Gigi's gray eyes. He knew that pain. He felt that pain. For a moment, he had wanted to hop over the counter and pull her into his arms and tell her it would be alright, even though he wasn't sure it would. It still wasn't alright for him, so who the hell was he to say anything?

When Gigi showed up later that afternoon, she looked like she had just stepped out of the mall in her skinny jeans, designer sweater, and matching shoes. She had been cute this morning at the coffee shop, but now as he watched her try and pull an oversized suitcase out of the back of a Jeep, she looked downright beautiful. With her gorgeous figure no longer hidden behind the apron from the café, Holden couldn't help but notice that this woman was curvy in all the right places. Her sweater was fitted just enough to leave him wondering if her breasts were as perfect as they seemed hidden under that soft fabric, and those jeans stretched across a pair of hips that led to an ass he couldn't help but want to take a bite of. After a moment of watching her, he ran over to help, worried that she might topple over from the weight of the luggage.

"Let me get that," he said, grabbing the handle of the bag. The smile she flashed him made his stomach do something weird as he drank her in. Her makeup was done simply, letting her natural beauty shine through. Holden couldn't help but wonder what her story was. Looking at her, he wouldn't have taken her for someone who was shy, yet she was decidedly guarded.

"Thanks. Kirk didn't really introduce us, huh? I'm Georgia-Grace Hawthorne, but everyone just calls me Gigi."

"Holden St. James," he said, nodding at her.

He helped her carry her stuff up the stairs and into the small studio apartment above the garage. Standing in the kitchenette when they finally had everything upstairs, he handed her the key. The area was small, forcing them to stand closer than he normally would to a stranger, but he didn't mind being this close to her. She, however, still seemed a little uneasy.

"This used to be a carriage house when the place was first built in 1853. They converted it into a garage around World War II and created this space for staff," he told her, trying to make the moment less awkward.

"Wow. We don't have a whole lot of stuff that's this old in Atlanta. The yankees kinda burned most of it down," she said, her southern accent in full swing.

"So that's where you're from? Atlanta?" he asked, letting his curiosity get the better of him. He knew he should just walk away, but he couldn't help himself.

"Yup, born and raised. Other than a few years in Tuscaloosa for college, I've never lived anywhere else."

"Tuscaloosa, huh?"

"Yup, Roll Tide!" she responded with a little giggle.

"We're gonna have to disagree there, Miss Hawthorne," he said, feeling the wry smile start to creep up his face. "It's Geaux Tigers!"

She rocked back a half step, looking almost affronted by his response. A ladylike hand flew to cover her chest as she mockingly gasped.

"OMG, you're not kiddin', are you?"

"I have family from down there. They made sure my allegiances were formed young."

She let out a little giggle, and the sound sent a feeling through Holden that he didn't recognize. Something he hadn't felt since Hannah. Was that…lust? He had no idea, but what he did know was that if he wasn't careful, he was going to try and make her make that sound again. He needed to get out of here. Needed to go retreat back into his space and be alone.

"Well, Miss Hawthorne..."

"Gigi, please," she corrected him.

"Gigi," he said. "I should leave you be to get settled. If something doesn't work, my number is on a sticky note on the fridge. You should have enough service to text me. If not, just knock on the door."

"Thanks again."

Holden nodded once more and stepped to the side to head to the door. In doing so his arm brushed up against hers, and Holden watched as Gigi flinched, crashing into the counter behind her as she tried to move out of his way. It struck him as an odd reaction to such a light touch, but he reminded himself that she'd been through a lot recently. He probably did weird things right after losing Hannah. Hell, he was still doing weird things if you asked his friends and family.

He had no idea what her story was. But there was something about Gigi Hawthorne that had him intrigued. He just hoped she wasn't going to be trouble.

3

GIGI

Without a doubt, this had been the most interesting week of Gigi's life. Which was saying something, because her very privileged life up until now had allowed her to go a lot of places and see a lot of things. Included in that list of things, however, had not been espresso machines, industrial kitchens, cash registers, or studio apartments. To say the learning curve was steep would be an understatement.

Not that she wasn't grateful—she was more than just grateful. She'd thought about leaving Bradley for years but never actually had the guts to do it. Every time she'd started to think about it, or even tried to think of a plan, she'd always come back to the same thing—how on earth would she support herself? But that question had seemingly been answered thanks to a random nail in her tire. It was still a little surreal to her how it all came together so quickly, but if she'd learned anything in her thirty-four years on this earth, it was that you did not question God's timing. His sense of humor, however, was something she was starting to wonder about. Sticking her in the middle of rural Vermont and having her work at a café had to be keeping Him all kinds of entertained.

Just like that first day at the café, her new landlord—who was sexy as all get-out with his tattoos and beard—came in every morning for coffee. She didn't fully understand why he didn't just have it at home, but Kirk told her it was the only time he knew of that Holden left the house. Who was she to question someone else's routine? Besides, she enjoyed seeing him. And not just because his was the only coffee order she had gotten correct that morning. There was something about Holden that made her feel like she was thirteen again and crushing on some boy in math class. And she really, really liked that feeling.

While she hadn't had to fiddle with the coffeemaking side of things after her first day, she did have a couple of run-ins with the register. Kirk hadn't told her not to hit the back button. Had he told her that, she wouldn't have done it, and it never would have resulted in the machine freezing to the point where the rest of the day was spent ringing customers up by hand. Kirk was more than happy to banish her to the kitchen so she could get to work on the cakes after that.

True to her word, Zara had been right about their kitchen having everything she would need. Between Audrey having been a professional chef and Roderick, the uber hot baking mastermind who kept the Bean stocked with all the savory baked goods, they knew all the right equipment for an operation like this. Not that a lot of them meant anything to Gigi, but she could tell that it had anything you could want if you actually knew what you were doing. She was holding her own though, or so she'd thought, until Audrey approached her this afternoon.

"Hey, Gigi, how are you settling in?" Audrey asked, as Gigi pulled a tray of cupcakes out of the oven.

The tops of each little cake hadn't risen the way she had expected. Instead of having a nice round top that crested over the top of the divot in the tray, each one was barely level with the little wrapping she'd placed the batter in. Had she not put in enough batter? *Oh, for heaven's sake...*

"Fine!" she replied, with maybe a little too much enthusiasm. She didn't want her new boss to have any idea that she didn't really know what she was doing and that underneath this very well put together exterior, she was nothing but a hot mess. Hell, these days she was the hot mess express. "It's been quite the week, but I think I'm starting to get my footing."

"Good! I'm so glad you found a place to stay so quickly. I stayed at the motor lodge myself for a moment when I first visited Colebury, and it's an experience!"

"That's a very nice way of putting it!"

"I just wanted to check in, because we've gotten some feedback on all the new stuff you've made. Everything is so pretty. The roses yesterday were just adorable!" Audrey started.

"Oh, I love those!" Gigi responded. The one thing that the Busy Bean didn't have on hand was fondant. Which was fine, because regular frosting was easy enough to make, and Gigi knew she wouldn't screw that up. It just meant being extra careful in piping a large rose on top of each one. "There wasn't any fondant in here, so I've had to keep things pretty basic for right now until we can get some in. Or I guess I could try and make some." She'd watched the chef who taught her class make some, and it looked easy enough. Maybe she could try that.

"I've got it on the list to order," Audrey continued. "But, we've had some...I don't want to say complaints, but...comments...that things have been a little undercooked."

"Undercooked?" Gigi repeated. Her heart sank. Here she thought she'd been doing so well, that she'd actually made a halfway decent cupcake. Sure, it was just a basic recipe off the internet, but everything had smelled so good when she pulled them out of the ovens. Maybe she should have tried one first. "I'm sorry, I hope I didn't make anyone sick!"

"No one got sick—nothing like that. The cake part is just a little gluey, you know? Look, I understand that industrial convection ovens take some getting used to, so don't worry about it. Even Roderick had to play around with some of his stuff when he started here. I just thought I'd let you know so that you could adjust your baking time."

Gigi knew she couldn't blame the oven, but she was not about to admit that out loud. She couldn't let on that she was faking her way through this. If the cupcakes needed to bake longer, then they would bake longer. That's all there was to it. Maybe she should practice at home.

"Thank you for letting me know. I'll leave them in for another minute or so and see what that does," Gigi said, hoping it sounded correct. Since Audrey simply smiled and told her she'd see her later, it must have been a satisfying enough answer. It just didn't leave Gigi feeling very good about herself.

HOLDEN

If Holden hadn't known any better, he would have thought that the blinking cursor on his screen was mocking him. Why was this so hard? He used to long for the days when he would have enough downtime to get all the ideas bouncing around his head onto the page. Inspiration always managed to hit when he was in the gym or out for a run—moments when he could do absolutely nothing about it. Thankfully, his muse had left him alone during matches so he wasn't distracted, but the second he stepped off that pitch, it'd been fair game.

It was another perfectly crisp fall day in Vermont, and Holden was sitting out on the front porch with his laptop. He'd been hoping that maybe some sunshine and fresh air would help knock something loose in his brain. As if the bright fall colors had magic powers. Turns out, they didn't provide anything other than a great view and a wonderful distraction.

The sound of his phone ringing stole his attention from the mostly blank Word document. Pulling it from his back pocket, he rolled his eyes playfully when he saw his godfather's name on the screen.

"Uncle Field..." he greeted him.

"Why do you already sound suspicious, young man?" the familiar voice on the other end said.

"Well, old man, it's the middle of the day. Some of us are working," Holden retorted, giving his godfather a hard time. If there was anyone on this planet he could be a smart-ass to, it was this man. In fact, it was Caulfield Montgomery who had taught Holden how to be a smart-ass in the first place.

"Working? Does that mean you've typed more than four words today?"

Ouch. Holden winced at the all too accurate accusation. Caulfield was an incredibly successful author in his own right, so he understood a thing or two about writer's block. Not that his understanding stopped him from harassing Holden about it, claiming it was all "part of the process." Looking down at his laptop screen, Holden counted the words written there.

"Six, thank you very much."

"Well, that's more than four," he laughed.

"I trust that mocking me about my word count isn't why you are calling?"

"It's October. I thought I'd check to make sure you remembered to winterize the pipes in the carriage house. Don't want anything to burst."

And there it was—the real reason he was calling. Mrs. Welch must have spilled the beans about the carriage house not only being occupied again, but by a very attractive woman. No, attractive wasn't the right word for Gigi. Stunning, beautiful, sexy—all of those worked to describe the shapely little blonde who had stumbled into his life last week.

"Carriage house isn't empty at the moment, so no need to winterize the pipes."

"Not empty? I thought the weird kid moved out?" There was a mock ignorance to his tone, and Holden barked out a laugh.

"Am I at least on speaker so that Mom and Dad can hear this too? Wouldn't want you to relay bad information," he teased, knowing that his parents were probably no more than ten feet away. After retiring from Dartmouth where he'd been a literature professor, Holden's father had found the perfect golf community in Florida where they could while away their days. Not surprisingly, since the two men had been joined at the hip since they became roommates in college, Caulfield had joined them six months later, buying a condo in the same building.

"Hi, honey!" his mom's voice called.

"Hi, Mom."

"How are you? Mrs. Welch mentioned that a sweet young lady moved into the carriage house. I didn't think you were planning on renting it out again after her nephew."

"I wasn't. But Gigi just moved to town after losing her husband and needed a place to stay," he told them, trying to keep it as simple as possible.

"She's a widow? Oh, poor girl. But it gives you two some common ground, which'll be nice."

"I don't need common ground with her, Mom. She lives above the garage, that's all."

"Son, would it kill you to have a friend?" his father chimed in.

Holden sighed audibly. Did everyone still have these kinds of calls with their family? He would have figured that by the time he turned thirty-nine they would have been over this, but apparently not. Apparently even though he was pushing middle age, his parents still felt the need to talk to him about the importance of friends like he was in kindergarten.

"I have friends, Dad. I just like being alone."

"Son, this isn't what Hannah would have wanted."

"Leave her out of this," Holden snapped.

"Enough, Heath. Go get us beers, let me talk to him," Holden heard Caulfield say. A moment later, after some shuffling,

Caulfield's voice came back on the line, much clearer than before. He must have taken him off speaker. "Holden, listen to me."

"I'm listening, old man."

"I know you miss Hannah and the life you were supposed to have together. Just like I miss your Aunt Viv. But you can't stay hidden away in that old house forever."

"Aunt Viv had an aneurysm. She wasn't murdered." Moving his laptop to the ground, Holden stood up and started to pace. His emotions were going to get the best of him if he didn't somehow take control of everything he was suddenly feeling flow through him.

"She was still taken from me unexpectedly. I still found her body in the garden. It still ripped my heart out of my chest and made my world come to a halt."

Holden thought back to the phone call from his mother letting him know that Aunt Viv had passed. She'd been not too far from where he stood now, tending to the flower gardens in the front yard closer to the carriage house. Caulfield arrived home from a run to the hardware store to find her lying there among her beloved tulips, already gone. Prior to Hannah's death, it was possibly the hardest moment of Holden's life. But for as heart-broken as Caulfield had been, a few short weeks after her death, he was back to his old routine and already talking to his publisher about his next book tour.

"Viv would have my balls if I didn't go through with this book because of her. Last thing I need is to get to heaven and have her waiting to bitch me out about it," he'd said when Holden had asked him why so soon. But it wasn't the same for Caulfield. He wasn't the reason his wife was dead.

"That's different."

"How? Explain to me how it's different," his godfather pushed back.

"You weren't the reason an artery burst in her brain."

"And you weren't the reason Hannah was stabbed."

"I need to get back to writing."

"You mean back to staring at years-old notes and a blank page? It's been six years, Holden. Your muse won't return until you forgive yourself and let yourself move on from Hannah."

Holden hung up without saying goodbye. He didn't need this lecture again. His family had made it perfectly clear how they felt about things. The reminder that it'd been as long as it had without any kind of inspiration really only added more salt to the wound. Because Caulfield was right—his muse was gone.

She had died right alongside his girls.

4

GIGI

"Oven's ready!" Gigi said to the empty apartment as the appliance beeped at her. Grabbing the muffin tray off the counter, she slipped it inside and closed the door with her hip. She set the timer, and then upped it a couple more minutes, wanting to make sure these were fully cooked.

See, you're getting the hang of this! It just takes practice.

Turning around, she frowned as she took inventory of the incredible mess she'd made. Working in this little space was so much harder than the giant kitchen at the Busy Bean. Her one little counter in this kitchenette only had a fraction of the space that the big, long prep tables there had. Trying to follow this recipe on her phone, while the counter was covered in flour, sugar, and every other ingredient she'd purchased on her way home this evening, was proving a lot more challenging than she'd thought.

The whole process had taken her a good bit longer than expected, but when she finally got the muffin tray into the oven, she heaved a huge sigh of relief. However, the idea of cleaning all this up seemed a little too daunting for the moment. Why was it so easy to make the mess, but so much harder to clean it all up? Not that she'd ever taken her staff for granted—she knew they worked hard—but she had a whole new level of respect and understanding for them after this week.

Sipping on a glass of limoncello, Gigi wandered over to the little window that looked over the yard and toward the big Victorian house. The stately looking home was painted a soft, light blue color with white trim and featured large, two story bow windows, one on either side of the front door. It looked exactly like something you'd see in a magazine about old houses, and Gigi couldn't help but wonder if the inside was decorated to match the classic New England exterior or if it was done up in a more modern way. Holden didn't exactly seem like someone who was particularly interested in all the latest and greatest gadgets, but what did she know? They'd had all of three conversations since she moved in here.

"Well, hello there, sir…" Gigi muttered, taking a long sip of her drink as Holden appeared in view of her window.

He was walking up the long driveway with what looked like the mail in his hand, his strides long and graceful like he was a lion who was lazily sauntering across the prairie. When he'd walked up to the counter last week at the coffee shop, Gigi had immediately been taken with him, although she had no idea why. He was nothing like her husband, or any of the men she'd dated before. At almost six feet tall, he had plenty of height on her, but that still made him shorter than her usual type. But his broad shoulders and muscular frame that always seemed to move so gracefully, no matter what she saw him doing, sent sparks through her body. His piercing blue eyes were guarded, giving away nothing about what he was feeling. Gigi couldn't read his face even the slightest bit, and that only served to intrigue her more. Oh, and that beard. Beards had never, ever been something that Gigi had found attractive, and yet on Holden, that long, somewhat ragged beard, with streaks of gray starting to weave their way through it, was such a turn-on.

And then there were his tattoos. She hadn't gotten to see them up close, other than the few that were poking out of his pushed up long-sleeved shirt, but both arms appeared to be covered in brightly colored art, and it left her wondering just how far up his arms they went and where else he might be inked. Watching him now, she was disappointed to see that those beautiful forearms were once again covered in long sleeves as he headed into the house.

Snap out of it, girl. Who are you? Thinking about beards and tattooed arms, she scolded herself. Just because he was tall, dark, and mysterious, with hair just long enough to always look perfectly mussed, didn't mean she should be standing here lusting after him. This was not how a recently widowed woman reacts to men who aren't their husband. Never mind that her husband wasn't actually dead. Regardless, she didn't need to be distracted. She was starting over and finding herself—and finding herself did not require a man in any way.

A fierce smell hit her nostrils, tearing her attention away from her daydreaming. Sniffing a couple of times, she tried to place the smell. It almost smelled like…like something was burning.

"Mother trucker!" she exclaimed, taking three large steps to land her back in the kitchenette.

Placing her glass on the stove and grabbing a kitchen towel, she flung open the oven door to find her cupcake tray on fire. The flames were small but still covered more than half of the items, and if she didn't do something quick, it would be all of them.

"No, no, no!" she yelled, looking around her, trying to figure out what to do. She just had to remember to breathe. No big deal. So the cupcakes were on fire. Grasping the oven rack with the towel, she pulled it out as far as it would go and started to blow on the flames as if they were candles on a birthday cake. This only seemed to make the flames grow, and panic started to rush through Gigi's body.

"Stop!" she told them, as if somehow food was suddenly going to talk back. "Sugar Honey Iced Tea!"

Unsure of how to make them stop, she swatted at them with the towel she was still holding. For a brief second this seemed to work, until she looked at the towel and noticed that it was now also on fire. Letting out another shriek, she threw it as hard as she could toward the sink. Missing the sink by just enough to be an issue, the towel brushed against the faded floral curtains that hung around the itty-bitty window just above it. Gigi's eyes went wide as she watched the flames jump from the towel to the cheap fabric of the curtains, which lit up faster than anything she'd ever seen.

"No, no, no!" she repeated, frozen in place, watching as the flames grew bigger. What did she do? Was she really that big of an idiot that she just set her kitchen on fire?

"Georgia, what were you thinking? You are not cut out for domesticity. Just stick with being pretty, would ya?" Bradley's voice said. She could feel the tears start to sting in her eyes at the thought. But she couldn't let him be right. She just didn't know what to do.

A loud pop resounded through the little studio apartment as one of the cabinets next to the flames splintered from the heat. The amount of smoke filling the room was starting to make Gigi's eyes burn. She needed to figure out how to put this fire out and fast. Water? Was that the answer? Yes, of course water was the answer. *Water plus fire equals no more fire, Gigi. That's how this works!*

She needed something to fill with water, and she didn't dare use any of the items that currently sat dirty in the sink. They probably had oil residue from the batter, and oil was bad for flames, right? Hadn't she read that somewhere at some point? Why couldn't she remember these things? She could feel her whole body shaking as she spun around to find something to fill up. Her lungs were starting to hurt from the smoke, and her eyes were burning even more now. Her heart was pounding and her breath was ragged, and she couldn't remember ever being this terrified. This was even worse than the tire blowing out last week. Just as she lifted her hand to reach for a cabinet door, she felt it come into contact with something.

Her glass.

She remembered she had left it on top of the stove just as she watched the pale yellow liquid spill out through the haze. As the alcohol hit the still burning tray of cupcakes, Gigi could feel the heat of the flames whoosh over her. The fire in the oven tripled in size thanks to the limoncello, and all Gigi could feel was the heat start to engulf her. She took a few steps back, trying to get away from it, when a loud bang startled her, causing her to trip and land on her rear end.

"What the fuck?" Holden called out, coughing as he entered her apartment. "Gigi!"

"Holden!" she shouted back, trying to push herself up.

Next thing she knew, he was right next to her, scooping her up off the floor. In a single movement he threw her over his shoulder, like she was nothing more than a sack of potatoes. He rushed through the door of the apartment and barreled down the stairs. She jostled a bit as he did so, but was thankful to no longer be anywhere near the flames. He had one arm wrapped around her knees and the other holding her in place on her back. His hands were warm and strong against her, and there was a feeling of comfort to them in this moment.

"But it's on fire!" she exclaimed a few steps from the stairs.

"I've called the fire department," he replied harshly, taking a few more steps before putting her down. He took in what a mess she was, still covered in cake ingredients and now smoke. "You okay?"

"I...I...I..." she stumbled, tears starting to trickle down her cheeks. She could hear the sirens of response vehicles approaching, and her heart skipped a beat thinking about how much damage there was going to be to the apartment.

"It's okay," Holden told her, his face grim. "You're safe."

"But the carriage house!"

Before Holden could respond any more, a small fire truck, followed by two pickups and a sedan, pulled up the driveway, lights and sirens blaring. Three men suited up in their fire-retardant gear piled out of the fire truck, and two of them headed straight up the carriage house stairs, extinguishers in hand. The two men who got out of the pickups ran over to the fire truck and helped the last guy unravel the fire hose and get it hooked up to a hydrant down by the street. Gigi watched in amazement as these men did everything in tandem at what felt like warp speed. The only place she'd ever seen anything like this was on TV, and she still couldn't believe she was witnessing it now. Had she really done this? How on earth did a kitchen fire get this out of hand so quick?

A short, stout redheaded woman in her early fifties walked over to them, a concerned look on her face. "Everyone get out?" she asked.

"Yeah, she was the only one inside," Holden said, tilting his head to indicate Gigi.

"Good, but we'll still need to get you checked out," she said as an ambulance pulled up behind the sedan she'd gotten out of. "I'm Chief Horrigan, and I'll let you know once we have things under control."

"Thanks, Chief," Holden replied, his own stony expression unchanged. Turning to Gigi, he said, "You go see the EMTs."

"I'm fine, just shaken up," she said, not wanting to be any more trouble.

"Not up for discussion," he barked. "Go see them. Now!"

Gigi flinched at his tone, stumbling back a step or two. His face was cold and mean, covered in a "don't mess with me" look. She knew that look. She'd seen it many times before, only instead of it being on the face of someone tall, dark, and mysteriously sexy, it had been on her husband's. So Gigi did the only thing she knew that she was good at.

Doing as I'm told…

HOLDEN

"So, Mister..." Chief Horrigan said as she approached Holden, who was still just standing in the middle of his yard. The fire department had managed to get the fire out relatively quickly, but the chief had spent the last thirty minutes in the carriage house checking everything out.

"St. James," he informed her, shaking her hand. "Holden St. James."

"Mr. St. James, thankfully it was just a small kitchen fire."

"Any idea on what started it?"

"From the looks of it, my guess is an over-greased baking pan. There seemed to be some charred paper on the bottom, so I'm thinking she must have set the pan down on the paper the butter comes in and not realized it was there before sticking it in the oven. If she bought some local stuff it'd be wrapped in wax paper rather than parchment, and that stuff isn't oven friendly. Although, with all that butter, even parchment is a risk," she told him with a definitive nod. "Add in the limoncello...well, let's just say gas ovens, flaming baked goods, and alcohol tend to be a bad combination. The cheap fabric the curtains were made of didn't help anything either. No structural damage though, just cosmetic. Could maybe even do it yourself if you're into that kind of thing," she said, looking him up and down.

"Good to know," he muttered, hoping he didn't come off as rude. He wasn't really looking for a home improvement project, but then again, he wasn't exactly writing either, so maybe it was something to consider. "So, she's fine to keep living there?"

They both looked over at Gigi who was sitting in the back of the ambulance wrapped in a large gray blanket. Her strawberry-blonde hair was a mess, pieces of ash weaving through it, and her face had black dirt streaks across it. Even sitting there with the remnants of the fire coating her, holding an oxygen mask to her face, she was cute. Something about her screamed to him to hold her and comfort her. But he'd also seen the shaken look in her eyes when he'd snapped at her a little bit ago. It was the same one she'd had when she had flinched after he accidentally made contact with her the other night in the apartment. There was definitely a lot more to Gigi Hawthorne than met the eye.

"Oh no. Not even close," the chief said, turning back to Holden. "The particles from the smoke and soot are wicked dangerous, even after the fire is out. You'll need to at least have the place professionally cleaned by a fire mitigation company before anyone inhabits that space again. I can give you the name of someone from Montpelier who can probably get that part taken care of in the next couple of weeks."

Holden glanced back over at Gigi, who hadn't moved at all. If she couldn't move back into the apartment, where was she going to go? There weren't a whole lot of options around here other than maybe the motor lodge, and that was probably not the best place for a single woman. Turning and looking back at the main house, he thought about the four unused bedrooms. Any one of those would be more than suitable for her to stay in. Hell, the room at the opposite end of the hall that connected to the hall bath was probably not much smaller than the carriage house apartment. But that would mean sharing common areas with her which, given the way his body reacted to her, might not be the best of ideas. He just didn't know what he disliked more—the idea of turning her out on the street or the idea of her under the same roof.

"Yeah, that'd be great," he said, turning back to the chief.

"Sure thing. And we're almost done here, so we'll be out of your hair soon."

Holden nodded his thanks and sucked in a deep breath. Running his fingers through his hair, he tried to find it within himself to tell Gigi that she was technically homeless. Again. But even he wasn't that much of an ass, was he?

Gigi looked up as he approached her, a defeated look in her eyes. That look immediately morphed into panic when he came to a stop in front of her. He hated that reaction.

"Hey, how ya feeling?" he asked.

"I'm fine!" she said, removing the oxygen mask. "I'm so sorry, Holden! I don't even know how it happened. I was just trying to get the cupcake recipe right because Audrey said that there were some complaints and I don't want to disappoint her and Zara! I'm so, so sorry!" she blurted out as she popped up from where she was sitting. The frantic look on her face seemed to radiate throughout her entire body, her petite frame shaking slightly as the blanket dropped to the ground.

"Is it ruined? I didn't ruin the carriage house, right? I didn't mean to, I promise!" she continued, seemingly oblivious to her own rambling. A tear slipped down her cheek, and Holden could tell she was fighting hard to not let any more show. "I'll pay for it! Whatever the damage is, I'll pay. I'm so, so sorry!"

"Whoa, whoa. Slow down," he said, placing his hands on her shoulders. Slowly guiding her back to the ambulance, he eased her into her seat and grabbed the blanket to wrap back around her. An EMT appeared from around the vehicle and handed her the mask again, giving her a look that could only be construed as, "don't move."

"The carriage house will be okay. Just smoke damage. Apparently nothing a professional cleaning and some trips to the hardware store can't fix."

"Oh, thank heavens," she said, her voice cracking slightly with emotion.

"But…the chief says it's uninhabitable for a while."

"Sugar Honey Iced Tea!"

Holden tried to bite back a laugh at her way of avoiding saying 'shit,' but it managed to escape anyway. Leave it to this cute little thing to find polite ways to swear.

"I can at least go inside and get my things, right? Or do I have to head to the motor lodge in just what I have on?" she asked, looking down at her yoga pants and T-shirt, covered in not only cupcake batter but also soot.

"I'll have to ask about getting your things, but if you'd

prefer…" he started, before pausing to get his words right. He had no idea why he was about to offer her a room in his house, but he was. He enjoyed being alone. Enjoyed keeping the world away. With Gigi in his house that was never going to happen. But he couldn't let her leave either. Clearing his throat, he started up again. "If you'd prefer, the big house does have five bedrooms. And there is one at the opposite end of the hall from me that connects to the bathroom, so you'd have your own space."

"Really? Holden, I couldn't intrude like that!"

"It's fine. There's plenty of room." Gigi's face lit up a little at his words, and a smile started to tug at the corner of her pretty pink lips. Why did he want to kiss them so bad? He was a married man—he shouldn't be thinking of his tenant like that. *You were a married man,* he corrected himself. *Hannah's been gone for six years…*

"We're just going to have to set some ground rules."

"Like?" she asked, looking at him like he might pull the rug out from under her.

"Like the only time you're allowed to use kitchen appliances is if I'm home. And the fire extinguisher remains on the counter at all times," he answered, laughing a little.

The look of defeat washed over Gigi faster than anything Holden had ever seen. He'd meant it as a joke, but everything about her body language currently told him that to her, it most certainly wasn't one. What had gone on in her life that she lacked any kind of confidence?

"Gigi, it was—"

"No, I think that's more than fair. I did almost burn down your hundred-something-year-old house. But I promise I'm not an idiot! It was an accident and—" she rambled.

"Gigi, I know it was an accident. Accidents happen. No one thinks you're an idiot. Now you sit here, rest, do what the EMTs tell you, and I'll go ask the chief about getting your things to move you into the big house," he said, turning to head toward the carriage house where he could see the chief talking with her crew.

Throwing a look back over his shoulder, he saw Gigi shudder, and she let out what must have been a sigh of relief. His heart ached a little, watching her like this, and he wished there was more that he could do to make her understand that he didn't blame her. He just wasn't sure he had the emotional capacity for it.

5

HOLDEN

It was another two hours before the chief would allow Holden to go into the carriage house to grab Gigi's items. She tried to insist that she could do it, but the chief had put a stop to that immediately, telling her that she wasn't allowed since she'd already inhaled too much smoke. It hadn't taken him very long to get everything she needed, since the only items it seemed she had unpacked were the toiletries in the bathroom. Once he'd gotten everything into the big house and Gigi had been officially released by the EMTs, they both made their way inside.

"Well, this is it. Montgomery Manor, as we call it," Holden said, suddenly feeling like he was thirteen and having a girl over for the first time. "Like I said the other day, it was built in 1853. There are five bedrooms and two bathrooms. Awkward note about that—both bathrooms are upstairs."

"That's…odd," she responded, seeming to relax a little. Her eyes still had a concerned look to them, like she was still feeling guilty about the accident and was worried that she was putting him out.

"Yeah, it's not something I've ever understood, but it's been that way my whole life, so at this point I'm just used to it."

"Did you grow up here?"

"No, this place belongs to my godfather. I grew up just across the border in New Hampshire, but I spent every summer here," he told her. "So, I know this weird old place pretty well at this point."

"I'd say so."

"This is the living room," he said, stepping out of the entryway and into the large room that took up most of the front of the house. The two large bow windows were surrounded by built-in bookshelves and sat across from a large fireplace. "Then through here is the dining room."

They walked into the connected room heading to the back of the house. The old house was the exact opposite of an open floor plan, but the idea of tearing down the wall between the two rooms just seemed like too much work. Holden watched as Gigi's eyes went wide, taking in the massive oak table that seated twelve as well as the built-in buffet that ran along the entire length of the wall that was shared with the living room. The room was massive and largely unused for years. Caulfield had stopped hosting dinner parties after Aunt Viv had passed, but no one could seem to find a better use for the space, so the table remained.

"Please don't think I'm crazy, but you know what this kind of reminds me of?" she asked, pointing to the buffet, holding back a giggle.

"What?" he asked, curious to see where her mind was taking her.

"All the arches in the buffet make me think of the opening to *The Muppet Show*. You know, where each Muppet is in their own little alcove swaying back and forth?" she said, mimicking the motion of the puppets from their childhood.

Holden barked out a laugh, realizing she was right. "I've never noticed that, but now I don't think I'm going to be able to think of anything else."

"Sorry. It's beautiful. I don't know why my mind went there."

"I like that it did," he said, giving her a gentle smile. He liked seeing this side of her. One that was a little more relaxed. She was letting her real personality show through, and damn if that didn't make her even sexier. He didn't need her getting sexier. "This is probably what you're most interested in though."

"Holy cow!" she exclaimed, rushing through the door to the attached kitchen. "It's stunning! I love the blue cabinets! That's so unique." She ran over to them and ran her hands along the counter top, taken aback by the simple beauty of it all.

White marble lay on top of the custom painted cabinets that ran along the length of the kitchen. A large, butcher block style prep table sat in the middle of the room, underneath a hanging rack full of dangling pots and pans. Holden had always wondered how he'd never managed to hit his head on any of the suspended kitchenware, but he was thankful every time he'd moved around the butcher block that he hadn't. A small kitchen table sat up against the far wall underneath a big picture window.

"Aunt Viv, my godmother, did that. When she and Uncle Field redid the kitchen about ten years ago, he gave her carte blanche to do whatever. His only instruction was 'just don't paint the cabinets blue.' So what did she do?"

"Turned around and painted them blue?"

"Yup. All he could do was laugh. When I asked him why he wasn't upset, he told me it was his own damn fault for giving her the idea."

"They sound like wonderful people. Why don't they live here anymore?"

"Aunt Viv passed away shortly after that, actually. It's why they are still blue, because Uncle Field couldn't bring himself to change it."

"I'm so sorry."

"It's okay. Let me show you upstairs," he told her, pointing to the staircase hidden in the corner of the room. When they reached the landing that led to the second floor, he pointed to another doorway. "This is your side of the hall. That door right there is your room, which connects to that bathroom. There are two more bedrooms along the hall, then a bathroom, and my room, which is at the top end of the stairs you saw in the living room. Looks the same as this end of the hall, just a different staircase, and then there is another small bedroom on the other side of it."

"Okay, that should be pretty easy to remember," she smiled, turning to look at the rest of the staircase. "Where does this go?"

"After you," he said, gesturing with his hand for her to lead the way. She gave him a cautious look, but started up the stairs anyway. Slowly making her way up the steep and narrow steps, she teetered a bit, her legs a little unsteady. Making sure to stay behind her, Holden got a great view of the glorious backside he'd been admiring from afar all week. His hands ached at the thought of holding on to her hips, feeling the way they curved under his grip. Watching her like this was doing things to him he didn't think were possible anymore, and he wasn't quite sure how he felt about it. Although his dick certainly seemed to have an opinion.

Three or four steps up, a floorboard creaked under her foot, catching Gigi off guard, causing her to stumble. Before he knew what he was doing, Holden lunged forward, his hands catching her in the exact spot he had just been distracted by. With one arm wrapped around her waist, holding her against him for balance, he felt his cock twitch as his groin made contact with her ass.

"Steady," he said, trying to sound reassuring. "Old house, so the steps are small and steep. Here, hold on to the railing." He guided her hand to the rail, placing his over hers for just a moment as she gripped tight.

"Thanks," she whispered, starting the climb again.

Her soft, feminine body had felt even better against him than he'd imagined. For as brief a moment as it was, it seemed to have awakened something inside him. Something he'd thought was long gone. Now he was going to have trouble not letting his mind wander into thinking about what she felt like underneath those yoga pants.

As they entered the open space at the top of the steps, he heard Gigi gasp softly. The vaulted ceilings and exposed beams gave the room a rustic look that Holden had always found peaceful. A large picture window, as well as several skylights, provided plenty of natural light during the day and some great views over the back of the property. The desk that Holden used during all those pretend writing sessions sat directly across from the picture window.

Gigi wandered through the room, finally stopping in front of the antique curio cabinet that housed a number of books and awards. She scanned the book titles curiously, holding up a finger and pointing to each one, as if she were taking inventory.

"You have Caulfield Montgomery's entire collection!" she squealed. This was the most excited he'd seen her. "And some of these are first editions!"

"Well, they should be. They're his," Holden said.

"His?"

"Yeah, that's his collection."

Gigi turned back to the hutch, this time looking at the awards nestled in among the books. When she turned back to him, her eyes were wide all over again, and a stunned look had taken over her face.

"How do you have his collection?" she asked, her voice sounding both impressed and unsure.

"Well, it's his house. Where else would you expect his collection to be?" Holden responded, trying to sound nonchalant.

"This...this is Caulfield Montgomery's house? *The* Caulfield Montgomery? As in the greatest southern gothic author of our time?"

"Don't let him hear you say that—it will go right to his head..."

"There is no way this is his house. We're in Vermont! He's from...Baton Rouge..." she said, the realization and connection to what he told her the other day coming together.

"He is. Then he went to Dartmouth, where he met his best

friend, Heathcliff. The two immediately bonded over being named after literary characters. Although, it should be noted that Caulfield was a family name and he wasn't directly named because of the book. They met and married a pair of locals and stayed here. But don't tell anyone you know that. He much prefers everyone thinks he wrote all his books in New Orleans, rather than a loft in Vermont."

"Heathcliff is your father?" she asked.

"And before you ask, yes, my mother's name is Catherine."

"It is not!"

"Oh, it is," Holden confirmed.

"So then you are named after *The Catcher in the Rye*?" she asked, her eyes lighting up. The sparkle that shone seemed to ignite something in him too. He had no idea why, but suddenly all he wanted was to make sure that look never left her eyes.

"Holden Hemingway St. James. Whatever else would you expect from a Lit professor and a special ed teacher?"

"I think it's fantastic," she said, smiling. It was the biggest smile he'd seen from her, and it made him feel warm and fuzzy inside that learning about his name and his family made it appear. "And I'm jealous of this collection. I love his books."

"Now you're really not allowed to meet him," he laughed. "You'll be bad for his ego."

Gigi giggled in response, and it sent a bolt straight to Holden's already struggling erection. Damn, that sound was going to be trouble.

"Well, I did write my senior capstone paper on the role of the color green in *At Midnight*," she offered.

Holden looked at her, puzzled. He would never have guessed her to be someone who would be into such a genre, much less to have actually studied it. Maybe she wouldn't be such bad company after all.

"You studied literature?" he asked, sounding more surprised than he'd intended. The only thing he knew about this woman was that she was starting over after her husband had a heart attack. There was no reason to think she wouldn't have liked to read. Just because she looked like she could be a cast member of one of the Real Housewives shows didn't mean anything. For all he knew, she didn't really come from money like he'd been assuming. He really needed to make more of an effort to get to know her.

"I'm not as stupid as I look," she answered softly. Instead of it coming off as a joke or even as if she were defending herself, it came off sounding defeated, almost as if she were reminding herself as much as anyone.

"I didn't mean..."

"I should probably head to my room. It's been a long day, and I need a shower," she said, looking down and gesturing to her soot-covered clothes. "I guess I'll see you in the morning. Night."

Gigi quickly made her way back to the stairs and scurried down them like she was on a mission. Holden figured she probably was—a mission to get away from him.

"Night," he replied, to the now empty room. So much for that.

GIGI

The ancient looking hardware in the shower took some fiddling with to get the hot water going, and Gigi figured there was probably some special trick or secret handshake she needed to do each time to get it just right. She probably should have asked Holden that before when he'd pointed out her room, but she didn't dare go back and ask him now. Not after that disaster of a conversation.

Stripping out of her clothes, she left them in a pile on the floor and stepped into the shower. Normally she would have made sure to take the extra special care of folding them and placing them on the counter, since Bradley hated clothes being left on the floor, but this was her chance to do things how she wanted. Steam billowed out from behind the shower curtain and engulfed her as she tugged it shut, filling Gigi's lungs as she inhaled deeply. The hot water felt so good against her skin, allowing her muscles to finally relax.

She replayed the day's events in her mind as she leaned her head back under the stream from the showerhead. From Audrey's feedback about her subpar cupcakes, to starting a kitchen fire and having to be rescued by her sexy-as-sin landlord, to the discovery that she was now staying in the home of her favorite author—it had been a hell of a day. At this point, she was pretty sure she couldn't be any more embarrassed if she tried. Her new life was not off to a very good start.

Am I in over my head? she wondered, lathering her hair. She'd felt so lucky to stumble into a job like she had, she hadn't even considered what it all meant. But baking shouldn't have been this much trouble, right? People did it every day, so how hard could it really be?

Then there was Holden. Goodness, that man did her in, and she had no idea why. But just looking at him made her forget how to breathe. No man had ever done that to her. Not even Bradley. Sure, she'd thought Bradley was incredibly handsome, and when he'd flirted back with her that night at the country club she'd felt giddy inside, but that was nothing compared to the butterflies Holden was giving her. Something about that broody stare of his and how his ice-blue eyes seemed haunted at times made her want to curl up in those beautifully tattooed arms and share secrets. The feel of those strong arms wrapped around her this afternoon as he carried her out of the carriage house had been incredible and left her wondering what it would be like to have them hold her while she slept. Or what his hands would be like as they explored her body, his gruff voice whispering her name. Just the thought of it was sending shivers down her spine, despite the temperature of the water.

But she needed to be careful. Just because this man made her girlie parts come alive in a way she wasn't sure they ever had didn't mean anything. She had no idea who he really was, or if he could be trusted. She couldn't let herself be swayed by his connection to famous authors, or by his beautiful old house. What if the truth got out? It was bad enough she was lying to everyone about her baking skills. What would happen if they found out her husband wasn't really dead?

Worse than that, though, was the thought of Bradley finding her. There was no way that he had handled it well when those church doors opened and she wasn't starting her descent down the aisle. His temper was unstable on a good day, and that would not have been a good day. She'd been on the receiving end of that temper enough over the last ten years to know just how he would react. The only question in her mind was, would she live to tell about said reaction?

A knock at the door as she was stepping out of the shower startled her. There was only one person it could be, but she was not about to greet him in a towel.

"Yes?" she called out hesitantly.

"Hi," Holden's voice came through the door, sounding just as hesitant. "I...I just wanted to apologize. I didn't mean to imply—"

"It's fine!" she said hurriedly, cutting him off. She knew she should probably let him finish, but she'd just been fantasizing about him in the shower. There was no way for him to know that, but even with the door between them, she felt like she'd been caught red-handed. Turns out she was wrong earlier—she *could* get more embarrassed.

"Okay, well then, I guess I'll just see you later," he responded. There was an awkwardness to his voice now, and she hated that she was causing it. But she needed to keep him at arm's length.

The new Gigi didn't need a man. She was a strong, independent woman. That was what she had told herself from the moment she created her plan to start over.

But, what if she *wanted* one?

6

GIGI

"What are those?" Kirk asked, warily eyeing the tray she was carrying.

"Scones," she replied brightly. "I thought they would be fun!"

It had been almost two weeks since what Gigi now referred to in her head as "disaster day." Colebury was a small town, and word traveled at a rapid pace, letting everyone know that the fire department had been called into action. Kirk had spoken to her more that next morning than he had her whole first week combined. He still treated her like she was in the way, but at least now a little less so.

"Roderick makes the scones."

"Well, today he let me make them," she quipped back, trying to sound polite.

"What happened to cupcakes? Those were finally starting to get good," he told her. His strange, semi-robotic tone had grown on her a bit, as weird as that sounded. Maybe Kirk wasn't ever going to be Mr. Personality, especially compared to Roderick who seemed to be nothing but personality, but Gigi could at least try to find some good in him.

He was right, however. She had finally figured out the perfect amount of time to bake the cupcakes and had yet to burn them here at the café. The fondant that Zara had ordered also came in, so she'd been able to work with that and create adorable little toppers for the cakes. Not only had the complaints stopped, but she was even starting to get compliments on her work. Maybe all she had needed was time.

"I've got some about to go into the oven right now. But I saw this recipe online and asked Roderick about it, and he said to have at it."

"Don't worry, I checked the bottom of the baking sheet first," Roderick joked, slipping back behind the counter, heading to the kitchen. He winked at Gigi, who just rolled her eyes in response. He'd been having way too much fun teasing her ever since he'd learned what had happened. It had all been in good fun though, and in a way made Gigi feel like she was starting to fit in.

"Oh, what are those?" an older gentleman asked as he approached the counter.

"Orange cranberry scones!" Gigi answered brightly.

"Those sound great. I'll take half a dozen for the store," the guy told Kirk. Gigi's heart soared hearing these words and she couldn't help letting a little giggle escape as she smiled at Kirk, trying to politely tell him "told you so!" with her eyes.

Heading back to the kitchen, she couldn't help but think that maybe, just maybe, things were starting to come together. On top of her finally feeling like she was getting her footing at the Busy Bean, life at home had settled as well. After that first eventful evening, she and Holden had managed to find a rhythm, making the whole situation only slightly less awkward. Gigi was up, out the door, and at the café before Holden seemed to even be out of bed. But every morning, right around nine fifteen, he walked into the Busy Bean, placed his order, and then found an open seat to eat his muffin and read something on his phone. Not that Gigi had been watching him or anything. She just liked knowing when to expect seeing him.

When she'd arrived home in the afternoons for the last few days, he'd been working on hauling some of the damaged stuff out of the carriage house. She'd been more than a little distracted when she saw him carrying a burnt cabinet down the stairs, his jeans slung low on his hips, white T-shirt hanging from his back pocket, and those muscular arms on display. It was a good thing the car was already in park, or she might have had another accident. His chest was as intoxicating as she had imagined, with well-defined pecs, a flat stomach, and a little patch of dark hair that drew her eyes south to some place else she'd been picturing. While his abs weren't chiseled like some underwear model on a billboard, it was apparent that he spent time keeping himself in shape, and the presence of the hip-V was more than prominent enough for her liking.

They made small talk if they saw each other in passing in the hall or the kitchen, but Holden spent most of his time up in the loft when she was home. She wondered what he did up there, but she didn't have the guts to go up there and try to get to know him. No matter how intrigued she was by him, she didn't want to push it. He was already going out of his way to let her stay in the house. She didn't need to annoy him by being all up in his space all the time.

"Miss Hawthorne," a familiar voice said, as she carried more scones out front. She looked up and found Officer Nelligan standing at the counter.

"Officer Nelligan, hi! And please, call me Gigi."

"Miss Gigi, I hear you gave our fire department something to do last week."

"Didn't you know that's why I was sent to Colebury?" she said, in her best super sweet, hostess voice. "I'm here to make sure that all your emergency services are in proper workin' order! So far, police, fire, and EMT have all passed with flyin' colors! If you have recommendations of who I should hit up next, you just let me know."

Officer Nelligan let out a laugh, and Gigi was glad that her attempt at a joke had landed such a response. She hadn't had very many opportunities to laugh and joke since she arrived, and it felt good to be able to make light of the situation.

"Are those scones?" he asked, once he'd composed himself.

"They are! Fresh baked!" She put one on a plate and slid it across the counter to him, before placing the rest of the tray in the display case. Out of the corner of her eye, she saw that Holden was sitting at one of the small tables directly in front of her, rather than the counter seats at the window overlooking the patio. The window seats were wide open, and she couldn't help but wonder why the change. Not that it was any of her business. Although when it came to Holden, she certainly liked trying to make it her business.

Sneaking another glance at him, she smiled to herself, noticing a scone on his plate. He hadn't taken a bite yet, and her chest filled with nerves as she thought about him trying it for the first time. She wanted everyone to like the goodies she was making for the café, but she really, really wanted Holden to like them. Maybe even like them so much that he'd ask her to make some just for him, at home. An image of the two of them in the kitchen together, covered in ingredients as he pressed her up against the blue cabinets, flitted across her mind, making the nerves in her chest morph into something else entirely. Was that…lust?

Stop it, Gigi…just because the way to a man's heart is through his stomach doesn't mean you need to make an attempt. Especially with that *man.*

The sound of coughing pulled her attention back to the counter, where Officer Nelligan was still standing. When he finally swallowed, he took a long swig of his coffee, blinking harshly, like he was trying to forget a taste.

"Miss Gigi, may I ask what you put in these?"

"Ummmm, usual scone ingredients?" she floundered. "Flour, salt, cream, baking powder, orange zest, cranberries…"

"I'm not much of a baker, but I think you might have mixed up your baking powder and your baking soda. A girl did that in my junior high home ec class, and it tasted much like this—kinda metallic," Officer Nelligan said.

"What?" Gigi said. All feelings of butterflies and lust were long gone now, replaced by sheer panic. She looked at Officer Nelligan in horror, taking in the scone he'd just bitten into. The apologetic look in his eye told her everything she needed to know —she'd screwed up. Big time.

"Georgia. I don't know what possesses you to even try these things. It's a well-established fact that you just are not capable of cooking. Please stop trying—you're just making yourself look ridiculous," Bradley's voice said. She shook her head, trying to clear his words from her mind, as she turned and ran into the kitchen.

Sure enough, the canisters labeled "baking powder" and "baking soda" were right next to each other. However, it was the baking soda whose lid was off and sitting in front of it. That was the one she'd used when measuring out her ingredients.

"Sugar Honey Iced Tea!" she exclaimed, stomping her foot in frustration. She could feel Roderick looking at her, but she didn't have the heart to turn around and see the expression on his face.

"Uh oh," she heard Roderick's voice say over her shoulder. "That's a bad day."

Was she ever not going to screw this up? When would she learn that she couldn't do this? No, what she couldn't do was let Bradley's words get to her.

At least it was just Officer Nelligan. He was used to seeing her at her worst at this point. He and Holden.

Holden.

Holden had also ordered a scone. But he hadn't eaten it yet. Right?

Racing back up front, she skidded to a stop in front of his table to find him midbite into the inedible treat.

"Nooo!" she cried. "Don't eat that—it's..."

"A bit salty..." he responded, choking it down.

Gigi could feel the tears starting to prick at her eyes, but she wasn't going to let anyone here see her cry. It was no big deal. So she got the canisters mixed up. Happens to everyone at some point, right?

"I'll get you a muffin," she told him, turning back to the counter. Looking between Holden and Officer Nelligan, she sighed. "At least it was just you two, right?"

"And Mr. Hughes," Kirk said, not looking up from the espresso machine.

"Who?"

"That older guy who bought six. Owns Hughes Hardware store up the street."

"Oh, for heaven's sake!" she exclaimed before turning and running out the front door. She had to get to him before he let his employees have any of them.

Deserting the café like this was probably not her best move, but she figured after this disaster, she was going to be lucky to even have a job.

HOLDEN

Holden hadn't quite realized just how out of shape he was until he'd started to demo the smoke-damaged kitchen in the carriage house. The company the chief had recommended had been out a few days after the fire and gotten the place cleaned up. It had taken them three days to take care of everything, but when they were done, they told him that it was safe enough for him to do the demo himself as long as he wore a mask to keep from inhaling anything that might break loose in the process. Doing this himself had sounded like a great idea, a way to distract him not only from all the words he wasn't currently writing, but from the insanely tempting little blonde that was now flitting around his house. That was, until he'd started to actually swing that sledgehammer.

It wasn't a secret that he'd gone a little soft after retiring from professional sports. Gone were the days where he spent six hours a day working out and watching every bite of food he took. But it wasn't like he'd let himself go completely. He still ran ten miles a day and did plenty of stuff around the house. So he didn't have the washboard stomach that Hannah used to refer to as his "fifteen pack"—didn't mean he wasn't still a stud. Other than how incredibly sore and tired he was from hauling cabinets out of the small apartment.

Walking into the kitchen to get a glass of water, he found Gigi standing in front of the open fridge. Clearing his throat to announce his presence, he watched as she gasped, jumping back from the fridge and slamming the door shut. Her beautiful gray eyes were red and swollen, and her normally rosy cheeks were tearstained. His heart ached at the sight. It was obvious she'd been crying for a while, and he was pretty sure it had to do with the scone incident this morning. She'd run out of the Busy Bean faster than he'd ever seen her move, looking like she might throw up. The whole thing would have been funny had he been watching a sitcom, rather than it playing out in real life.

"What's the matter?" he asked, stepping closer to her.

"Nothing," she answered, wiping her hands against her cheeks, trying to making it look like she hadn't been upset. "I'm fine. I'll get out of your way."

She turned to go, but he caught her by the elbow, stopping her. He could feel her body go rigid as she froze in place when his hand made contact with her skin. He hadn't meant to scare her, so he quickly let go, letting her arm fall back by her side. The startled look on her face, paired with her puffy eyes, made her look so vulnerable just then. Holden's heart ached even more, and he had to stop himself from wrapping his arms around her in a bear hug. It was an urge he hadn't felt in years, but it was just as strong as the last time it had rushed through him.

"No, don't go. Talk to me. What's wrong?"

"What's wrong? Holden, you witnessed it. Please don't make me recount it—it was bad enough the first time," she said, walking back toward him and resting against the counter.

"Can I ask what happened after you ran out of the coffee shop? Did you catch up with the guy from the hardware store?"

"I did," she sighed. "I did not realize just how far Hughes Hardware was from the Busy Bean, at least in terms of walking distance. Luckily, Officer Nelligan caught up with me and gave me a ride. When I got to the store, I found Mr. Hughes, and I told him that I was sorry, but I needed those scones back because there was a problem with them and I offered him cash to refund him, but he just looked at me like I was crazy. Told me he didn't know what I was talking about, and he didn't buy any scones this morning. We went in circles for a good couple of minutes until one of his sons, Gabe, came in, walked back to the office, and found the box."

"At least you got to him before they had any?" Holden offered, trying to help her find a silver lining.

"Ha!" she barked. It came out half as a sob, and he could tell the tears were about to return. "He'd eaten two. Gabe didn't say it outright, but I get the impression that Mr. Hughes has some memory issues. He didn't remember eating them."

"Then he doesn't remember how bad they tasted."

His last words made her lower lip start to quiver, and that's when he knew he'd said the wrong thing. A single tear escaped from her eye and slowly slid down her cheek, making Holden feel like he'd just taken a punch to the gut. He'd forgotten how powerful a woman's tears were, and knowing that it was his fault that they'd started up again only made it worse.

"Oh Gigi, please don't cry. They weren't that bad," he assured her. "It's a mistake everyone has made at some point. So you grabbed the wrong container. It's no big deal."

"It's a huge deal! How am I supposed to be the cake lady-boss if I don't even know the difference between baking powder and baking soda? Or if I'm just one step away from burning the whole place down?" she cried, the rest of her tears coming in earnest now. "Spoiler alert, I don't actually know what I'm doing. I've never actually baked anything before."

"Huh, coulda fooled me," he said under his breath. Or so he'd thought, because Gigi just shot daggers in his direction with her eyes, letting him know his sarcasm was not appreciated in the moment. "So, why'd you take the job if you can't bake? And where'd you learn to make all the little frosting thingys?"

"I won a cake decorating class at a charity auction a bunch of years ago. It didn't focus on the baking part, just the making things pretty part. I'm good at pretty. The chef taught us how to sculpt fondant," she sighed. "So when I got that flat tire and was sitting in the Busy Bean waiting for it to get patched, I overheard Zara and Audrey talking about adding cakes to the menu, and I showed them some of the ones I had 'made.' And by 'made,' I mean 'decorated.' I left out the part about not actually baking them. They offered me the job, and I took it."

"Even though you had no idea what you were doing?"

"Yes! I thought I could figure it out. I *needed* to figure it out. That was the whole point of starting over without Bradley. To prove to myself and everyone that I'm a strong, independent woman. I left Atlanta to have a new life. One where no one knew me, and I wasn't expected to be anything. I spent so many years doing as I was told and following all these rules because 'that's how it's done.' I just wanted to be able to figure out who I am outside of all of that and do what I want to do. But apparently the only thing I'm capable of doing is messing this up."

"I think you're being too hard on yourself."

"Yeah? And what would you know about it?" she snarked, her southern accent taking out some of the bite. He looked her up and down, taking in her stylish outfit. Her jeans fit her like they were custom made for her curves and the long-sleeved knit top she was wearing hugged her just right as well. Once again, she looked like she was ready for a luncheon, rather than an evening in. Come to think of it, though, even when she'd been wearing sweats she looked put together, and it made him wonder if she knew how to just let go. From the sounds of it, she was so used to keeping up appearances, he was starting to think she didn't. If he could only help her realize that she could let it all go and be whomever she wanted. That's when the idea hit him.

"Go grab your jacket. We're going for a ride," he told her.

"What?"

"Grab your jacket. It'll be cold once the sun goes down. And put on shoes you're comfortable walking in."

"Where are we going?" she asked, questioning his sudden change of subject.

"You'll see."

7

HOLDEN

The drive had taken a little longer than Holden had expected, but the sun hadn't set completely yet, so he knew there was still plenty of time. Finding a parking spot had also been a lot easier than he'd thought, since this year the festival organizers had made an attempt at a parking lot. The fact that it was also the first night of the event helped as well, since the majority of the crowds wouldn't be showing up until tomorrow.

"Are you going to tell me where we are now?" she asked as they climbed out of his truck. When he had told her to put on shoes she would be comfortable walking in, he didn't know what he was expecting, but a pair of sneakers hadn't been it. Hell, he'd been more than a little surprised to see she even owned a pair of sneakers. She also had busted out an old crimson hoodie, the front emblazoned with that unmistakable Alabama A. The whole outfit made her look absolutely adorable, and Holden was having a hard time keeping his eyes off of her.

"This is the Moose Mountain Fall Festival," he told her, a wry smile on his face. He'd always loved this event, although he wasn't really sure why. Truth be told, it wasn't much more than a bunch of food and arts and crafts vendors set up in an open field, but there was something about it that he'd loved ever since he was a kid. It had been at least fifteen years since he'd been here, however. He and Hannah had taken a day trip up here while he was playing for the New England Revolution, the professional soccer team in Boston. Once they'd moved to London, the fall was the start of his season, so getting away for a trip back to the states just hadn't been possible.

"Moose?" Gigi froze in her tracks, her eyes as big as plates as she looked around her as if she were expecting the large creatures to appear out of nowhere.

"Moose Mountain is actually quite a ways that way," Holden explained, gesturing off to his left. "And while yes, it's named that because people often see moose up there, we're not going to see any here tonight. They aren't interested in cider donuts and handmade soap."

Gigi nodded as she caught up to him. The two fell into step with each other as they approached the main row of vendors.

"Tonight's the first night, so it's a little slower, but I think it's more fun to check it all out without all the people. This event has been going on since the sixties. You've got your standard local arts and crafts, soaps, and that kind of stuff. Plus all sorts of different food vendors. During the day there are field day games. You know, the three-legged races, and the egg on the spoon thing. Once upon a time there was a dunk tank, but I think they stopped that."

"Seems a little cold for a dunk tank," she said, rubbing her hands up and down her arms.

"That's why they stopped it," he said with a little bit of a laugh. Guiding her over to a big white tent, they ducked inside, the smell of freshly fried dough surrounding them. "First things first, cider donuts."

"What's a cider donut?"

"Only the best fall tradition ever," he replied. Turning to the girl behind the counter, he ordered them both a couple of donuts and a cup of hot cider. He handed Gigi hers and waited as she took her first bite of the cinnamon- and sugarcoated goodness.

"Holy cow, this is yummy!" she said, almost jumping up and down as they exited the tent. She looked so cute, with the pastry in one hand and a to-go cup in the other, cinnamon and sugar smeared across her pretty pink lips. Holden told himself he needed to stop staring. If he didn't, he was likely to lean in and kiss the mess right off her. "I wish I could make something this good."

"I bet you could. I've never actually made them myself, but my mom and Aunt Viv used to do it every fall, and I don't remember it being an overly involved process."

"Holden, that's very kind of you to say, but you've experienced my baked goods," she said, her sweet southern voice sounding defeated. The ache Holden felt earlier returned, and he longed to be able to fix this. He had no idea why—no one had made him feel like this since Hannah.

"I have...*experienced* them, as you put it," he said, nodding his head in the direction of the other end of the festival, indicating which way to turn. "And those scones were not the worst thing I have ever put in my mouth."

Gigi looked at him with wide eyes, a slightly embarrassed look on her face. He could see a little bit of a blush spreading across her cheeks as she fought back a little giggle at his words.

"Okay, that came out dirtier than I intended," he said, trying to recover. "I just meant that I spent years in London, and the Brits aren't known for their food."

"Nice recovery," she retorted, still holding in a giggle.

They walked side by side, embracing a companionable silence, arms lightly brushing every couple of steps. Each time they made contact, Holden felt a zing rush through him, even with the layers of clothing separating them. His first reaction had been to pull away, to ever so slightly direct his steps to the right so that there were more than a few centimeters between them. But he couldn't bring himself to do it. He liked the feel of her so close to him. Her presence was oddly comforting—like when you've been outside for so long that you don't realize how cold you've gotten until you're back inside by the fire. Gigi was that fire, and he was drawn to her like a moth to a flame.

"Oh, look!" she said, pointing to a booth with a bunch of oddly-shaped little jars. She grabbed his hand and pulled him over to it. Her fingers were a bit cold from the fall air, but the feel of her hand in his sent a heatwave through his body. When they reached the booth and she let go of him, he missed the touch almost instantly, making him wonder what he needed to do to get her to hold it again.

The banner loosely draped on the front of the table read "Hunnie's Honey." The table itself was covered in all sorts of jars filled with the amber substance, each jar looking a little different from the last. Holden picked up one that looked like it had a twig in it, trying to figure out exactly what was inside there.

"Hi there!" a brunette said, approaching them. She looked to be about thirty and was every inch the Vermont hippie, with her hair in two braids, well-worn jeans, a flannel shirt, and Birkenstocks. "I'm Hunnie! Welcome to Hunnie's Honey!"

"Hi!" Gigi said, showing off a bright smile that Holden hadn't seen yet. "This is so cool. Do you make all this?"

"I do! My family's run a honey farm for more generations than I can count, and this is just my spin on it!"

"Is that a twig in there?" Holden asked, holding up the little jar that looked like an upside down V. He didn't want to sound too skeptical. They were here to show Gigi that anyone could learn to make something new, and this little hippie might just be his golden ticket.

"It's rosemary," she told him. "You can infuse honey with pretty much anything, and getting creative with it is half the fun."

"These all sound yummy," Gigi said, that illuminating smile still spread across her face. It lit her up in all new ways, and damn, was she pretty. If he'd thought there was something pulling him toward her before when she was sullen, now seeing her like that, there was no denying it. His own desire stirred deep within him, and if it wasn't for a bit of unease at feeling such a thing, he'd be having a much harder time resisting the urge to hold her. "Do you have a favorite?"

"That's a toughie...but right now I'd say the elderberry," Hunnie told her.

"I wish I could do something this creative," Gigi lamented, letting the smile fall from her face. "I'm kind of a disaster in the kitchen."

Holden opened his mouth to comment, but Hunnie beat him to it.

"Oh please, you totally could do it!" Hunnie responded. "I'm not saying it's without a learning curve, but there's no reason you couldn't figure it out."

"That's so sweet of you to say, but I've recently tried to take up baking, and it's not going very well. I mixed up a couple of ingredients this morning and about made everyone choke," Gigi told her, a strangled little laugh at the end.

"Baking is hard. I once mixed up the salt and sugar, and boy, were we all in for a rude surprise on that first bite!"

"I mixed up the baking powder and the baking soda."

"I've done that too!"

A feeling of relief washed over Holden as he watched the exchange between Gigi and Hunnie. He tried to hide his smile as he listened to this complete stranger tell her all about how she had made the exact mistake Gigi had this morning, and how her family now laughs about it. A sense of hope filled him, wanting to make sure that Gigi heard every word that Hunnie was telling her. When the idea came to him that talking with some of the vendors here about their process might help Gigi find some inspiration, he'd never thought that the first vendor they came upon would be this helpful. Had he known what a gold mine Hunnie's Honey was going to be, they would have made a beeline for here and gotten donuts later.

"Really?" Gigi asked.

"Yes!" Hunnie exclaimed.

Jackpot…

GIGI

"There's lots of trial and error in everything," Hunnie continued. "You should have seen me trying to learn this process. First time I played around with the chili pepper honey, I left the chilis in too long. I couldn't taste anything else for *days*. I've just now gotten to a place where I can laugh about it."

Gigi couldn't believe what she was hearing. Was this adorable hippie really telling her all about her failures? It had already been a relief to hear that someone else had made the same mistake with the baking powder and baking soda. But listening to Hunnie talk about how it had taken a bunch of failed attempts to get her product right made Gigi feel a glimmer of hope. Like maybe she really could be good at this.

Sneaking a glance at Holden, she felt her insides warm up. He stood only a few inches from her, picking up jar after jar and looking at each one curiously. She knew he was trying to look nonchalant, like he wasn't listening to the conversation she was having with Hunnie, but she would bet anything he was. The heat that was radiating off his body made her want to snuggle into his side, but she reminded herself that this wasn't a date. Not only did she barely know the guy, he was her landlord. Oh yeah, and she was still married. Still, she couldn't help but wonder what it would be like to have those strong arms wrap around her or what his beard would feel like against her lips.

You did not just think about kissing another man, Gigi!

"I'm happy to hear that I'm not the only one who has had a couple of mishaps," Gigi said, bringing her thoughts back to the matter at hand.

"Not even close! Here, take this," Hunnie said, handing her a small jar of honey. "And here's my card. My number is on there—call any time you need to share a kitchen disaster! Don't be shy!"

"Thank you! I might just take you up on that."

Gigi stuck the jar in the front pocket of her hoodie as they walked away from Hunnie's booth, making room for more customers. She could feel Holden's big hand on the small of her back as he guided her back to the walking path, and she reveled in the comfort of it. It'd been a long time since a man had placed his hand there simply out of being a gentleman, rather than trying to control her. She wanted to lean back into his touch but didn't want to make things awkward. What would she even tell him if he questioned her behavior? Sorry, it's been forever since someone else's skin on mine wasn't leaving a bruise? No, she couldn't say that. She didn't need him knowing that about her. Right now it was enough to simply not be afraid of his touch.

"I'd ask if you put her up to that, but you don't really seem like the type to orchestrate such a thing," Gigi said, turning to look at Holden once they were out of hearing distance from the booth. He removed his hand from her back, sticking it in his pocket, and she instantly missed it. She had to remind herself that it would be rude to ask him to put it back, no matter how much she craved the feeling.

"I've never seen her before in my life," Holden laughed. "However, she makes some excellent points."

"I guess," Gigi said, shrugging slightly.

"You guess? Gigi, did you not hear her talk about how she couldn't taste anything for *days* after trying to make a honey with chili peppers?"

"Yes, I did," she sighed. "But that's different. She already knew about honey. Her family runs a honey farm! You know what my family does? I come from a long line of socialites. We excel at making lunch reservations and going shopping."

The words sounded a lot more condescending than she had intended. She had wanted to try and make a joke out of the sad situation she was in, but apparently, she couldn't even do that. A desire to open up to Holden bubbled within her, but every time she went to say something, she lost her nerve. She felt so foolish around him. Here he was, this beautiful, confident man, who'd now seen her through two major failures. She was lucky he wasn't laughing at her. Or worse, kicking her to the curb. She had no idea what his story was, but it was obvious he didn't *need* a tenant to make ends meet.

The sounds of shouts made them turn just in time to see a group of preteen boys speed toward them on bicycles. Gigi froze in place, so taken aback by their sudden presence that she had no idea how to respond. Holden grabbed her hand and pulled her out of the way, just as the boys went whizzing by. Just as before, his skin was warm against hers, and there was a tingle from the contact. She felt her whole body react to the small gesture, and took a long, deep breath, trying to steady her racing heart.

"You okay?" he asked, looking into her eyes, his own full of concern. For the first time since they'd met, she took a moment to stare into his eyes, noticing all the different shades woven together to create a beautiful aqua hue. The strands of blue with a touch of green mixed together so perfectly, and she knew that it wouldn't take much to get lost in his gaze. He gave her hand a light squeeze, sending a jolt rushing through her, breaking the spell she was under from being so close to him.

"Yeah, they just startled me," she said, turning to start walking again. He followed her lead but kept her hand in his. She couldn't tell if it was because he felt the need to hold on to her like a parent did a small child or if it was because he enjoyed the closeness as much as she did. Allowing herself to think it was the latter, she smiled secretly, hoping he didn't notice her slightly giddy expression.

"I think you just need some more trial and error," he finally said after a few moments of walking in silence.

"There is only so much trial and error I can have before I lose my job. After today I think Roderick might be on to me, and all I can do is pray he doesn't tell Audrey and Zara."

"What if you had a test subject? Someone you could use as your guinea pig to try out recipes on. That way you wouldn't have to do it at the café?"

"I'm not sure I know anyone who is that much of a glutton for punishment," she said, laughing. "Unless you're volunteering for the job."

"I am."

His words stopped her in her tracks. Did he really just say that? He had to be joking. There was no way he'd subject himself to being her taste tester. If he knew what was good for him, he'd run the other way.

"What?"

"I'll be your test subject," he offered. "Just don't poison me."

"Not funny, Holden!" she said. She knew he meant it as a joke, not realizing how afraid she was of that actually happening.

"Sorry," he said, a coy smile taking up his face. His eyes lit up in a way she'd never seen from him, highlighting those blue strands again. The expression in them had always been so solemn that she had no idea they could light up like this. She had no idea why, but hearing this idea excited her even more, sending a whole new rush through her. "But really, how hard can it be? We can watch some YouTube videos, pick out some recipes—we'll figure it out together."

"Really?" she squealed.

"Really."

Before she knew what she was doing, Gigi launched herself at Holden, wrapping her arms around his neck and pulling him close. Why on earth he would volunteer to do this was beyond her, but she was so excited that he was willing to help that his motives didn't really matter. When he returned the embrace, she took a moment to relax into him, enjoying the closeness. His body was hard against hers, yet soft and welcoming. Those strong arms felt even better wrapped around her than she imagined, only adding to this moment. Bradley's arms had never felt like this.

Coming back to her senses, she released him and took a step

back, hoping that he couldn't see her blushing. "I promise you won't regret this!"

"That's the part that my pants are concerned about," he said with another laugh.

Gigi pressed her lips together, stopping herself from making some sort of quip about his pants. It was perfectly obvious that he meant gaining weight, and *not* something sexual, but she couldn't help herself. That hug had knocked something loose deep inside her, and the blush she could feel creeping up her neck was more than telling. She was going to spend the rest of the night thinking about just what Holden St. James had in his pants.

8

GIGI

Sitting at the kitchen table with both their heads huddled over Holden's tablet felt oddly natural. Like this is how they spent all their Saturday afternoons. More than once in the hour they'd been sitting here, Gigi had let her mind wander, picturing the scene as if it were some kind of Norman Rockwell painting. Is this the kind of thing she'd been missing her whole life? That maybe if she'd spent a few more Saturdays like this, just hanging out, that her life might not have gotten so far off track.

Oh, who was she kidding? This was never the track of her life. No one in her family would have ever spent a day searching for recipes and laughing about some of the names people had created for dishes. Not to mention, Bradley wouldn't have been caught dead helping her with such a project.

"Georgia, I don't have time for whatever silly little pet project you're working on now," he would have told her. "I have actual important things to focus on."

Yeah, like schmoozing clients on the golf course...

"Earth to Gigi," Holden said, snapping his fingers in front of her face, trying to get her attention. She hadn't realized that she had slipped off so deeply into her own thoughts. Poor Holden must think she was a space cadet.

"Sorry, lost in thought," she replied, smiling innocently.

"The grasshopper cake sounds easy enough, yes?" he said, acting as if he were repeating it.

"Yeah, but Bradley doesn't really like mint, so…" she started, but then trailed off as the realization hit her. It didn't really matter what he liked, now did it? He had absolutely no say in any of this. A spark of excitement lit inside her, and she shivered at the thought. This is why she had done all this—so she didn't have to consider him in everything—and she liked that more than she could say. "Except he's not here, so I guess his opinion doesn't matter. So yes, let's do the grasshopper!"

"How long has he been gone?" Holden asked.

"Oh, um, just a few months," she answered. She had always known that she would be asked at some point, and she had the whole story practiced and ready. But the longer she'd been here in town without having to tell her tale, the more she thought she'd never have to.

"So you left right after he passed."

"Well, not the split second, but shortly after. I needed out," she answered. *I needed out* were the three most truthful words she'd said in a long time, and it felt good to have them out there. Even if the full weight of them was still a secret.

"How long were you married?"

"Ten years. I was just out of college when our parents introduced us. Well, 'introduced' maybe isn't the right word. I knew who he was. Our families have known each other for years, but Bradley was four years older than me, so we never overlapped in school. He was one of those older guys that every girl crushed on, even though they didn't really have any idea that we existed. Bradley had started working for my father's investment firm while I was at Alabama, and then when I graduated, our parents thought it would be a good idea for us to 'officially meet.' He asked me out, and two years later we were married."

"Sounds more like a business transaction than a love affair," Holden murmured. Gigi's heart sank at his words, not wanting to admit just how right he was.

"Sometimes it was in our social circles," she said. "But not for me. I was head over heels for that man. He was good-looking and charming, had a good job. All the things a young southern socialite looks for in a husband. We were happy, at least in the beginning."

"Things changed?"

"Don't they always?" she shrugged. Holden's blue eyes had a look in them she couldn't place. It was one of concern and comfort, yet wary at the same time. She wanted to know what was going through his head, if he was really interested in knowing about her and Bradley's story or if he was just making conversation. Either way, she knew she had to be careful with what she said. As amazing as Holden was proving to be, she still wasn't sure she could trust anyone with the truth. "But that's all behind me now."

"Should I be worried about who is currently sitting at my kitchen table? You're not on the run from the law, are you?" he joked.

"No, I'm not running from the *law*," she retorted. *Just my abusive husband*. Gigi looked Holden up and down, taking him in for what must have been the hundredth time since they sat down at this table. He seemed so trustworthy, and he'd already done so much for her. "Truth?"

"That is generally preferable."

Keep it simple and as close to the truth as possible...she reminded herself.

"I knew my family would not be supportive of putting Bradley behind me. Of wanting to find myself and be independent. I had the chance to walk away and prove that I am more than just a pretty face and a great hostess, and I took it. But that choice is not one that everyone understands." And it was the truth. Abbot and Marnie Shaw were not the kind of people to understand wanting to go your own way. Which was probably why they had made no effort to contact her in the weeks since she'd taken off. Or at least she assumed they had made no effort—it's not as if she left a forwarding address. However, after the embarrassment she was sure she'd caused them by disappearing the way she had, she was positive that there would be no welcome back into their good graces. If it wasn't for her already cashed out trust fund, she had no doubt she would be completely defunded as well. "Besides, the Shaws aren't those kind of people."

"And just what kind of people are the Shaws?" he asked, leaning back in his chair. His ice-blue eyes were curious, yet welcoming, and made Gigi want to continue to spill all her secrets.

"The Shaws and the Hawthornes are see and be seen kind of people," she laughed, trying to brush it off. For as much as she wanted to open up to Holden, she knew she couldn't tell him everything.

Holden's face was still for a moment as he took in her words. A nervous feeling took over Gigi as she waited for some kind of reaction from him. Would he understand it? Or would he just look at her like so many others and think "poor little rich girl." Gigi didn't think she could stand it if he did think that. He was the first person in a long time that she felt could maybe see her for, well, her. But the longer that blank expression sat on his face, the more she thought maybe she was wrong. It wouldn't have been the first time she'd been wrong about a man. It had taken her years to see her mistake with Bradley though.

"I get it," he finally said. Gigi let out a sigh of relief, hoping she wasn't too obvious about how much she'd been awaiting his answer. "Families don't always understand the choices you make, even if you know it's for your own good."

"You say that like you have experience in the subject," Gigi said, trying to turn the conversation off of her. She still knew very little about Holden, and all this sharing about her situation made her want to start asking questions of her own.

"I have some. My family doesn't fully understand why I left the game."

"The game?"

"Soccer, football, whatever you want to call it. I played for Chelsea over in the UK for a while."

"You played professional soccer?" she said, trying to hide the shock in her voice. Narrowing her eyes, she looked at him closer, trying to figure out if she recognized him. Bradley had watched a lot of soccer a number of years ago when he was trying to win over some big deal British client. Liverpool had been the team of choice. In fact, it was their loss in the championship that had led to....

"I did," he answered. His simple words pulled her back into the moment, and away from memories she had no business revisiting.

"And you just up and quit?"

"Something like that."

"But why?" She knew she was prying, but she couldn't help herself. She wanted to know everything about this man sitting across from her.

"It just didn't seem right to keep playing after...." he trailed off.

"After..."

"After losing my wife."

HOLDEN

Well, that was something Holden hadn't expected to reveal this afternoon. Hell, it wasn't something he'd ever expected to tell Gigi. But there was something about her and the vulnerability she was showing him that made him want to show her she wasn't alone. That there was someone else who understood her.

"You lost your wife? You're a widower?" she asked, her face paling slightly.

"Yeah," he managed to get out. Now that it was out there it just hung like a heavy cloud, and he didn't know what else to say. Maybe this was not the way he should have gone about this. It's not like he needed this to be something they had in common, something for them to bond over. He hadn't talked about Hannah to anyone in years. Not since that last therapist he'd seen. The one who had suggested he find a hobby—to cultivate a new passion. Except there was no passion without Hannah.

"Can I ask what happened?" Gigi reached across the table, taking his hand as if they were old friends. The warmth of her touch was welcoming and spread throughout his entire body, catching him off guard. It'd been so long since another person's touch had made him feel anything, and he had no idea what to do with it.

"Home invasion gone wrong. Police believe it was a bunch of druggies looking for cash, or something easy enough to convert into cash, and didn't realize anyone was home," he told her. Closing his eyes, he let the usual feeling of guilt wash over him as he thought about how she shouldn't have been home alone that night. That if he'd been there with her, how everything would be different now. He felt a light squeeze on his hand and realized that Gigi was still holding it. Looking down at the connection, he noticed just how dainty her hand was. It fit so perfectly into his, and he liked the idea of it staying right there.

"I'm so sorry, Holden," Gigi said, tears filling her eyes. Gone was the skittish look she'd had earlier when talking about her own family. But what replaced it surprised him more than a little. It wasn't the same look of pity that most people gave him. It was one of simple sadness that only someone else who mourned a partner could understand.

"What was her name?" Gigi asked, just above a whisper after a long moment of silence.

"Hannah," he whispered in return. Usually just the mention of her name brought along with it an unescapable pain. However, in this moment, with Gigi's hand in his, the pain was somehow less. Like she had some magical powers absorbing it. Before he knew what he was doing, the words started tumbling out of his mouth. "First time I saw her was across the quad our sophomore year. I was kicking around a ball with some teammates, and she was leaning up against a tree drawing. I went up to her, made a bad joke about 'drawing me like one of your French girls' and when she actually laughed, I asked if I could buy her coffee. We got married a couple of weeks after graduation and moved over to London a couple of years later. Life was pretty good."

"Until it wasn't?"

"Until it wasn't," he responded. He could feel the weight of it all starting to close in on him. Pressing his fingertips over his heart, he tried to rub away some of the ache he felt. He could still see the nursery they had set up in the London flat. Hannah had promised not to go too overboard with the pink when they had found out they were having a girl. What he hadn't accounted for was Hannah's love of children's literature and for her nesting to take the form of a massive mural on the wall opposite the window. She'd spent weeks debating which theme to go with, before finally settling on Winnie the Pooh.

Pushing up from the table, it only took him a few strides before reaching the butcher block. He wanted to slam his fist down on the hard wood, making him feel something other than the pain ripping through his chest at the loss of his girls. But he didn't want to scare Gigi. Poor, sweet Gigi who had no idea who she was really dealing with. The thought flitted through his head, wondering if she would trust him so much to help her if she knew just how much he had failed Hannah.

"Holden, you don't have to talk about it if it hurts too much,"

Gigi told him, her sweet southern accent washing over him, comforting him in a way.

"No, it's fine," he gritted out. "You opened up to me. It's only fair."

A look flashed over her face, making him think for a moment that there was something she still wasn't telling him. But it was gone before he could comment, replaced with a sympathetic smile. "This isn't a competition, Holden."

Ignoring her words, he turned around to face her, taking in her beautiful features. There was a part of him that wanted to rush over and kiss her for being so understanding, and another part of him that wanted to scream at her. Kissing Gigi was the last thing he needed to be doing while thinking about Hannah.

"Hannah was seven and a half months pregnant." The sound of her gasp filled his ears, but it wasn't enough to stop him. He needed to get this out. "After they were killed, I couldn't stay there. I couldn't play the game anymore. My heart just wasn't in it. So I came back here."

"To your family?"

"Oh no," he said, a sad chuckle escaping. "Don't get me wrong. My family was nothing but supportive. Maybe a little too much so. Uncle Field had lost Aunt Viv a few years prior, so of course he was the expert on dealing with loss and moving on. None of them were willing to just let me grieve in my own way."

"Which was?"

"Holing up in this old house and hiding from the world," he shrugged in response as he rejoined her at the table, not knowing what else to tell her. It was the truth. He wanted nothing to do with the outside world anymore, and up until she arrived in town a couple of weeks ago, he'd had no interest in ever talking to anyone either. What she had done to change that, he still wasn't sure. This was really not where he had seen the afternoon going. This was supposed to be about picking out recipes to help her. Not about them learning each other's deepest secrets. He wasn't supposed to be sitting here wondering what else this beauty had up her sleeve and why on earth she made him feel so alive.

"Don't shrug it off," she said, squeezing his hand again. The same warmth from earlier flooded his system again, and he had to take a deep breath, trying to keep calm. "I get it. Picking up the pieces isn't easy."

The pang of understanding that hit Holden made his pulse race. He liked knowing that Gigi got it—that she got him. He liked it maybe a little too much. Looking at her now, he saw more than just the hapless widow who'd almost burned down his carriage house. He saw someone much stronger.

"That it's not," he said, pulling his hand away from hers. He needed to get a grip. He needed to get them back on track. Back into whatever zone it was where he wasn't picturing holding Gigi against him like he had the other night at the festival. Just because she had felt better than he could have possibly imagined didn't mean that he was allowed to keep thinking about it. Especially after he'd just told her all about Hannah. "So, back to recipes."

"Right," she agreed, a little too quickly for his liking.

See, she's not interested in you like that, so stop it.

"I think we've got some good ones. I can run to the store tomorrow morning, and we can try the first one out after that?" she asked.

"Do you want me to go to the store with you?" he asked.

"No, I got it," she said, pushing up from the table. "I mean, how much damage can I do at a grocery store?" Laughing lightly, she added, "Actually, maybe I should take that back. I best not tempt fate."

"Well, you know where to find me if you change your mind."

"I do, thank you," she said, turning to head up the stairs to her room before pausing and turning back around. "And thank you for opening up to me about Hannah. I know that wasn't easy."

9

HOLDEN

Never in his life had Holden ended a run more confused than when he'd started it. Running had always served as a method to clear out the cobwebs or whatever was clouding his brain in the moment. Apparently not today, however. Of course, most of those runs had been before he'd met GeorgiaGrace Hawthorne as well.

Yesterday had not gone how he had envisioned. They were just supposed to pick out recipes. Maybe have a few laughs to help brighten her mood. It wasn't supposed to turn into them opening the door into their lives, their histories, and learning about each other. He hadn't meant to unload on her about Hannah that way. He also certainly hadn't meant to spend the rest of the night thinking about holding Gigi close and kissing away the pain he saw in her eyes. No good could come of him thinking about how she was just the right size to fit in his arms—and about all the things he wanted to do to her while she was there.

Still, he felt like he'd only scratched the surface with Gigi. He wanted to know more about her, about everything she'd left behind and what she wanted for her future. He even almost wanted to tell her about himself. She'd thanked him for opening up to her. Who did that? Only other people who knew what it was like to go through such a loss. Except, no matter which way he thought about it, Holden got the distinct impression that maybe Gigi's loss wasn't quite like his. Like her losing her husband was actually a good thing. He'd lost his entire world when his girls were stolen from him—Gigi seemed to be determined to find her world now that Bradley was gone. From the very little she'd told him, her late husband did not seem like a nice guy. Even if she'd never come out and said it, he saw it in her eyes and in her skittish actions whenever she was around others. There was a fear there that he didn't quite understand and probably never would.

Opening the front door to the house, he was immediately assaulted by the sounds of some bubble-gum pop music blasting from the kitchen. It was a complete one-eighty from the heavy metal he'd been listening to on his run, and he couldn't help but bristle a little from the change. Although the sweet, female voice that was singing along with the auto–tuned pop artist did have the rest of his body alert and paying very close attention.

"Hey!" Gigi called out enthusiastically as he walked into the kitchen. She was already wearing a frilly teal apron over her T-shirt and jeans, her beautiful blonde hair pulled up into a messy bun, looking like she was ready to tackle whatever the kitchen threw at her. All sorts of ingredients were strewn across the counter, haphazardly placed, with what seemed like little to no organization at all. "How was your run?"

"Fine," he answered, still taking in the whole scene in the kitchen. He wanted to laugh, because every inch of this disorganization screamed Gigi to him, but he knew that would not be received well. Looking back at her, he gave her a bright smile. She looked so fucking cute in that apron. *Stop it, she's not here for you to ogle her.* "I see you made it to the grocery okay."

"I can grocery shop!" she said defensively.

"I didn't realize that real housewives went grocery shopping," he joked.

"I was not a real housewife! Those women are…something else entirely."

Holden barked out a laugh at her response. It was the first time that Gigi had said something even remotely disparaging about someone else, and even in her attempt, she was still nice as could be about it.

"I was going to put everything away, but I wasn't a hundred percent sure where it all went, and I didn't want to do it wrong."

"There is so little in these cupboards these days that I'm not really sure there is a system. So, have at it!" he told her. The smile that took over her face could have rivaled a kid at Christmas, and Holden couldn't stop himself from laughing a little. Had he known all it would take to get that kind of smile out of her was to let her organize a kitchen, he would have done that the day she moved in. "I'm going to take a shower and then we can start. Cool?"

"Cool," she repeated.

Turning to head up the back stairs, he paused on the first step, turning back to her. "Think we could listen to something a little… a little less teenybopper when I get back though?"

"You did not just say that about Queen Tay. Hashtag T Swift for life!" she told him.

"Got it!" he replied, as he finished making his way up the stairs.

After the quickest shower he could manage, Holden rushed back down the stairs into the kitchen. He was surprised to find the whole place looking like a scene from a magazine. All the bags and boxes that had been strewn about just moments before were now tucked away in their new homes, and all the counters seemed to have been wiped down. The only things that were still out were all the basic ingredients for a chocolate cake.

"I thought this recipe called for box cake mix? Or did you decide not to start with the Better Than Sex cake?" he asked, watching Gigi mix the ingredients together. Her cheeks flushed as he said the cake's name, just as they had yesterday. Watching her blush like this was easily one of the cutest things he'd ever seen, and like hell if he wasn't going to keep trying to make it happen.

"It does, but that felt like cheating. Besides, it's not like I can use a box at the Busy Bean. Trust me, I've considered it."

"That's fair. So, not to tell you how to do this, Gigi, but you know the oven isn't on, right?"

"Yeah, I was a little afraid to touch it. Didn't want to burn down this house too," she admitted. Her words came out sounding sassy, but the slightly sheepish look on her face betrayed that there was at least some truth to her statement.

"You're not going to burn down the house by pre-heating an oven," he told her as he pressed the button on the appliance.

Gigi stopped mixing and just stared at him, a blank expression on her face. After a moment, she stretched out her hand to him, as if they were meeting for the first time.

"Hi, I'm GeorgiaGrace Elyse Hawthorne, née Shaw. Like Shaw Investments, not Shaw flooring. That's a whole different set of Shaws," she giggled. He could tell that this was a very well-rehearsed line of hers, and she could have recited it in her sleep. He also had no idea where she was going with this. "Anyway, when I fail, I do it *spectacularly*, as evidenced by your carriage house. Also, you told me I wasn't allowed to bake anything unless you were here." The saccharine smile she shot him as she finished screamed "so there!"

Holden shifted slightly on his feet as he felt a rush of blood head straight for his dick. He had no idea where this version of her had come from, but fuck if he didn't like it. The smile still tugging at her pretty pink lips made him want to reach over the butcher block and kiss it right off of her and show her just what she could do with all this sass. Instead, he opted to play into it and see if maybe she felt the sizzle in the air too.

"Admit it. You were really just worried that this cake isn't better than sex, and that you were going to need me for research," he said, giving her a wink.

"I'm sure the cake is indeed better than sex," she replied, her tone just as cheeky as his.

Holden opened his mouth to respond and then stopped himself. *Did she just say that she thinks the cake is going to be better than sex? No, you misheard her. There was no way cake was better than sex…*

"I seem to have misheard you. You think a cake is going to be better than sex?" he asked, dumbfounded.

"I've never understood the hype around sex. I mean, who cares? It's not that good," she told him with a shrug, pouring the cake batter into the glass pan she'd pulled out.

"You don't like sex?"

"Nope."

Holden blinked a couple of times, still not fully understanding. How was it that this stunning creature didn't like sex? Had her marriage been *that* bad?

"How do you not like sex? Everyone likes sex."

"No, not everyone," she said, like it was completely obvious. "What's there to get so excited about? It's not like it is on TV…all passionate and sweaty. He climbs on top, goes 'uh uh' a couple of times, and it's over. Big deal!"

Is that what she thought sex was? He'd gotten the impression that her marriage hadn't been something that romance novels were made of, but it couldn't have been that devoid, could it?

"Um, foreplay?" he suggested, letting his mind wander to all the dirty things one could possibly do. Images of Gigi splayed out on his bed filled his mind, as he kissed and worshipped her body. His dick twitched again just thinking about how she would taste and feel underneath him, writhing in pleasure. The urge to kiss her returned, and it was taking way more self-control than it should to hold himself back in this moment.

"Bradley wasn't into that. He was just a 'main event' kind of guy." She shrugged, almost as if in defeat, and it was more than Holden could take.

It took him two steps to round the butcher block and pull Gigi into him. For a brief moment he wondered if he should stop, but the look in her eyes and the gasp that escaped her as their bodies met told him that she was feeling this too. Her hands met his chest, slowly inching up his pecs, as if he had braille printed there and she wanted to make sure she felt every word. He tightened his grip on her hips and gazed into her gray eyes. They were filled with wonder, seemingly excited about where this was going to lead. He had no idea what he was doing, but listening to her talk about sex like it had been some kind of marital obligation left him feeling like he needed to do something.

"Bradley was a dumbass," Holden said, not daring to unlock their gaze. The electricity surrounding them now was palpable, and feeling Gigi relax into him only fueled his fire even more. "Sex isn't just mechanically inserting P into V. It's heat, and passion, and desire. It's communicating with your body what words can't say."

"Yeah?" she asked, breathless. "Like what?"

"Like this…" he said, tilting his head, lowering it slowly. The anticipation was killing him. He wanted nothing more in this moment than to devour her. But he wouldn't do that. This was the first time she hadn't shied away from his touch, and he wanted to make it good. So fucking good that she spent the rest of the day thinking about it. He paused, their lips a breath away from each other, stretching the moment out.

BEEEEEP!

GIGI

Gigi startled at the sound of the oven, jumping back from Holden. Cold air rushed around her, making her instantly miss the heat from his body, but she knew it was for the best. Letting herself get so caught up in the moment was a bad idea.

"Oven's preheated," she managed to say, sounding a lot more

breathless than she intended. She was feeling more than a little pre-heated herself in this moment.

Get it together, Gigi. This is not how an independent woman acts. She does not get all weak-kneed and giddy just because some guy got flirty with her and maybe almost kissed her.

Grabbing the cake pan, she slid it in the oven, ignoring Holden's presence. Maybe if she pretended it didn't happen, then she could get her heart to stop racing. Oh, who was she kidding? Her heart was always beating a little faster if he was around. He did things to her she hadn't felt since college. Hell, he'd brought out a sassy side she hadn't let fully show since…well, longer than she cared to try to think about.

"Okay, so while that's baking, I need to make the whipped cream," she said, trying to get her head back on straight. Holden grabbed the carton of cream from the fridge and poured it into a mixing bowl before handing her the whisk. Their fingers grazed each other's lightly as she took the utensil from him, sending shocks through her body. How was it that an almost kiss had left her so on edge? "Now, says here to just beat it until it's stiff," she read from the recipe on the tablet.

Holden bit back a laugh just as Gigi realized what she had said. Well darn it, now he was going to think that her mind was in the gutter.

"Beat it until it's stiff and you'll have cream alright," he muttered, still trying not to laugh.

"Holden!"

"Sorry, I couldn't help it. You walked right into that one."

"I was just reading the directions!" she said, blushing even more. The giddiness that she had felt earlier rushed through her again, and this time she let herself enjoy it. She liked seeing this side of Holden, and she liked that she could let this side of her out. Maybe the new Gigi could be fun and flirty. She certainly didn't have to worry about who might be offended by a colorful comment or innuendo. Holden certainly wasn't holding back. Deciding to embrace the moment, she winked at him, letting a cheeky look take hold, and said, "Besides, I thought that if you beat it too hard then the whole thing collapsed."

The look Holden gave her was one of both shock and appreciation. There was no mistaking the fire in his eyes as he looked at her, trying to figure out his next move as if this were a game of chess. All Gigi could do was smirk in response and turn back to the task at hand.

"And here I was thinking that you were some sweet southern belle," he commented. "Underneath all that sugar is something a little more savory, huh?"

"There might be," she quipped playfully, still whisking away at the cream. She was having way more fun with this conversation than she should, but she was still amped up from that almost kiss. She really wanted to know what his lips tasted like. "Or maybe it's something more…spicy."

"I somehow doubt there is anything *spicy* about your *cupcakes*," he told her, that fire in his eyes still burning.

A flush of heat washed over her, making her stumble slightly in her whisking. There were so many things she wanted to say in return, but she also didn't want to push this too far. Not that she was really sure where the line actually was. The most flirtatious thing she'd done in the last ten years was the requisite good business-wife giggle. That was what they were doing here, right? Flirting? She was pretty sure. He *had* almost kissed her.

"Maybe I'll let you have a bite so you can see for yourself."

"Gigi, I'll gladly taste whatever you give me," he said, his voice suddenly low and rough. It sent a thrill through her, and she licked her lips just thinking about what he could mean by that.

Turning back to the oven, not wanting to get caught off guard by the timer again, her heart sank a little when she saw there were only thirty seconds left. That didn't really leave any more time for coded messages and innuendos, even though she was dying to see what else they could come up with. When the timer dinged, she pulled the cake out and put it on top of the oven, so it could cool like the recipe called for. Grabbing the mixing bowl and whisk from where she had set them next to the oven, she spun back around, trying to think of a clever comeback to Holden's last statement about tasting. All thoughts about being cute and sassy disappeared a half second later though, when she lost her balance mid-twist, sending her straight to the floor.

Gigi landed on her side with a thump and the sound of the mixing bowl shattering. She felt the cool, whipped cream splash across her entire body and face as she landed, making the moment that much more embarrassing. Only she could screw up something as simple as turning around. Before she had a chance to react, Holden was crouched down by her side, helping her sit up.

"Oh, for heaven's sake!" she cursed.

"You okay?" he asked, a look of concern having replaced the heat in his eyes from a moment ago.

"Never better!" she said, trying to wipe the mess off her face. "That was totally my signature move. Don't act like you're not impressed."

"Totally impressed. You really nailed the landing. Although we're still waiting on the score from the French judge—they may deduct a few points for style," he joked.

"Leave it to the French," she laughed, loving that he was going along with her on this and not making her feel like she'd failed at something else. "But I made a mess."

"Don't worry about it. It's not something that can't be cleaned," he said, swiping at her cheek with his thumb. When he pulled his hand back, she saw it was covered in whipped cream. He slowly brought his thumb to his mouth and licked the cream right off. No, licking wasn't the right term. It was somewhere between a lick and a kiss. Gigi had no idea what to call it, but watching those lips caress the pads of his thumb like that made her all kinds of hot and bothered. Her eyes locked on his as he did this, and for the life of her, she couldn't look away. She wanted him to do exactly that to her. More than she wanted her next breath.

Slowly, Holden leaned in, closing the gap between them. Gigi sucked in a breath, hoping, praying that this time he didn't hesitate like he did before. As if he could hear her thoughts, Holden slipped the hand that had just been at his lips behind her head and pulled her into him, their lips meeting fast and hard.

For as sudden as his initial move had been, his next was soft and tentative as he slowly moved his lips against hers. Gigi felt as if her insides were going to burst into flames as he continued to move like this, drawing her in even closer. His lips were tender and rough all at the same time, and he tasted like nothing she had ever experienced before, but now that she had, she couldn't imagine not having it again. The tickle of his beard against her face sent her soaring, one new sensation after another. Is this what kissing someone was supposed to feel like? Like she was floating off somewhere, tethered to nothing but this other person, sending new pulse waves of delight through her? Each second this continued got better and better, and Gigi thought that she would be more than happy to never, ever let this moment end.

After a long moment that still was not long enough, Holden pulled back. Gigi hated for the kiss to end, but at the same time, she needed a moment to recover. No one had ever kissed her like that. Not even on her wedding day. She ran her fingers along her lips, which felt a tad swollen from Holden's attention. But she didn't care. She was still too high from it all.

"You had some whipped cream on your lip," he said, clearing his throat. He suddenly seemed nervous and unsure how to act around her. It was the complete opposite to how he'd been all afternoon, and Gigi suddenly worried she had done something wrong. What if he didn't think the kiss was as good as she did? What if she did something wrong? Pushing up to his feet, he pulled her up as well. A small, almost shy smile tugged at his beautiful mouth as he looked at her and said, "But don't worry. I think I got it all."

10

GIGI

"Hi!" Audrey's voice called out as she entered the Busy Bean's kitchen.

"Hey!" Gigi said back, her southern drawl such a contrast to Audrey's northern accent. At least it was her accent making her stand out this time, though, and not a kitchen failure.

She was two weeks into her personal baking challenge and was actually feeling pretty good about herself. These two weeks had been filled with cakes, cupcakes, muffins, and other such treats, most of which had turned out spectacularly. Other than one slight mix-up with the salt and sugar in a batch of lemon poppy seed muffins, she hadn't messed up a recipe or burnt anything. She also hadn't poisoned Holden yet, which was a major win in her book.

It had also been two weeks since the "Better Than Sex" cake had almost led to actual sex. Or well, something that resembled it. That kiss had been the closest thing to sex that Gigi had experienced in months and was still infinitely better than every previous encounter she'd ever had. Kissing Holden had been unlike anything she'd ever experienced. It had been all-consuming. She had felt that kiss in every inch of her body, and it left her wanting more. So, so much more. She wanted to get lost in him and his kisses for the rest of time. How his strong hand had been so soft and gentle, so reassuring as he'd pulled her close, and yet had also been fierce and possessive was something she had replayed over and over in her head. She had felt safe in his hands. And safe was not something she had been used to feeling in regard to a man's hands. On top of that, the unique taste of him had lingered on her tongue for hours, so much so she'd almost been afraid to brush her teeth that night in fear of washing it away. Forget the cake. Holden was the best thing she'd ever tasted.

The only problem was it had also been two weeks without a repeat performance.

Carefully placing the little embellishments on the last of the cupcakes she was working on, Gigi stood up to find her boss staring at the tray, wide-eyed. The beautiful blonde's face lit up as she picked up one of the cupcakes, twisting her wrist around to look at the baked good.

"This is adorable! Is that a pumpkin?" Audrey asked.

"Sure is!" Gigi said proudly. "These are a spiced cake with a cream cheese frosting. So nothing weird, but I thought they could use a little seasonal décor."

She'd gotten the idea to sculpt little mini pumpkins and leaves to place on the treats while she and Holden had been watching TV the other night. Something about the combination of their awkward heart to heart about their spouses and the kiss that followed had opened the door to something she had never seen coming. A friendship.

"What do you mean you've never seen *It's the Great Pumpkin, Charlie Brown*?" he'd asked her the other night as she had been pulling a tray of muffins out of the oven.

"I mean I've never seen it. Why is that so hard to believe?" she asked in return, confused by how appalled he was over her never seeing a cartoon that was decades older than they were.

"Because everyone has seen the great pumpkin. It's a rite of passage!"

"Well, I haven't seen it," she sassed back at him.

Out of nowhere, Holden appeared behind her and swooped her up, like a groom carrying his bride over the threshold. She let out a little shriek of surprise as he did so, her arms flying around his neck, holding on tighter than she probably needed to. But the comforting feeling of his arms around her was not something she was going to take for granted.

"Where are you taking me?" she asked, as he walked through the dining room and into the front living room. He placed her on the old, worn sofa that was almost hidden up against the wall just past the door from the dining room.

"We're gonna watch it," he told her.

"There isn't a TV in here," she pointed out. She felt stupid for stating the obvious, but he was not making any kind of sense.

As if he hadn't even heard her, he crossed the room and grabbed a laptop from the table that sat adjacent to the front door. He wiggled it slightly, showing it off as he walked back toward her and slumped down on the couch.

"The Internet is an amazing thing, sweetheart," he said with a wink. She could feel herself flush slightly at the moniker, but she loved it all the same. It made her feel special. It made her feel like she maybe was becoming as important to him as he was to her. She knew that it had taken a lot for him to share what he had about Hannah as well, which only served in solidifying that feeling.

Not that either one had dared broach the subject of their marriages since that first conversation, but there was an understanding there that they both had some pain in the past that the other knew about. Gigi could tell there was more to the story of Hannah's death than Holden had told her, but she didn't want to push the issue. It wasn't like she was being completely forthcoming about Bradley only being dead in the metaphorical sense.

Nonetheless, going home to Holden every evening had become the highlight of her day. She loved telling him all about what had happened at the Busy Bean and swapping stories with him about some strange thing Kirk had done or something off the wall and colorful Roderick had said. Inevitably their conversation would turn to one or the other talking about their childhood or college, laughing the whole time. She never had this kind of camaraderie with Bradley, who'd never shared anything with her unless he was barking some kind of order. Holden, however, had no problem opening up. For as much as he wanted to let everyone think he was some kind of recluse who didn't need anyone, the man who sat at the kitchen table every night as she flitted around him showed her otherwise.

"They're adorable!" Audrey cooed. "And just what I came in to talk to you about!"

Gigi's stomach sank at Audrey's words. What had she messed up this time? Everything she had tasted herself had been good. All the comments she'd gotten from the customers had been positive as well. Even Kirk had told her yesterday that he liked the strawberry lemonade mini cake she'd made. Whatever it was though, she wasn't going to let it get to her. She had come a long way in becoming the independent woman she'd set sights on when she left Atlanta, and she wasn't about to slide backward now.

"Oh?" she asked as casually as she could manage, steeling herself for whatever came next.

"Yes! I've gotten a couple of requests from people wanting to buy desserts for Thanksgiving and wondering if we took orders for cakes. I wasn't sure what your schedule was or if you would be comfortable with that, so I wanted to check before I made a sign and started advertising it."

"Thanksgiving? Orders?" Gigi choked out. People wanted her to make the desserts for their Thanksgiving? *Holy cow...*

"Right?! It's so hard to believe that Thanksgiving is a little more than a week away. I swear yesterday was the Fourth of July!" Audrey said. "So, if it's cool with you, I was thinking we wouldn't overcomplicate this, but offer the option to purchase six or twelve cupcakes, and then a small cake or a bigger one? You can tell me what sizes you think would be easiest for you to bust out. I know this is kind of short notice, but I'd love it if you thought we could pull it off. Roderick makes cookies for every major holiday, and they're incredibly popular, but ever since Crumbs closed down, Colebury hasn't had anything like this. I'd love it if we could fill that hole. And maybe take some burden off of him. Last year I'm pretty sure he didn't sleep for a week trying to finish Christmas cookies." The smile that spread across her face was contagious, and Gigi couldn't stop herself from returning one just as big.

"Of course!" Gigi exclaimed, her mind still reeling from what her boss just told her. "Can we limit flavors as well? That way I can just make large batches of everything."

"Absolutely! I can't wait to tell Zara—she's going to be stoked!"

A thrill rushed through Gigi as this all started to sink in. She'd done it. She'd turned it all around and was making this whole baking thing a success. People wanted to special order her cakes—that was something that she would have laughed at just a month ago, and now…well, now it was a reality. She couldn't wait to get home and tell Holden.

"What are your Thanksgiving plans?" Audrey asked, plucking Gigi out of her thoughts. "If you don't have any, you're more than welcome to come join us."

The offer made Gigi stop in her tracks. She hadn't even considered what she would do for the holiday. She and Bradley had always joined their parents at the country club for the day, enjoying the large buffet and mingling with a number of personal and business acquaintances. She knew Audrey had married into a large family and that they lived just outside of town, but the idea of joining the Shipleys made her uneasy. Thinking of all those people who would be curious about her and her story. No, she would prefer a small meal with just her and Holden at the kitchen table.

Holden.

Suddenly an idea struck her, and a different kind of thrill rushed through her. She'd mastered the baking part of it, so how hard could the cooking part of it be?

"Thanks, but I already have plans."

Now, she just had to pull it off.

HOLDEN

The damn blinking cursor was taunting him again and Holden had no idea how to stop it. He'd spent the better part of the afternoon staring at the open document in front of him but hadn't typed more than a handful of words—all of which he'd then deleted—since he'd sat down. At this point, he'd give any one of his organs if he could just write *something*.

Mindlessly, he picked up the last of the crumbs from the Harvey Wallbanger cake that Gigi had made the other night and tossed them into his mouth. This cake had turned out incredible, and he had already told her at least twice that she needed to make it again. Of course, pretty much everything she had made these last couple of weeks had been good, causing him to add an extra mile to his daily run just to make sure it didn't start to catch up to him.

"Holden! Holden!" Gigi's sweet southern accent rang out from downstairs, the front door slamming behind her. Glancing down at the clock on his computer, he realized it was a lot later in the day than he thought. *Another day wasted on not writing.*

"Up in the loft," he hollered, hoping that his voice would carry down to her.

His life had changed so much since she'd waltzed her way into it—but he wouldn't change it for a second. Much to his surprise, he was enjoying having her around. He liked having the company inside the house. And not just the company, *her* company to be specific. Her bright smile and bubbly personality had come out more and more ever since he'd kissed her that day, and he was enjoying every second of getting to know her.

And then there was that kiss.

He knew he shouldn't have kissed her. But she had been so damn cute sitting on the kitchen floor, covered in whipping cream. The almost dejected look on her face had broken his heart, and the only thing he could think to do in that moment was kiss it off her. He'd been so amped up from all their flirting and innuendos all afternoon that he just couldn't help it. There hadn't been any blood left in his head for thinking—it had all rushed to his dick. But it wasn't fair to her. She'd just lost her husband; she didn't need another man kissing her. Even if the guy had been the biggest prick on earth—which from the very little Gigi had told Holden about him, he was pretty sure that he *had* been the biggest prick on earth—he didn't need to be making moves on her like that. Not to mention, he had his own wife's memory to be respecting.

But it had been one hell of a fucking kiss.

Footsteps on the stairs to the loft drew his eyes away from the screen in time to see Gigi pop up into the room. She looked as beautiful as always in her skinny jeans and fitted purple knit top. Her long blonde hair was falling loosely around her shoulders. She looked like some kind of angel as she skipped toward him.

"Oh my goodness, Holden! Guess what! Guess what! Guess what!" she squealed, almost jumping up and down as she reached his desk.

"What?" he said, sitting back in his chair. He'd never seen her anywhere near this excited, and he had no idea what could have possibly set her off like this.

"People want my cakes! The Busy Bean is going to be taking

orders for cakes and cupcakes for Thanksgiving! Isn't that amazing?!"

"Wow," he said. He suddenly felt nauseous at the mention of Thanksgiving. Was that already next week?

"It's gonna mean a bunch of extra hours this weekend, but still. People like my stuff enough to want to have it at their holiday meal!"

"That's incredible, Gigi. I'm excited for you."

Holden sucked in a deep breath as the room started to spin around him. He could hear that Gigi was still talking, but he had no idea what she was saying. It was like she was the teacher in a Peanuts cartoon—all he could hear was noise.

Thanksgiving had always been a big deal to Hannah. Holden had never understood exactly where her love of the holiday had come from, but there was no stopping it. She treated Thanksgiving like some people treated Christmas, with wreaths, pumpkins, gourds, and all sorts of other decorations that seemed to cover every inch of their home. If there had been such a thing as Thanksgiving music, Holden was sure she would have listened to it at full blast the second it was socially acceptable—and maybe even a little before. Even after they had moved to London, where traditional American Thanksgiving wasn't celebrated, she had found a way. She'd called it "friendsgiving" and gathered together a bunch of their neighbors and his teammates for a great big dinner the third weekend in November.

"This year's theme is Indian," she had told him as they sat at the breakfast bar in their kitchen, sipping on a glass of wine one night.

"That seems a little inappropriate," Holden had remarked, knowing full well what she really meant, but unable to stop himself from teasing her. He was also unsure of how she thought she was going to pull it off. She had taken to finding a new theme these last few years for what she started referring to as her "signature event." While the French food a couple of years prior had been very well received, last year's choice of Ethiopian had left something to be desired by most guests. Himself included. "Not sure they really condone the holiday."

"As in the Asian subcontinent, not Native Americans," she'd corrected him, giving him a look like she couldn't believe he went there. He laughed at her, taking a sip of his own drink and letting her continue. "I talked with Priti and Jatin from upstairs, and she gave me a bunch of recipes to try! It's gonna be so much fun!"

True to her word, the event had turned out to be a lot of fun. Holden couldn't remember the last time he had laughed as hard as that moment when his team captain, Nate Van Ryper, attempted to swallow that first bite of vindaloo. After managing to choke it down and immediately chugging his entire beer, the Dutchman had taken a moment to catch his breath before turning to Hannah.

"Just so I know, is everything on this table going to make me feel as if I'm swallowing fire?" he'd asked. Van Ryper's wife had smacked him with the back of her hand, as their goalkeeper and a pair of defensemen at the other end of the table started to snicker. "Because if it feels like that going in, I can't imagine what it's going to feel like coming out!"

The whole table had erupted into laughter as Hannah's face paled. Taking a bite of it herself, she'd quickly spit it out and muttered a not-so-quiet "fuck me!"

"I followed Priti's recipe to the letter!" she'd exclaimed in between gulps of water. "It never occurred to me that it would be this…this…"

"Potent?" Holden offered up.

"Yes!"

The table had erupted again, this time with not just laughter, but Hannah's profuse apologies and jokes about her almost killing half the starting line-up. When Van Ryper suggested that they box it up and send it up to Liverpool, who they believed to be the only team standing between them and the Cup that year, the howls of laughter probably could have been heard from space. After running to the local takeaway joint down the block and getting them something that the group wasn't afraid to eat, they'd settled in for some of the most fun they'd had since moving overseas.

"That'll teach me to get adventurous with food ever again," Hannah said that night as they had climbed into bed. Snuggling into him, she sighed softly, a sweet smile on her face. He pulled her close, kissing the top of her head.

"It was not one of your finer culinary achievements," he'd told her. "But I think we still had a pretty good night."

"Next year, I promise, we'll do that traditional thing," she'd told him. "And maybe not with so many people. I think I want our first one as a family to be just us."

"First one as a family?"

Hannah looked up at him, her eyes full of hope and a glow he'd never seen. The smile tugging on her lips was the one she had whenever she was about to spill a secret, and his heart skipped a beat as he started to process her words.

"I'm pregnant," she had whispered.

It was as if Holden's heart had stopped and sped up simultaneously. Pregnant. He was going to be a father.

"Seriously?" he'd asked, shifting to get a better look at her. She nodded slowly, that secret-spilling smile now taking over her entire face. "Then I am the luckiest fucking man on earth, and I already can't wait for next Thanksgiving."

A sinking feeling overwhelmed Holden as he thought back on his words that night. Had he known what he did now, he would have done so many things differently. He would never have gone out with the guys that night, never let Hannah convince him that she was fine to go home by herself. If he had just been a little less selfish, then he and Hannah could have had not only that first family Thanksgiving, but a whole bunch more.

"Does that sound like something you might want to do?" he heard Gigi ask through the fog in his head.

"Um, yeah. Sure," he said, not having any idea what he just agreed to.

"Squeeee!" she shrieked, bounding over to him and throwing

her arms around his neck. She smelled of baked goods, and he inhaled deeply, trying to chase away the monsters in his mind. Her warmth surrounded him, and he wanted to get lost in it. *No, dumbass, you cannot get lost in her. Not after thinking about your* wife. *Get it together.*

If only he had a way to do that.

11

HOLDEN

The sound of banging from the direction of the kitchen dragged Holden out of his nice, peaceful sleep. It had been a week since Gigi showed up in his office, bouncing up and down about he still didn't know what, sending him reeling back in time, leaving him in a funk ever since. Gigi had spent most of her time since at the Busy Bean, and while he'd missed their evenings together, he knew he probably would not have been the best of company.

Forcing himself into a half-sitting position, he glanced over at the clock. Nine sixteen, it told him. Why wasn't Gigi at the café? Had she mentioned a day off in the middle of the week and he'd just missed it? He needed to get his head together and fast. He snuggled back down into the pillows and closed his eyes, hoping that he could easily slip back into his slumber.

A heavy beat followed by the warble of a feminine voice abruptly started up, taking him from a state of still semi-asleep, to full-on awake. Forcing himself out of bed, he figured it was for the best anyway. The funk he'd been in had drained him to the point he hadn't been on a run in days, and he was starting to feel the effects. He needed to get out there and pound the pavement.

Maybe he could even add some distance to his normal route today, giving him more of a chance to clear his head. He quickly found his running gear, changed, and headed down to the kitchen.

Holden hit the bottom stair just as the song changed over to something a little slower, with a little more twang. He didn't know the details of Taylor Swift's back catalog, but if he had to guess, this one must have been from back when she still claimed to be a country artist. Either way, watching Gigi's gorgeous figure dance around to the melody was a sight that he was more than happy to see first thing. She stood up against the countertop, carefully reading a cookbook, dragging her finger across the page while swaying her luscious hips in time to the music. His hands itched to hold on to those curves as she moved, feeling the flow of her body against his.

"Hey, you," he said, flexing his hands as a reminder to keep them to himself.

"Ahhh!" she shrieked, turning around and clutching her chest. A bright smile spread across her face as she drank him in, making him feel all warm and fuzzy. It seemed impossible to him that she was doing this to him, in a way only one other woman had before, but he couldn't deny the attraction he felt for her. There was something special about Gigi Hawthorne, and whatever it was, he was damn glad it was being discovered in his kitchen. She reached for her phone and turned down the music before looking back up at him. "Are you just now heading out for your run? I figured you had left already."

"Got a bit of a late start this morning," he said. "What are you up to?"

"I chopped all the veggies last night, so I just need to finished prepping the bird and get it into the roasting pan and slide that into the oven. Then I can start on the sides. If all goes as planned, dinner should be around two-ish."

"Bird? Dinner?" Holden asked, his head starting to spin. She wasn't...

"It's Thanksgiving."

Thanksgiving.

It was like a switch flipped inside him. Holden clutched onto the counter as he looked around him, taking in everything she had laid out. He'd been so busy staring at her ass when he walked into the room, he hadn't noticed what she was surrounded by. Sure enough, a small turkey sat resting in a roasting pan on the butcher block. It looked like it had been slathered in butter mixed with herbs. Three distinct kitchen bowls sat next to the pan, filled with chopped carrots and celery, potatoes, and onion. Over on the counter by the cookbook she'd been reading was a bag of what appeared to be stale bread chunks for stuffing and a handful of sweet potatoes. He bet that if he looked in the fridge, he'd find she'd made a cake for dessert.

He could feel his blood start to boil as his eyes flicked between the items. Gigi was making *Thanksgiving*. What the fuck had given her that idea? Clenching his fists, he told himself to calm down. But the waves of rage that were rising inside were coming faster, and it didn't matter the reason. This was not happening in his house. How could she do this? How could she disrespect him in such a way and flaunt this holiday in his face? Nothing good came from this day, from this meal.

"Thanksgiving," he repeated, his teeth gritted. The word tasted vile in his mouth, leaving an aftertaste he was almost afraid he'd never get out. He swallowed hard, trying to replace that taste with something—anything—else, but he couldn't. The more he looked at the items on the counter, the angrier he got. They were just potatoes, for God's sake, but they taunted him just the same.

"I have all the traditional fixins. Roast turkey, stuffing, sweet potatoes, rolls, cranberry sauce, and of course, green bean casserole!"

Her voice was sweet, and the glow on her face was something that moments ago he would have done almost anything to see, but now, it only served to set him off more. He could feel something inside him snap, and all that rage he was trying to tamp down erupted from his veins.

"What the actual *fuck*." His palms came down hard on the butcher block. The pan and bowls rattled, their contents shifting from the disturbance.

"What?" she asked, a terrified look in her eyes.

"Are you kidding me?"

"I just...I just thought..." she squeaked, her voice trembling. He could see the fear in her as she cowered away from him, but there was no stopping him now.

"You just thought *what?*"

GIGI

"Holden, I..." Gigi trailed off, too afraid to finish the sentence.

The look in his eye was one she knew all too well. Nothing good ever came from that look.

"It's just Thanksgiving," she began again, fighting back the tears she could feel coming. She had no idea what she had done to upset him like this. But the man standing before her was not the Holden she had come to know. "I asked you last week if you'd want to celebrate, and you said yes."

"I said no such thing! I don't do Thanksgiving!" he hollered in response. His face was hard as he glowered at her.

"But...but...last week, we were up in the loft, I asked you—"

"You did *not* ask me about this. I would not have told you this was okay."

"Holden, I swear. I would not have done this if you hadn't agreed. If you changed your mind, then we don't have to—"

BANG!

Holden slammed his fist down on the butcher block, making it rattle again. Some of the chopped vegetables tumbled out of their bowls onto the floor, but Gigi didn't dare try to pick them up. She was too afraid to move. Too afraid of where that fist was going to be aimed next.

A deep growl from Holden made the hair on Gigi's arms stand on edge, her gaze returning to his face. His hands were now fisted in his hair, as if he were considering ripping it from his scalp. A vein bulged over his left eye, making her wonder if at any moment he would turn green and quadruple in size.

"I can't...I can't believe this," he growled, letting go of his hair and throwing his arms out to the sides. Gigi flinched at the motion, looking around her trying to figure out the best way out of the kitchen.

"I'm sorry, I didn't think it would be a problem," she responded, the tears finally letting loose. She tried as hard as she could to stop them, but she couldn't. Every inch of her wanted to believe that Holden wasn't like Bradley, that he was just mad and that this wasn't going to escalate further. But she'd also believed that Bradley would never hurt her, and she'd been very, very wrong about that. So how could she trust that this was any different?

"Of *course* it's a fucking problem," he shouted, stepping toward her. "This is a bullshit fucking holiday. The only thing it does is remind people of what they don't have. Pretending to be grateful, and happy, and like everything is just fine."

"Is...is this about Hannah?" she choked out. Holden hadn't shared much about her, other than that she passed, along with their unborn child. The only thing she knew about her death was that it'd been a home invasion gone wrong. Had that happened on Thanksgiving?

Holden jerked at the sound of her name, and Gigi knew she was right. But also so very wrong. Because the sound of his wife's name seemed to hurt him like a physical blow. He staggered sideways, colliding with the counter. His elbow made contact with the roasting pan. It jerked sideways, skidding, and then hit the tile floor with a deafening clatter. The greased-up turkey popped out of the pan and slid across the floor, like the stone along the ice in a curling match. It hit the wall on the far side of the kitchen with a thud, leaving a greasy mark on the wall.

Holden let out a loud, primal yell, raking his hands through his hair again. Part of him looked like he couldn't believe he'd just caused so much chaos, while another part of him looked like he wanted to cause even more. Gigi didn't wait to see what he did next. She didn't need to be a part of this rage or stand around trying to help. She knew better than to be in the way.

Turning on her heel as fast as she could, she bolted out of the kitchen, through the dining and living room, and straight up to her room. As soon as she had her bedroom door closed, she twisted the old-fashioned key that sat in the keyhole and locked the door. Turning around so her back was against it, she slid down to the floor, her body shaking as she fought back the sobs.

I just left the devil I knew, only to find the devil I didn't…

12

GIGI

The sound of the front door slamming shut didn't do much to stop Gigi's heart from racing. Sitting there, crumpled up against her locked bedroom door, she tried to remind herself that this was not the same as what she left behind in Atlanta. Holden was not Bradley.

Although what had just gone down in the kitchen was still running through her mind, trying to convince her otherwise.

Gigi had learned quickly enough what Bradley's triggers were. The problem was, the list was extensive. Anything from being cut off in traffic to something having gone wrong at the office was enough to set off his temper. His usual outburst generally only consisted of some harsh words about just how much of a failure Gigi was in his eyes. How the only thing she was good for was looking pretty and making him look good in the process. He'd cut her down every chance he got. No matter what it was she was doing, he told her all about how she was probably going to fail at that.

Unless he was drinking.

If Bradley had alcohol flowing through him, all bets were off.

And in the last couple of years of their marriage, there were very few times he was home and *didn't* have some kind of drink in his hand. All he needed was a little "liquid courage" to strip away all sense of decency and unleash the monster inside him.

"Are you incapable of doing anything correctly?" Bradley had blustered as he stormed into the library of their Atlanta townhouse.

Gigi slowly placed her bookmark in her well-loved copy of Caulfield Montgomery's *At Midnight*, before she slid it onto the small table next to her. She had no idea what he was upset about now, but it didn't really matter. She managed to find a new way to screw up every day it seemed like, so it really could have been anything.

"What's the matter?" she'd asked, trying to make herself sound more concerned than frightened. Fear only seemed to fuel his anger even more. As if she should somehow not be afraid of him and his moods. It was her fault after all, or at least that was what he liked to tell her. If she could only do things properly, then he wouldn't have to be the bad guy.

"What's the matter? How dare you ask that. How dare you sit in here and act like you don't know."

"I don't know, Bradley," she'd told him, her mind scrambling to figure out what it could possibly be. She had spent all day with the committee for the Southern Children's Comfort Fund going over last-minute details for their annual event, Hearts and Heels, that coming weekend. She'd been gone longer than she had expected, since there had almost been an issue with the table settings, but she'd still made it home in time to make sure that everything had been cleaned or fixed as needed that day. Dinner had also been ready promptly at seven, just the way Bradley insisted. Not that he had been home until well over an hour later.

"My crimson pinstripe shirt, ring a bell?"

"It's at the dry cleaners. It will be ready tomorrow." She had pushed up from the chair and taken a step closer to him. She knew it was a risky move, but she also had to show him she was paying attention to his needs. It was the only way to possibly avoid what she had feared was coming next. "It's the first thing on my to-do list."

"I fucking need it for tomorrow, you dumb bitch!" Bradley had exploded. "How are you so fucking stupid?!"

"I'm…I'm not. You said you didn't need it this week."

"You can't even listen, can you? I told you I needed it for the Richter meeting, and that's tomorrow. What the fuck am I supposed to wear now?"

"You have plenty of options, I'll go pick something out," she'd told him, maneuvering around his large frame to head to their bedroom. She knew that he had expressly stated that he didn't need that shirt—that he could never wear crimson around the Richters, since they were diehard Texas Longhorn fans—but she didn't bother correcting him. Correcting him would just end poorly.

As soon as she thought she was out of his reach, she had felt his hand clamp down on her arm and pull her back to him. His fingers had squeezed tightly around her elbow, causing a whimper to escape her lips from the pain. A growl rumbled in his throat as he'd gripped her tighter, holding her in front of him.

"You think you can just walk away from me?"

"No, I was going to—"

Smack!

She'd felt the sting from the back of his hand making contact with her face only milliseconds before she felt the scrape of his class ring against her skin. As much as she wanted to cry out, she hadn't. The tears pricking at her eyes would betray her soon enough and push Bradley over another edge. She'd lived through enough of these moments to know she just needed to let him get it out of his system. A few more hits and he'd storm off, lock himself in his study, and drink until he passed out. She'd survived up until now, she could survive this too, right? That was what she would continue to tell herself, ignoring the fear that someday she wouldn't.

"It's a good thing you're pretty, Georgia. You're not really good for much else," Bradley had said, taking her face in his hand and pinching it, like he was holding a taco. "Life woulda been real tough had you been ugly and had to fend for yourself. Although your daddy's got enough money that he probably coulda paid someone off."

Swallowing hard, Gigi had continued to fight back the tears. They were what he wanted, but she wouldn't give in to it. Wouldn't let him know that he was getting to her. She might not be strong enough to fight back or even to leave, but that didn't mean she would let him see her cry.

When he'd finally let her go with another shove, she let out a breath—one she hadn't fully realized she was holding. The fear that had coursed through her veins was paralyzing, forcing her to remain right there in front of him, instead of running away like she knew she probably should. She didn't need to give him any more reason to be upset, but she still couldn't move. Bradley let out a loud huff, sneered at her, and then stormed out of the library, leaving her to collapse back into the chair she'd been sitting in.

Everything she was feeling now, resting against the bedroom door, was nothing compared to the apprehension and dread that she used to feel every time her husband walked into a room. But it also wasn't the same excitement she had felt even just a few hours ago when thinking about Holden. Letting out a sigh, she took a deep breath, trying to figure it all out. She didn't know what to do. She could pack up and go, but where? Colebury was a small town—it wasn't like there were a lot of options. Not to mention, it was a holiday. She could take Audrey up on her offer for Thanksgiving, and see if she could crash on their couch, but that wasn't a long-term solution. Plus it would lead to a lot more questions than she was prepared to answer.

More than anything, her heart was breaking over the thought that her newfound life was not working out the way she thought it was. Despite her serious attraction to Holden, the two of them had really started to build a friendship, or so she thought. And it had been a really, really long time since she'd felt that kind of connection with anyone.

Pushing up away from the door, she double-checked both doors to her room were locked and then lay down on her bed. It was way too early in the day to go back to bed, but there was always one thing that made her feel better. She reached under the pillow on the side of the bed she didn't sleep on and pulled out her old paperback of *At Midnight*.

If nothing else, she had Caulfield Montgomery's words to comfort her.

HOLDEN

Holden hadn't even made it all the way down the drive before he regretted everything. Just what kind of douchebaggery was that? If it had been at all possible, he'd kick his own ass for acting like that. No matter the reason, Gigi didn't deserve to be treated that way.

The look of fear that had been on her beautiful face gnawed at him as he thought about what must have been going through her mind. She was always a little on edge, and after this, he couldn't blame her if she never got near him again. She'd been so full of joy and excitement when he came down the stairs, dancing around the kitchen, and he'd killed all that with just a few words.

Turning right toward town as he reached the road, he replayed her words in his mind. "I asked you last week if you'd want to celebrate, and you said yes." Had she brought it up and he just missed it? He really didn't remember her talking about it at all. They'd talked about her cakes and how people wanted to special order them, so she was going to have to work longer hours, but that was it. Right? Nothing else had come up. Except, the reason people would have been special ordering cakes could only have been one thing.

Thanksgiving.

"Well, you really fucked that up, buddy," he muttered out loud.

The feel of his phone buzzing in his pocket made his spirits perk up for a second. He reached into his running shorts, hoping to see Gigi's name on his screen, however it was only his godfather. His heart sank, knowing that he shouldn't have even thought that maybe it could be her after his horrible words.

"Uncle Field," he said as he answered the call.

"Happy Thanksgiving!" the older man called from the other end of the phone.

"Yeah, that."

"Why do you sound so dejected? I know this day brings up some tough memories, but you sound more crabass than normal."

"It's nothing," Holden told him. He really did not want to talk about this with his godfather. He wanted to be able to wallow in his own feelings on the matter, even if he didn't fully know what they were.

"Ahhhh, so it's something," Caulfield said. "This have anything to do with the pretty little roommate of yours?"

"How do you know she's pretty?" Holden asked defensively. Had there been a conversation with Caulfield that he didn't remember too? He couldn't imagine having admitted his attraction to Gigi, but he also didn't seem to remember a bunch of important conversations recently.

"It's in your voice, my boy. You sound different when you talk about her. Just like you did with Hannah."

The mention of his wife made his chest ache. Not only for the loss of her, but for his reaction to Gigi asking about her. The two of them had been building a friendship these last few weeks, opening up to each other about their late partners. He'd told her about Hannah. Well, mostly. But Gigi didn't have to pry it out of him—he'd told her because he wanted her to know he understood her pain. Her asking about Hannah this morning hadn't been anything other than her returning that sentiment. And he repaid her concern by *losing his fucking mind.*

"It's not betraying her by thinking another woman is pretty, you know," his godfather said after he didn't respond. "So tell me, this Gigi, she's pretty, isn't she?"

"Beautiful," Holden admitted. "Different from Hannah, but absolutely beautiful."

"So, then…why are you talking to me and not putting the moves on her?" he asked with a laugh.

Holden huffed out a small laugh. His godfather had always been an instigator, and age was not slowing the man down one bit. "I'm not really sure she's talking to me right about now."

"What'd you do?"

"I *badly* overreacted when I found her cooking Thanksgiving."

"She was cooking you Thanksgiving? Did you not tell her?"

Holden searched his memory again. For the life of him, he didn't remember her asking. But this was Gigi, and if he'd learned anything about her in their short time together, it was just how considerate she was of others. There was no way she would have done all that unless he had told her it was okay. Guilt surged inside him again for not remembering the conversation, on top of the embarrassment he was feeling for his tantrum.

"She sure was. And I guess I didn't, because I'm sure she wouldn't have done it had she known. Hell, if she'd known, she would have done something to take my mind off of it," Holden said, the realization hitting him. *You really, really fucked up, dude.* "She went all out too, attempting to make it all from scratch. Then, I lost it."

"Lost it how, Holden?" he asked, his voice almost accusatory.

"I yelled…and…" Holden paused, swallowing hard. He was so ashamed by how he acted, he could barely get the words out. "I knocked the turkey off the counter."

"Holden Hemingway St. James," Caulfield said slowly, drawing out each syllable of his name. Now he knew he was in trouble. "You are not the Incredible Hulk. What the hell were you thinking?"

That was a damn good question. One he didn't really have a good answer for.

"I wasn't, Uncle Field. I came downstairs, and she was dancing around the kitchen, getting ready to make this whole big meal, and the only thing crossing my mind was Hannah and how she was stolen from me and how this bullshit holiday does nothing but rub my face in that fact."

"Holden, you can't keep living like this. Hannah would not have wanted it. You need to move on. Moving on doesn't mean forgetting her. It just means that you learn to accept that she's not here anymore. I gotta believe that she's looking down on you right now, and she's hurting that you're still in this much pain. And she's probably quite pissed off that you're spending her favorite holiday acting like a jackass. Did it ever occur to you that maybe Hannah sent you Gigi?"

The question caught him off guard. Could that even be possible? That from somewhere beyond the grave Hannah was trying to show him something? He'd lost everything when he'd lost Hannah. Ever since her death he had felt like he was drowning, like he would never be able to fully breathe ever again. Until Gigi walked into his life and provided the fresh air he needed. It hadn't been one-sided either—the Gigi dancing in the kitchen this morning, the one who had bounded into his office last week, was a different woman than the one he'd met at the Busy Bean that first morning. She was definitely a different Gigi than the one who had started a kitchen fire in the carriage house. Maybe they were exactly what the other needed.

"Sounds like something that would happen in one of your books, old man," Holden responded, trying to deflect the question.

"Holden, listen to me. You have a chance here to reenter the land of the living. You've done everything you can to avoid it, but you can't anymore. So march your ass up the stairs, or back into the house to wherever that southern beauty is, and apologize."

"I'm not sure she'll talk to me. The look in her eyes, how afraid she was…that's gonna haunt me."

Holden sucked in a deep breath, holding it for a moment before slowly exhaling. He wasn't sure there was an apology big enough to fix what he did. Gigi had never come out and said it, but her skittishness had been enough for him to know that her marriage wasn't a good one, and he'd gone and acted like a rabid dog.

"Regardless of whether or not she'll talk to you, you owe the lady an apology. From there, it's up to her. But Holden, if she lets you back into her life, then you better cherish her for the angel that she is. Treat her so well she won't remember a time before you were in her life. And then take her to bed and blow her mind."

"Caulfield Montgomery!" Holden exclaimed.

"What? You can't deny you want to. I told you, I can hear it in your voice."

"I'm not having that conversation with you, Uncle Field."

"Don't act like such a prude!" he said, blowing off the comment. "Some good lovin' goes a long way in the forgiveness department."

"I'm hanging up now!"

Holden could hear his godfather laughing as he tapped the end button on his phone. Shaking his head in disbelief, he started back toward the house, thinking about the advice he was just given. Gigi would need space, that was a given, but the old man was right. He owed her an apology. A great big one.

When he got back inside, he surveyed the mess in the kitchen. The raw turkey sat in the middle of the floor, right where it had come to a halt after bouncing off the wall. The scattered chopped veggies and shattered glass from the bowls covered most of the room, each one sitting there as if it were a dead soldier on a battlefield. A stark reminder of just what an asshole he'd been not even an hour ago. A loud sigh escaped from him at the thought of cleaning it up, but cleaning would have to wait.

First things first.

He rapped his knuckle against the old wooden door to Gigi's room, hoping she was in there. A small sliver of light snuck out from under the door, giving him hope. Her car was still in the drive, and the bathroom door was open, limiting the places she could have run to.

"Gigi?" he called out. When she didn't answer, he knocked again. Could she be asleep? Glancing at his watch, he saw it still wasn't even noon, so sleep was not likely, although he had no idea what time she had gotten up to start prepping the meal. "Gigi?"

Still no answer.

"Gigi, I'm sorry. What I did…how I reacted…it's unforgiveable. I didn't mean to scare you. I don't remember you asking about Thanksgiving, and that's on me. This whole thing is on me. It's not your fault. I'm so, so sorry."

Holden waited, but still no response. He didn't know what he was expecting, but he knew he'd been hoping for something more than this. If he were being fully honest with himself, what he wanted was for her to open the door, throw her arms around his neck, and kiss him like she had a few weeks ago in the kitchen, even though what he really deserved was for her to open the door and smack him. Hell, even that would be better than the silent treatment.

He retreated away from the door and headed back to the kitchen to start the cleanup process and figure out a way to win back Gigi's trust.

If he could win back her trust.

13

GIGI

"Oh for heaven's sake!" Gigi exclaimed, turning the key in the ignition of her Jeep, listening to it click over and over again. She wasn't quite sure why she expected it to start after almost thirty minutes of trying, but she was still holding out hope. This was the last thing she needed right now.

Two days since the incident in the kitchen and Gigi was still on edge. She'd managed to avoid Holden since, happy to not have to face him. She believed him when he'd told her he was sorry through the door, but that didn't mean that she wanted to have to look him in the eye or talk to him. Right about now she could go the rest of her life without talking to Holden St. James.

Flipping the key one last time, Gigi said a little prayer. If this didn't work, she was going to be forced to walk home from the Busy Bean. She'd gotten here at the crack of dawn, as part of Operation: Avoid Holden, and the last thing she wanted to do was walk back in this cold, dreary winter weather. The engine cranked like it wanted to start for a split second, but then returned to the same clicking as earlier. Gigi's heart sank as she collapsed back into the driver's seat.

It's okay, Gigi, just call the tow truck and have it taken to the garage. Things like this happen to people all the time...

A knock on her driver side window startled her, causing her to jump and hit the horn on the steering wheel. The obnoxious noise that followed made both her and her visitor recoil, and she turned to see Holden cautiously approaching again. What is he doing here? She thought, taking in his muscular form, that he looked even bigger under the parka he had on. He moved his hand in a circular motion, indicating he wanted her to roll down the window. Gigi swallowed hard, suddenly nervous at being this close to the man who had knocked a turkey across the room the last time they had been together, but did as he asked.

"Sorry, I didn't mean to scare you," he said, a nervous smile tugging at his lips.

"What are you doing here?" she asked, confused. This was way too late in the day for him to be going for his run. Had he been out running errands and saw her sitting here? O*h please, please, please don't let him have witnessed today's calamity...*

"Kirk called, said your car wouldn't start."

Stupid Kirk. Why couldn't he have just minded his own business. It was bad enough that she'd had to ask him if he could drive her home, only for him to look at her like she was crazy. How was she to know he had sold his car and walked everywhere to "reduce carbon emissions"? But now she also had to deal with the fact that he called and told on her? She had no idea when he was leaving for Costa Rica, but right about now it couldn't be soon enough.

"Um, yeah. It just keeps making this clicking noise," she offered up.

"Probably the alternator. Guys down at the garage will have to look at it."

"Okay, good to know."

"C'mon, I'll give you a ride home." He nodded his head in the direction of his truck across the parking lot. Had he really come into town just to pick her up?

"I have to call the tow truck," she said, trying to make an excuse. It was a lame one—they both knew it—but it was all she could think of. While there was a part of her that was thrilled to see him and wanted to launch herself into his arms and cry, another part of her wanted more than just a car door between them.

"I already took care of that. Kirk is gonna watch for them. Just leave the keys in the visor."

"And just what makes you think I'm going to get into a car with you?" she spat. The words were sudden and harsher than she intended, but she didn't regret it. He needed to know that showing up like a white knight with a working vehicle didn't mean that he was out of the doghouse.

Holden's face fell at her reaction, a look of hurt taking over. Gigi steeled herself, trying to remember that she didn't care if she hurt him. He'd hurt her worse.

"After the way I acted the other day, you have every right to not trust me. I was an ogre, and I am so, so sorry. But if you'll just give me a chance, let me drive you home and I'll explain everything. And if you still hate me, then I'll help you find another place to live and move you there myself."

Gigi looked him up and down. The sincere expression on his face made her just want to melt into his arms. Even after the events of the last couple of days, she did still trust him, even if she didn't know why. But she was curious as to what set him off, and it seemed the only way she was going to get her answer was to take him up on his offer.

Nodding, she opened the door and slid out, placing her keys between the visor and the roof of the car. Holden helped her up into his truck, which he had left running so it was nice and warm. The short drive back to the house was silent and awkward, but no part of Gigi could bring herself to say anything. There was nothing to say.

Once they were inside the house, Gigi only felt more awkward. The fireplace in the living room was lit, giving the room a warm glow that was more inviting than she wanted to admit. Holden had moved the overstuffed couch closer to the fireplace, between the two large armchairs that normally flanked it, making it look like a scene from a magazine showing off the perfect New England fall Saturday night.

"Okay if we talk in here?" he asked, walking into the living room. "Fire feels good."

Gigi nodded and headed toward the fire. Holden was right—the heat coming off of it did feel good. She watched as he sat down on one end of the couch, motioning for her to join him. Instead of taking the other end of the couch, though, she sat in one of the chairs—the one farthest from him, trying to put some space between them. A hurt look flashed across Holden's face as he watched her purposefully sit as far as she could from him, but she didn't care. She needed the space.

"Gigi, I'm so, so sorry. I shouldn't have snapped the way that I did. I don't know what came over me. I've never acted like that in my life. Which probably isn't much of a consolation, but it's the truth."

"It's not a consolation at all." Everyone had a first time; she knew this all too well.

Holden nodded solemnly, turning on the couch so that he faced her. Running his hands through his hair, an almost tortured look crossed his face as he searched for the words, like he was unsure exactly where to start.

"Six and a half years ago my team won the league. Soccer in other countries is different than American sports. There isn't a playoff system. It's whatever team has the most points at the end of the season wins. We'd been in a battle with Liverpool all season long, and they were our last match of the season. We had one point on them in the standings, so as long as we didn't lose that game, we won the cup. They were a tough team, with some of the best players in the world, but we managed to edge them out one nothing, and we won the cup," Holden began, his voice tense. Gigi's mind flashed back to the game—she knew it well. Bradley had taken to following the English Premier League that season due to a client of his being a big Liverpool supporter. Things had not ended well in their house when they lost that game. "It was one of the happiest moments of my life. Right up there with my wedding day and Hannah telling me she was pregnant. We were all kinds of hyped up after the game, and a bunch of my teammates wanted to go out and celebrate. Hannah was exhausted, and being seven months pregnant I couldn't blame her. I told her I'd skip the celebrating and we'd just go home, but she was insistent that I go out with the guys. So I went out with them."

Holden swallowed hard, and Gigi could see the tears glistening in his eyes. His large frame shook as he tried to steady himself. Gigi felt her heart ache already, anticipating what was coming next.

"I stumbled my way back to our flat sometime in the ungodly hours of the morning. My only concern was that I didn't want to wake Hannah. That was until I walked down the hall to our condo and found the door wide open. I rushed inside, no idea what I was expecting to find, but whatever I thought, it wasn't my wife lying in a pool of her own blood." A sob escaped from Holden as he closed his eyes, turning to look away from her as he tried not to let the tears take over. Gigi could feel tears of her own starting to fall, watching him, trying to even begin to understand the pain. She wanted to tell him it was okay, that crying was okay, but she didn't want to interrupt his story. "I rushed to her and tried to find a pulse, but couldn't. There was so much blood everywhere. When the EMTs and everyone got there, they told me there was nothing they could do. She'd been dead for a couple of hours by that point."

"Holden..."

"So while I was out celebrating a stupid championship, letting random people buy us drinks and congratulate us, my wife and daughter were at home, dying. Autopsy showed that she was stabbed three times in the abdomen and slowly bled to death. Her and the baby," he continued, his voice breaking with emotion. He sucked in a long breath, seeming to hold it as he fought through the pain that was obviously tearing through him. Turning back to Gigi, he looked her in the eye, emotion written all over his face. "Hannah told me she was pregnant on Thanksgiving—her favorite holiday. Throughout her pregnancy, she talked about how she couldn't wait for us to celebrate 'as a family.'"

"So when..."

"So when I came downstairs and you were cooking, it brought it all back. Her announcement, her death, and how I wasn't there to protect them. I swear I didn't hear you say anything about it last week. I would have told you that I don't do Thanksgiving had I heard you ask. It's my fault for not protecting you from myself, just like I wasn't there for Hannah."

Gigi held her breath, taking in his words. "It's my fault for not protecting you." She'd spent the last two nights lying awake trying to figure out if Holden was a wolf in sheep's clothing, just as her husband had been. But that one sentence told her that she'd been wrong for jumping to that conclusion. He was running from painful memories, just as she was—their ghosts simply haunted them a little differently.

She got up and moved over to the couch, still keeping a distance between them. His tears left streaks down his cheeks leading to his scruffy beard, and Gigi fought the urge to brush them away. As much as her body was craving him, she wasn't quite ready for what touching him would mean. But maybe it was time for another type of intimacy. He'd come clean to her, maybe it was time she let him into her world as well.

"You weren't the only one who lost something that night."

HOLDEN

"I don't follow," Holden said. He swiped away at the tears that were making their way down his face. Crying was one of those things that men never admitted to doing, yet in this moment he felt no embarrassment about crying in front of Gigi. He was still much more ashamed of his anger earlier.

"It sounds like you and Hannah were really, really happy. Which is not something I can say about Bradley and me. We started off that way, I think. Or at least, I did. But over time, things changed," she said, looking away from him and into her lap. She picked at her fingernail, and Holden could feel the nerves radiating off of her. "I could do very little right in the eyes of my husband. I realize I'm not the smartest girl in the world, but I like to think I'm not a complete idiot. Except, to Bradley I was. Everything was my fault, even if I didn't actually have anything to do with it. It started out with him telling me that I should just stick to what I'm good at, or that it was a good thing I'm pretty. That was one of his favorites, actually."

"Did he..." Holden started, but then stopped himself. How exactly did one finish that sentence? Beat you? Abuse you? Either way, it sounded trite. He had no idea if she would confirm his suspicions, but if she did, he didn't want her to think for a second that this was something he didn't take to heart.

Gigi nodded, but didn't look up at him, a heavy sigh escaping her lips. "He was okay if he was sober. Then the worst he would do was just yell. But mostly it was little digs here and there. If he had been drinking, however...well then, all bets were off. First time he did it was after a client dinner. He said I embarrassed him because I called the client's wife Laura, and her name was Laurie. I told myself that it was just because he was stressed about landing this client, and really, I should have known the woman's name. But then he did it again, and again. And I kept making excuses."

"There is no excuse for that, Gigi," he told her. He wanted so badly to reach for her, pull her into his arms, or even just hold her hand. To let her know that someone else's touch could be gentle and soothing.

"You'd be amazed what you can justify," she whispered. "Something I've always wanted was to be a mom. I know that sounds cliché, but, I dunno, I've just always pictured myself with a little mini me. Playing dress-up, painting our nails, hanging out at the pool, that kind of thing. I know being a parent is more than that, but no one dreams of dirty diapers—just the fun stuff. Bradley and I had talked about starting a family, and he seemed excited about the idea. Even told me that I had finally done something right, preparing to give him an heir. You'd have thought it was the 1800s with the way he talked about it, but it was enough to curb his temper for a bit." She paused again, as if she were trying to prepare herself. "A couple of months into trying, he was working on landing this major client, who it just so happened was a Brit, and was really, really into soccer. His team of choice was Liverpool. I don't pretend to know anything about sports, but I do know that they lost the championship that year. I made the mistake of getting in Bradley's way shortly after the game ended. He lost his temper, and I ended up at the bottom of the stairs."

Gigi barely got the last words out before a sob wracked her body and she collapsed forward, her head falling into her hands as she cried. Holden felt his heart break into pieces, and he couldn't hold back any longer. He rushed to her, kneeling down in front of her, placing his hands on her upper arms. He moved his hands up and down lightly, trying to comfort her as she cried. He didn't take for granted the fact that she didn't flinch under his touch. If anything, it just made his heart ache even more.

"Gigi..."

"That was the day I lost my hope. If I had been honest with myself, maybe I would have lost it sooner, or at least not held on to it so tightly. But there was a part of me that really thought that a baby would fix things. Like somehow if I gave him that heir, that it would be a turning point for us. But after that, I knew I couldn't bring a baby into that house. I couldn't do that to my child. So, I secretly got an IUD put in—that way he would never have to know I'd changed my mind and was working against it. After a few more months, our lack of success was just one more way I was a failure. I couldn't even have a baby. 'The most basic female function,' as he put it. He started to spend a lot more nights out after that."

"Was he unfaithful?"

"I had my suspicions, but the one time that I actually worked up the nerve to ask, he denied it. He threw me up against the wall, shoving the accusations back in my face. Because why would I think that unless I was sneaking around on him? The bruises he left on my arms that night meant I had to wear long-sleeved shirts for a week, in the July heat, just so no one would see. I knew better than to ask ever again."

"Gigi, I'm so, so sorry. You didn't deserve my temper the other day, and fuck…I must have scared you shitless when I threw the turkey. That's all on me, sweetheart. I'm so, so sorry."

"I was so afraid that you were just like him," she said, looking up at him, tears still running down her face. Even with her tear-stained cheeks and red, puffy eyes, she was still beautiful. "But it's my fault for not double-checking with you about the meal. It was stupid of me."

"No, no, no. You're not stupid. So far from it. I shouldn't have said that. You are anything but stupid. *None* of it is your fault, Gigi. Real men don't do that shit. It was his flaw, not yours," he told her, hoping she heard his words. "And it's on me for the way I reacted. You did nothing wrong. Not yesterday, not six years ago."

"You didn't do anything wrong either, Holden," she said softly, looking into his eyes.

"I did a lot of things very wrong on Thursday, sweetheart."

"No. Six years ago. You didn't do anything wrong then. Hannah's death isn't your fault."

Her eyes never left his as she said those words. They hit Holden like a truck, and he had to catch his breath. It wasn't anything that his family, teammates, and even the therapists hadn't been telling him for years. But for some reason, when Gigi said it, it was different. Like she had been sent to him by Hannah, just to make him believe it.

"I know," he whispered in return, meaning it for the first time. "It's just hard to accept."

"I know."

They sat there for a long moment in silence, Gigi sitting on the couch with him kneeling in front of her. The fire behind him crackled as the wood settled a bit, causing a whoosh of heat to hit them. It felt good against his back, like the moment was embracing them.

"I really like you, Gigi," Holden said, breaking the silence.

"I really like you too, Holden."

Pushing up from his knees, he moved onto the couch so he was sitting next to her, their legs touching.

"Please forgive me," he whispered, turning toward her and leaning in so their foreheads were touching.

"I do."

Her words felt like salve on an open wound that he didn't know he had. How was it that two simple words could mean so much? Leaning in more, he brought his mouth to hers, until they were just a whisper apart. He could feel his heart start to race at just the thought of kissing her again, wondering if she wanted the same thing he did. When he felt her lean in just a bit more, he wasted no time in capturing her mouth with his. Her lips were soft and tender and felt absolutely perfect. He reached up and wrapped an arm around her, pulling her closer. He needed to feel her body against his. Needed to know if her heart was beating at the same furious pace. When she was seated in his lap, he deepened the kiss. She mewed as his hands caressed her back, moving her own hands into his hair. Fuck, she felt good in his arms. How was it that he could feel so much for her? He could feel his dick starting to get hard as she wiggled in his lap, continuing to kiss him back with the same fervor that he kissed her. But even with a raging hard-on, he was more than content to stay just like this—Gigi curled up in his lap, feeding him her addictive kisses.

Gigi pulled back slowly, a flirty little grin tugging at the corner of her lips. For a brief second, she almost looked drunk, and Holden couldn't help but feel a little bit of pride at the thought of her getting drunk from his kiss.

"Holden," she whispered, her eyelids still heavy.

"Yes, sweetheart?"

There was a beat of silence as he waited for her to respond. But instead of using her words, Gigi surprised him by leaning in and kissing him again.

14

HOLDEN

Metallica's "Enter Sandman" might not be most people's choice to pound the pavement to, but Holden found that the oldie but goodie served him quite well. At a tempo of a hundred and twenty-three beats per minute, for a full five and a half minutes, it provided just the rhythm he needed to maintain his pace. The guitar riffs also seemed to provide the perfect gateway to lead his mind down whatever road it needed to clear his thoughts.

His thoughts that had really only been filled with one thing since Saturday night—Gigi Hawthorne.

After kissing until both of them couldn't see straight, they'd rearranged themselves on the couch, pulling out Holden's laptop to watch a movie. Although if Holden had to guess, they'd maybe only watched about half of the movie, the rest of the time spent cuddling and kissing some more. However, when Holden had woken up the next morning, curled around Gigi, both of them still on the couch, he was left not knowing how to act. Sure, they'd both admitted to each other that they "liked" each other, but what did that even mean? It's not like they were in junior high and going to hang out with each other at the mall. They were adults, sharing a house.

And then there was everything they had admitted to each other the other night. Both of them had revealed some heavy stuff, and Holden didn't feel right making a move on her so soon after she let him in on her secret. Not that he didn't want to. Oh, did he want to. He wanted nothing more than to feel her curves underneath his hands again. He longed to see just how perfect her bare breasts were and to worship her whole body with his tongue.

Slowing down as he turned back up the driveway, he thought for what felt like the millionth time in the last six days that he didn't know what to do or even what to say to her. While things between them weren't full-on awkward, they were still…weird. It was as if neither of them wanted to be the one to cross the line but were still hoping the other one would. Not that Holden really had any idea what that line was. All he knew was that he wanted Gigi —on every level imaginable.

"Hello?" he called out, walking into the house.

The sound of the oven timer greeted him, followed shortly by Gigi's sweet, southern, "Hey!" It made him giggle every time she said it, all drawn out into two syllables, "hay-ay."

"Whatcha making?" he asked, still trying to catch his breath. He was sticking to the extra distance on his run, which was helping counteract all the amazing things Gigi was baking but was also showing off that he was still not in the shape he once was. Even with his heart still racing from his run, it managed to skip a beat when Gigi flashed him an excited smile, showing off her latest creation.

"Honey sticky buns," she said, a lightness to her voice that had recently appeared when she was talking about baking. "Hunnie gave me some of her cinnamon infused honey the other day when we had lunch, and it sparked an idea."

He crossed the kitchen, watching as she bent over to place the baking dish in the oven. Her backside always looked incredible, but when she bent over like that, he had to stop himself from grabbing ahold of her hips. Unable to tear his eyes away from her gorgeous ass, he mentally scolded himself before finally clearing his throat to speak. "I don't know that I've ever had sticky buns with honey."

"Neither have I, but I thought it would be something fun to try out. It took a little bit to get the consistency right, based off what the recipe said it should be like with the real ingredients, but I think it tasted okay when I tried it before going into the oven."

"How long until I can have a taste?" he asked, unsure if he was talking about the sticky buns or her buns.

"About thirty minutes or so?" she said with a little shrug. While there still seemed to be a tension between then, it was different now. It was one based on desire, rather than fear. Everything about her seemed so much more at ease now, like she was finally able to relax and not have to worry about what might lurk around the corner. Standing here now, a few feet from him, her stance was easy, and her body language was light, like this was her home—their home—and they were just a normal couple hanging out in the kitchen.

"Perfect, then I'm gonna hit the shower," he said, starting to lean in but stopping himself. For as much as he wanted to kiss her right now, he had no idea if she wanted that in return. Just because such a gesture felt natural to him didn't mean anything. Despite it feeling like they were a normal couple, they weren't actually one, were they? After all, she hadn't said anything to him about Saturday night either.

With a nod, he walked out of the kitchen and bounded up the stairs, shaking his head and scolding himself for not taking the chance. Maybe she was waiting on him to make the move. Or maybe he should have just manned up and said something to her. But what exactly did one say in this situation? "Hi, I know we're technically living together, but can I take you on a date?"

Once the water was finally warm enough, Holden stripped

down and stepped into the hot shower. The steady stream felt good against his skin, still chilled from the December air. Taking in a deep breath and letting his lungs fill with steam, he let his mind drift back to Gigi. Everything about her seemed to get under his skin, like her very essence was trying to make a home there. And everything about her, from the knot of blonde hair she piled on top of her head while she was baking, to her chic looking "comfy clothes," to her seemingly never-ending shoe collection, was just so damn adorable.

But it wasn't just her looks that got to him. It really was *everything*. Her smile, her laughter. The fact that she had all sorts of strange little expressions she used instead of swearing. It was her drive to better herself and to be her own person. He admired her spirit for starting over after her dick-wad of a husband's death. The strength required to move someplace new and take on a job she knew nothing about was something that he couldn't even imagine, and yet she possessed it all in the stunning little body of hers. He had no idea why their paths had crossed, but he wasn't going to take another second of it for granted.

Grabbing the bar of soap, he worked it into a lather all over his body. Not for the first time, he wished it was Gigi's hands that were working their way across his chest and down toward his hips. The thought of her soft, delicate fingers dancing across his skin sent the blood flowing straight for his dick. Closing his eyes, all he could picture was her standing in front of him now, the water rushing over the both of them, as they caressed each other's bodies. He wanted so badly to feel her up against him, skin on skin, exploring the electricity between them. His hand found his rock-hard length and slowly began to stroke as he thought about Gigi—about touching her, feeling her, worshipping her in ways that she'd never experienced. Showing her just how special she was.

Holden let out a long groan as his release hit him, sending a shudder throughout his entire body. Part of him felt guilty for conjuring up the image of Gigi as he took matters into his own hand—she deserved better than to be someone's spank bank material. She deserved a man in her life who treated her like she was his entire world. Someone who didn't use her or take advantage of everything she had to offer. A man she could trust to be honest and true, who was man enough to admit his feelings to the woman in his life. In order to be that man, he knew he was going to have to step it up.

That started right now.

GIGI

Gigi listened to the pipes rattle as the hot water for Holden's shower kicked in. This old house had a lot of weird little quirks, but she was finding that she loved each and every one—the only exception maybe being the way the second to last stair from the top of the back stairs squeaked if you stepped in just the right place. There was so much comfort to be found here, and she basked in the warmth of it all. Even with Holden's outburst last week, she felt infinitely more at home here than she ever had in the townhouse in Atlanta.

A pang of guilt hit her again, thinking about Holden and everything he'd been through. It was no wonder he'd been so upset over everything on Thanksgiving. She knew as well as anyone what a flashback could do to you, and she wished she had known more about Hannah prior to the incident. She wanted to be able to help him. Neither of them could replace the spouse that they lost, but having someone else who understood was no small matter. Her heart ached at the thought of everything he'd lost and how much guilt he still carried around about it. She wished that there was something she could do to magically erase all the pain.

If only kisses really did heal boo-boos, she thought as she loaded the dishwasher. She would gladly kiss him over and over again if it helped relieve the pain. Oh, who was she kidding, she would gladly kiss him regardless.

Her insides fluttered with the memory of his touch from Saturday night. If she had thought the feel of his lips against her was spectacular that afternoon in the kitchen, he had proven to her now that it only got better. And yet, the idea of kissing again had her tied in knots.

It wasn't that she was afraid of him, because she certainly wasn't. If anything, her mind wandered to the thought of those strong arms wrapping around her and holding her close a little too often. What she was afraid of was how she felt. The feelings she was starting to develop were more than just that of a horny teenager who wanted to jump the class bad boy. She genuinely cared about him and valued the friendship they had built. She just also wanted more.

The question rattling around in her brain was, did he? When he'd arrived back from his run moments ago, she felt his gaze on her before she even looked up to find him walking into the kitchen. The look in his eyes told her he was happy to see her, and when he stepped into her asking about the sticky buns, she would have bet money that he was finally going to kiss her again. But then he backed off and hightailed it for the shower. Had she done something wrong? It had been a long time since she'd kissed anyone other than Bradley, and he wasn't exactly the kissing-bandit. Was she just out of practice? Or worse, was she just bad?

The sound of her phone ringing startled her. Gigi couldn't remember the last time her phone had actually rung. There were only a handful of people who even had this number, and since it seemed everyone up here preferred to text, a real phone call was rare. Wiping her hands on her apron, she picked up the phone and smiled when she saw Hunnie's name.

"Hi!" she said into the phone.

"Hey! How did the sticky buns turn out?" Hunnie's sweet voice asked over the line.

"They are in the oven now—should be finished in a couple of minutes," she responded.

"I'm so excited to hear how they turned out. If they're good, I'm gonna need that recipe!"

The pipes stopped their rattling, and Gigi lifted her eyes to the ceiling as if she could somehow see through it and into Holden's bathroom. Images of Holden's muscular body filled her head as she pictured him stepping out of the shower. Just thinking of his hard chest, still wet from the shower, water droplets slowly dripping down his hot skin, made her mouth water, wanting to lick at each one of those drops.

"Earth to Gigi!" Hunnie's voice called through the phone again.

"Sorry, got lost in my own head for a moment. Yes, if they turn out good, I'll totally give you the recipe."

"Everything okay?"

"Yeah, I'm just..." Gigi trailed off. Just what? A little obsessed with the idea of my housemate/landlord naked and wondering why he hasn't kissed me in six days? There were just some things you didn't say, even to girlfriends.

The oven timer trilled, and Gigi was thankful that she didn't have to figure out just how to finish that sentence. *Saved by the bell!*

"That's them, gotta go! I'll send you a picture!"

"Sounds good, bye!" Hunnie said as they hung up.

Turning back to the oven, Gigi pulled out the baking dish, watching the gooey honey glaze bubbling from the heat. The golden-brown spirals oozed the sticky goodness, and Gigi's mouth watered all over again. Placing the dish down on the trivet that she'd put on the butcher block, she waited a moment before carefully removing one of the buns, slowly blowing on it to help cool it off. After a few more huffs and puffs, she bit into the sticky bun, hoping for the best.

The intense flavor that burst in her mouth caught her off guard. Chewing slowly, she let the cinnamon sugar filling melt on her tongue, allowing it to take over all her senses. Everything about what she was experiencing was new and incredible, and she suddenly fully understood what people meant when they used the term foodgasm. This was quite possibly one of the best things she'd ever tasted. And there was only one person she wanted to share it with.

Holden.

Rushing up the back stairs, she almost tripped on the long carpet runner that sat in the hallway between their rooms. The door to both his room and his bathroom were open, with the lights turned on, so she took a guess at where he was, crossing her fingers she got it right.

"Holden!" she hollered, as she rounded the corner into his room, looking around for him.

When he appeared from the adjoining bathroom door, with nothing but a white towel slung low around his hips, Gigi forgot why she was even there. He was still wet from his shower, just like she had been imagining moments ago, but looked even better than her mind could have ever pictured. His long torso was lean and taut, showing off a nicely defined chest. Gigi could see the faint outline of what was probably once a six pack, but was now just a smooth flat stomach, leading to a powerful set of hips, a dark happy trail, and a V that made her lick her lips. His whole upper body called out to her, like some weird siren song, and the desire to run her hands all over him waged a war within her.

"What's the matter, sweetheart?" he asked, a concerned look on his face. He stepped toward her, pushing his wet hair out of his eyes, and Gigi felt herself swoon just a little. She didn't know how much longer she was going to be able to control herself if he didn't put on some clothes.

"He...here...try this," she stumbled, holding up the half-eaten sticky bun.

Holden licked his lips, his eyes never leaving hers. Only instead of a concerned look, a fire burned within them, one Gigi hoped was for her. Lightly grabbing hold of her wrist, he drew it to his mouth, taking a generous bite of the baked good. He licked his lips again as he chewed. Gigi's breath hitched, and she was pretty sure he heard it too, but she didn't care.

"That's fucking delicious," he said, still not looking away from her. His hand was still around her wrist, and she could feel her pulse vibrating in that spot.

"I did it! I really did it. I created my own recipe," she said. She could feel the dopey smile taking over her face, but she was too proud of herself in this moment to try to change it.

"You sure did, sweetheart." The flame in his eyes flashed again, forcing Gigi to remind herself to breathe. The last thing she needed right now was to faint.

Opening his mouth wide, Holden took the last bite of sticky bun in his mouth, capturing her fingers as he did so. He swallowed it whole but then took his time, licking her fingers, making sure to get every last bit of honey off of them. Gigi shuddered from the contact, watching his mouth on her, a rush of desire flooding through her. He could apparently do a whole lot more than just kiss with that mouth, and every inch of her wanted to find out what else he had up his sleeve.

Releasing her hand, he slipped his arm around her waist and pulled her in close, so their bodies were flush together. Gigi shuddered again, her eyes glued to his mouth. More than anything she wanted him to kiss her—to take her in his arms and show her that he was feeling the exact same things she was.

"Gigi," he murmured, lowering his head so his forehead was pressed against her hairline. Their breathing seemed to fall into a rhythm, the two of them inhaling and exhaling in sync.

"Holden," she whispered back. She wasn't sure that she would be able to find many more words than that right now. Her mind was too cloudy with lust. She wanted him to kiss her, wanted to feel his bare skin against hers. She had never been this turned on in her life, and each breath only heightened her senses even more.

"I meant what I said the other night, sweetheart. I really, really like you. And to be honest, it freaks me out a little, since I never thought I'd feel like this about anyone ever again."

"I meant it too. I really like you. And…same…"

"But I want you to know that I respect you. You are so beautiful, Gigi, inside and out, and I don't want to do anything to make you feel uncomfortable. This is all in your hands, sweetheart. We won't do anything you don't want to. You just let me know what you want."

"You," she said, her voice coming out breathy. "I want you."

15

HOLDEN

"I want you." Those three little words were music to Holden's ears and set his entire body on fire. He could feel his skin grow warmer as his heart rate picked up and his dick twitched. Gigi's whispers were so delicate and soft, yet they packed a hell of a punch.

He wasted no time in moving his hands to her luscious ass, giving it a good squeeze. The feel of it in his hands was better than every one of his fantasies. Gigi gasped lightly under his grasp, pushing her breasts into him. His cock hardened even more with this new contact, and he let out a groan. Gigi had no idea what she did to him. Tilting her head back, she arched up onto her toes, and Holden captured her mouth in his, kissing her hard. She tasted sweet, like honey with an undertone of cinnamon, just like the sticky buns, but better.

There were so many things he wanted to do to her in this moment, but he knew he needed to control himself. More than anything, what he wanted was to make Gigi feel special, to feel adored. He wanted to show her just how much pleasure she could experience at the hands of someone else, rather than the pain he knew she'd been caused. In order to do that, he needed to go slow, and be steady and gentle. They could be frenzied later. Now was the time for tenderness.

Slipping his hands underneath her shirt, he trailed his fingertips up her sides, earning him a shiver and even more kisses. It was as if just the touch of his skin to hers lit sparks under her skin and, in return, fueled his own fire. When he reached her bra, he guided his hands up under it until his thumbs found her nipples, which pebbled almost instantly under his touch. Circling the little peaks with his thumb, he started to kiss along her jaw and made his way down her neck. Gigi mewled underneath his touch. Her breasts felt perfect in his hands, like they were made to fit right there. He hadn't even seen her naked yet, and he was already as hard as he'd ever been. If he wasn't careful, they weren't going to make it very far.

"Holden..." she gasped as he lightly pinched a nipple with his thumb and forefinger.

"You like that, sweetheart?" he asked, his voice gruff and full of desire. He wanted to make her feel so good that she forgot everything around her. He just needed to figure out what she liked.

"Mmmhhmmm," she moaned in response.

"How about if I do this..." he trailed off, dragging his right hand down her front and slipping it into her yoga pants. When he discovered that she wasn't wearing any panties, he felt his cock surge all over again. It was a good thing he hadn't known this before, or he would have had a much harder time behaving himself.

He continued to lower his hand until he found her already damp with desire. She cried out when his fingers found her wetness, her knees wobbling slightly. Slowly, he spread his fingers through her pussy, massaging her, making sure to avoid any direct contact with the spot he knew she wanted it most. This was about making her feel wanted and drawing out her pleasure, not about how fast he could get her off. Holden could feel her pulse pick up as he continued to play with her, teasing her. The look on her face told him that she was enjoying this as much as he was, and he never wanted her to forget this moment. Hell, he never wanted to forget this moment either.

Returning to her mouth for another long, hard kiss, he shifted his hand slightly and slipped a finger inside her. Gigi cried out again, louder this time, throwing her head back. Holden kissed along her exposed neck, nibbling lightly where her neck and shoulder met. He felt like the most powerful man in the world, having Gigi blissed out in his arms like this. But it wasn't enough. He wanted to see her face as she fell apart from his touch, to know what she looked like when she went soaring into space.

Without a word, he adjusted his hand, slipping a second finger inside her, finding her clit with his thumb. He only brushed against it ever so lightly at first, but it was more than enough to get the kind of reaction he was looking for.

"Oh my God!" Gigi exclaimed, grabbing on to his upper arms for balance as her whole body shuddered.

Holden ignored her outburst, continuing his efforts. His thumb circled the little bundle of nerves over and over, rubbing it like one would a wishing stone, until he knew she was so close that it was only a matter of moments until she came undone. Stroking her insides with his two fingers, he searched for the spot that he knew would push her over the edge. Just listening to her breathing and feeling how responsive she was to his touch was such a turn-on. His dick ached to be touched, to be given the relief it craved, but not until Gigi got hers. It didn't matter to him if this led to more or if this was it and he would be left to deal with his raging hard-on by himself. His goal here was simple—to take Gigi somewhere no man had ever taken her before.

"Faaaaaaa," Gigi screamed, her entire body convulsing underneath him. He captured her scream with his mouth as she held on to him for dear life. He could feel her insides clamp down on his hand as he furiously worked to keep her orgasm going as long as possible. She moaned, kissing him harder and harder as she rode his hand, like it was the only thing keeping her alive at the moment.

When she finally inched back from the kiss, Holden couldn't stop the shit-eating grin from taking over his face. The look of sheer ecstasy that washed over Gigi was more than enough for him to know that he'd succeeded. Except it wasn't enough. He wanted more. He wanted her, all of her. His cock twitched again, but he ignored it—Gigi was still his first priority.

Giving her a moment to catch her breath, he led her over to the bed and sat down on the edge. He tugged her in between his spread legs and kissed her again. This time it was soft and sweet, again trying to communicate to her that she was safe, and this was about her feeling good, not some obligation.

She was silent for a moment, tracing her fingers along the lines of the star tattoo on his left shoulder. There were so many things he wanted to say to her. His heart was bursting full of emotion, and his own desire still rushed through him like a bull. But he calmly waited for her lead, softly running his hands up and down along her glorious hips.

"Holden," she said, finally breaking the silence.

"Yes, sweetheart," he answered. With him sitting, he was only a few inches shorter than she was, so he had to look up to meet her eyes, unsure of what they were telling him.

"I'm…I'm not very good at this," she replied, quickly looking down at her feet.

Slipping a finger underneath her chin, he lifted it up until their gazes met. He could see the apprehension in her eyes, and his heart tugged. He hated that she felt this way about herself, especially after the powerful moment they'd just experienced. He was now on a mission to prove to her that she was wrong.

"Why don't you let me be the judge of that," he told her softly. Grabbing her hand again, he placed it on his barely concealed erection. She gasped again when she felt how hard he was, looking at him with wide eyes. "From where I'm sitting, you're doing everything perfectly."

"Really?" she asked.

"Really."

"Then why are you still wearing that towel?"

GIGI

Gigi was just as surprised as Holden when the question sprang from her lips. She had no idea where she had found the courage to say such a thing, but no part of her regretted it. Maybe it was the earth-shattering orgasm she had just experienced at his hand, or maybe it was the desire she felt—a desire she'd never felt for anyone ever before—but she was feeling like a whole new woman.

"Consider it gone," Holden said, winking at her. In a flash, he stood up, tugging the towel as he went. It fell to the floor, but Gigi couldn't be bothered to watch. She was too taken with the view in front of her. A naked Holden St. James was easily the most amazing thing she'd ever seen. The hip V that she'd been admiring earlier as it disappeared into the towel led her down to the most beautiful dick she'd ever laid eyes on. No wonder it was called a happy trail.

Prior to this moment, she wasn't sure she'd ever say that a penis was pretty, but with Holden standing there like this, in all his glory, it was the only word she could think of. It was long and thick, and she suddenly had the urge to take it in her hand. Reaching out to do so, she hesitated slightly. What if she did this wrong? Holden had just fingered her into oblivion, without so much as a second thought. What if she hurt him?

As if he knew what she was thinking, he took her hands and placed them on his cock. Holden slowly moved her hands up and down his length before letting go and wrapping his arms around her, drawing her in for another soul-searing kiss. Everything about this man drove her crazy.

"Umm, Gigi, that feels so fucking good," Holden moaned. "There's just one small problem."

"What?" she asked, quickly letting go of him.

"Not that, sweetheart," he said, placing her hand back on his dick. "It's that I'm naked and you're still fully dressed. I think we need to fix that." A wicked glint in his eyes sparkled, as a sly grin moved across his face.

"You...you want to see me naked?" she asked, surprised.

"More than anything," he answered. "Unless you don't want to."

"No, I do. I'm just surprised..." she started, stopping herself before she said something stupid. She didn't want to sound ridiculous in this moment but was afraid it was too late. So much for the confidence she was feeling a moment ago.

"Don't be. I think you're gorgeous," he told her, moving in closer and grabbing the hem of her shirt.

Gigi raised her arms, letting him pull her shirt up over her head. Licking her lips, more out of nervousness than trying to be sexy, she reached behind and unclasped her bra, letting her breasts fall from the cups. Holden's eyes grew wide like a small child who'd just come downstairs on Christmas morning to see that Santa had arrived. Taking a breast in each hand, he gave them a squeeze, sending a jolt through her. When his thumbs found her nipples a moment later, just as they had earlier, she couldn't help but moan. She could feel them pebble underneath his touch, and more than anything she wanted to feel his mouth on them. Arching her back, she sighed, letting herself get lost in the sensation.

Holden removed his hands from her chest, replacing them with his mouth as his hands found the waistband of her yoga pants. Gigi shivered and pressed herself into him more, not sure if it was the feel of his tongue circling her nipple or the excitement of him lowering her pants that was getting her so worked up.

Either way, she didn't want any of it to end. When he'd lowered the pants to her ankles, she stepped out of them and away from Holden, putting herself on display. For a moment she felt exposed and vulnerable, but that feeling vanished as soon as she saw Holden watching her. He was licking his lips, looking like he wanted to devour her. It sent a new wave of nerves through her, one that was a mix of insecurity and excitement.

"You are stunning, Gigi," Holden whispered as he stepped into her and picked her up, like a new bride being carried over the threshold.

He walked her the few steps to the bed and laid her down gently before joining her. He kissed and caressed her, his hands everywhere at once. Every place he touched her lit up like he was branding her with his fingers. She ran her hands up and down his hard chest and stroked his dick, hoping that he craved her touch as much as she did his. Everything about this moment was perfect.

"I don't have any condoms," Holden said between kisses. Gigi could hear the disappointment in his voice, like he couldn't believe he let them get this far without thinking about that detail. She smiled to herself, loving that was where his mind went in this moment. As crazy as it would sound to anyone else, it was romantic to her that he put her and her safety first. That he wasn't going to do anything that made her feel uncomfortable. It was just one more thing about Holden that made her melt.

"I still have that IUD," she said, not wanting to bring that ugliness into this beautiful moment. "I didn't want to risk anything."

"Are you sure?" he asked, thankfully following where she was going with this.

She nodded. "I've never been more sure of anything."

Pushing up to his knees, Holden leaned over her and slowly started kissing his way down her body. He paused briefly to toy with her nipples, sending new sparks through her body. When he got to her hips, he placed a kiss on each one before moving back up to her mouth. Settling himself between her legs, he placed his cock at her entrance and slowly guided himself in. Gigi groaned, feeling herself adjusting to him inside her. It'd been a long time since she'd had sex, and never with anyone as impressive as Holden. Just as carefully as he'd entered her, he slid back out, and Gigi whimpered at the loss of him. A few more strokes and Holden found a steady rhythm, driving her crazy with each one. His actions were unhurried, easy, as if he had nowhere else to be, and loving her was his only priority.

Was this what this was supposed to be like? Every movement sent her further and further into oblivion, like nothing else she'd ever experienced. She craved his touch and everything it made her feel. Her entire body was on fire, almost as if every nerve was sitting along her skin waiting to be ignited. Shifting her hips, she ground herself against him, chasing the delicious friction their conjoined bodies were creating. Holden thrust harder, his dick hitting her in all the right places.

Gigi could feel another orgasm building inside of her. Arching her back, she whimpered, trying to meet him thrust for thrust, wanting to find her release. Holden reached down and found her clit with his fingers, rubbing it furiously. A second later, Gigi exploded, her climax washing over her, sending her reeling. For the first time in her life, she saw stars, and her eyes slammed shut, her entire body vibrating. The sound that escaped from her was something she'd never heard before, and the only reason she knew it came from her was that it was soon drowned out by a guttural groan coming from Holden as his own release hit.

After a few more strokes, he collapsed back onto the bed beside her. Gigi only had a few seconds to try and catch her breath before Holden rolled her onto her side and pulled her into him. The warmth coming off of his skin was welcoming, and Gigi couldn't help but snuggle into him as he wrapped his large body around her. Her heart was still racing, despite how calm and relaxed she felt. Sex had never felt this good, this right. If this is how it was supposed to be, she now understood why Holden questioned the name of the cake. No baked good in the world came close to what she'd just experienced.

Gigi felt the tickle of Holden's beard against her bare shoulder as he placed a few soft kisses there. She giggled from the feel of it, hoping it encouraged him to continue.

"I don't know about you, sweetheart, but I think we might need to make sticky buns more often."

16

GIGI

Thoughts whizzed through Gigi's brain at a speed that she'd never experienced. It was almost enough to make her dizzy. But she couldn't stop them, and they just kept coming.

Did that really just happen? Did he enjoy it? He must have if he made the sticky bun comment, right? What if he was just saying that? What if I was bad? He's still cuddling me, so that's a good sign, right? What does this make us? Are we a couple? Dating? What if he doesn't want that?

She told herself to take a deep breath. Answers were not going to come from freaking out. And nothing good could come from being that girl. Was it still considered "being that girl" in your thirties? Gigi had no idea.

What she did know, however, was that was easily the best sexual experience of her life. And she wanted to experience it again and again. She just also wanted the *more* that came with a relationship.

Holden shifted behind her, still keeping her in his arms as he kissed his way up her neck. Nipping lightly at her earlobe, he pulled her hips closer into him, and Gigi couldn't help but let herself melt into him. Despite all the questions in her head, the rest of her was consumed with all the feels, as if she were floating on some white fluffy cloud.

"You remembered to turn the oven off, right?" Holden said, not letting up on his kisses.

Gigi could hear the lightness in his voice, but it didn't stop her heart from jumping into her throat.

"Yes…" she told him. She *had* turned the oven off, right? "I think…"

She quickly ran through her motions before running up here to have him taste her creation. It felt like forever ago now and for the life of her, she couldn't remember. Panic took over her, and she jerked away from Holden, popping up out of the bed.

"Oh for heaven's sake!"

"Gigi!" Holden said, grabbing her around the waist and pulling her back into him. "I was joking. If the oven is still on it's fine. We can turn it off later."

"But what if it catches fire!" she exclaimed, her voice sounding a lot more fragile than she wanted it to. She would never, ever forgive herself if she burned down this house too.

"Would it make you feel better if I went and looked?" he asked, a look of concern in his eyes. She wasn't sure if it was over the oven or just because she was maybe coming off a little insane.

"Do I sound crazy if I say yes?"

"No," he said, placing a kiss on her temple. "Be right back."

Holden squeezed her tight, planting a sloppy, wet kiss on her cheek before pushing himself off the bed and sauntering out of the room. Gigi watched his stunning backside as he strolled down the hall toward the back stairs fully naked. *Damn, he's got a nice ass.* All that running had toned him in all the right places, making for quite the view. She felt herself flush, slightly embarrassed by how unashamedly she'd been watching him, and looked down at her own naked body. No part of her had thought anything about it just a moment ago, when she was wrapped up in Holden's arms, but now the moment was gone, and she was just the naked girl in his bed.

Unsure of what came next in situations like these, Gigi grabbed her clothes off the floor and held them up to her chest, shielding herself, like the only other person in this house hadn't just kissed his way up and down her body, making her see stars in the process. This was all so new to her, leaving her to wonder what protocol was here—was there even one? Did she stay and wait for him to come back? Was this her cue to leave? Leaving was probably the better idea. It was only a dozen or so steps to her room, and if she hurried, she could make it there before he returned and she had to face him. She tiptoed out of his bedroom, trying to be as quiet as possible, still holding her clothes up against herself.

"It was off," Holden said, as he crested the top of the back staircase. His voice startled her, and she froze, halfway to her room. The deer in headlights look that she knew was painted on her face made her feel self-conscious all over again, but she couldn't move. "Where are you going?"

"Oh, ummm, just back to my room," she stammered, taking in his glorious naked form, this time from the front. It was like staring at the David, in awe of his beauty, just with tattoos and a much better package.

"Why?"

"Well...I...mean...we can't spend the rest of the day in bed..."

"Sure we can," he said, a look on his face like that should have been a given. He studied her for a moment before stepping closer and placing his hands on her bare hips. She hugged her clothes tighter to her, gasping at the contact. "Have you never done that? No wonder you thought cake was better than sex."

"We just had sex!" she whisper shouted, unable to contain the word vomit she'd been holding back. "What now? Are...are we... something? Or was that just sex to you? Because I'm not really that kind of girl, Holden. I mean, I've never just slept with anyone before. I'm not saying you have to be my boyfriend, but...that meant something, right? Or maybe it didn't. That's okay too. I get it. I know it's different for guys. But I do like you…and it did mean something to me. But if you don't like me, that's fine. I don't want to assume. So, if you don't want to again, I understand. Just please don't tell me that you regret—"

Holden cut off her ramblings with a kiss. His mouth seared to hers before she even had time to think, much less react, but it felt good. Damn good. Dropping her clothing, Gigi's hands flew around his neck, drawing him in even closer. His kisses were spicy and sweet all at the same time, and it created a need inside of her that she hadn't even realized existed. Moving his hands to her ass, he lifted her up in one swift motion, never breaking the kiss. Goodness, was there anything this man wasn't capable of? With her arms and legs wrapped around him, he walked them back into his room, where he sat down on the bed.

"Sweetheart, there is absolutely no part of me that regrets what we just did," he said after a long moment filled with fevered kisses. "In fact, I look forward to doing it again. And again…and again." A wicked grin tugged at his lips, making the butterflies in Gigi's tummy come back to life. "I told you the other night, I really like you. I know you're not that kind of girl, and I'm not that kind of guy. There's been no one for me since Hannah."

"No one?"

"No one," he confirmed. "I hope that shows you just how special you are to me, Gigi. I don't know what this makes us, because this is all new to me too. But what I do know is that I want to explore it. Let me take you on a date tonight."

"A…a date?" He wanted to take her on a date?

"Yes, a date. It's Friday night, and that's what a guy does on a Friday night. He takes his girl on a date."

His girl. The words almost made Gigi melt on the spot.

"I like that idea," she whispered, lowering her head until it was resting against his.

"Good. Now, we have some time to kill before we need to

shower to head into town...and I have a couple of ideas on how to spend that time."

HOLDEN

Holden slammed the door of his truck closed, having just finished setting up everything he and Gigi would need for the evening. It had been so long since he'd planned a date that he almost wasn't sure he remembered how. The idea of driving all the way to Montpelier for dinner seemed mundane, and while the diner in Colebury could be a fun experience, what he wanted tonight was something a little more, well, romantic.

Dusting himself off so he would look presentable, he glanced up to see Gigi come through the front door, greeting him with a huge smile. She looked too cute for words in her formfitting jeans, puffy teal winter coat, and a white knit hat and matching mittens. It was almost as if she stepped off the set of a movie and into his house.

"I was going to come pick you up at your door," he said. He placed his hands on her hips and tugged her into him, placing a soft kiss on her lips.

"My bedroom door?" she questioned, a little giggle to her voice.

"It sounds a lot more ridiculous when you say it like that," he answered, returning the laugh.

"I can go back upstairs if you want me to," she offered, biting her bottom lip. The nervous habit made her even cuter, and Holden could feel himself starting to get hard just watching her.

"I don't want to waste any more time. Let's get this date started." He took her mitten-clad hand firmly in his and led her to the truck. He loved the way her hand felt in his—even through the protective layers. Helping her up into the truck, he kissed her again, unable to help himself. Part of him had wondered if it would feel weird or wrong to take this step with Gigi, like he was somehow cheating on Hannah. But now that he was in the moment, it felt more right than anything had in a long time. This afternoon had officially pushed them over the line. She was one hundred percent his girl now, and he was going to make sure she knew it.

Just before they reached the road, Holden took a slight right-hand turn, driving down a long, winding trail.

"Where are we going? I thought we were going into town?" she asked.

"I had a better idea. But don't worry, we're not going far, you'll see."

A minute later he slowed to a stop and put the truck in park in front of an old, rundown gazebo overlooking a small pond. The small structure had certainly seen better days, since no one had given it much thought in the last decade, but Holden had checked earlier that it was still structurally sound, at least enough for them to hang out for a couple of hours. The moon was full and bright above them, reflecting perfectly off the water of the pond. Gigi took it all in with wide eyes and an equally big smile as he led her over to the gazebo, where he'd laid out a bunch of pillows and blankets for them to use. The built-in bench was lined with candles, which once lit would hopefully give off enough of a glow for them to be able to see each other, even if they didn't give off much heat.

"I had no idea this was over here," she commented, amazed by her surroundings.

"Well, as you can tell, it's in need of some repair, but it's been here since the twenties, I believe. It was one of my favorite places to come and read as a kid."

"Did you ever go swimming in the pond?"

"Uh, no. That thing is gross. You'd probably come out all covered in leeches, like in *Stand By Me*," he told her, a shiver running through his body at the thought. He led her to the blanket and motioned for her to sit, while he lit the candles surrounding them. Once they were all settled and tucked in, Holden reached behind him, grabbing a thermos.

"I've never seen it," she admitted as he poured hot chocolate into two camping mugs.

"Adding that to our movie list!" he laughed. "Are you warm enough?" Putting his arm around her, he closed the small gap between them. He rubbed his hand up and down her arm, enjoying the feel of her body against his.

"I am now," she said, snuggling into him. She took a sip of her drink, a soft moan escaping from her lips. "Can I ask you something?"

"Anything."

"You spend a lot of time up in the loft in front of either the computer or a typewriter. Are you writing a book? Like your godfather?"

"I'm pretending to write a book," he corrected her. "It should come as no surprise based on what I've told you about my family that I've always wanted to be a writer. That was always my plan. But then I got drafted, and it was too good of an opportunity to turn down. Financially we'd be set for a very, very long time, and I figured I could still write in my downtime. That proved a lot harder than I thought. Then everything happened with Hannah, and I haven't been able to write since. My muse died with her."

"Holden," Gigi gasped. The tears forming in her eyes about broke his heart, while still somehow endearing her to him. How was it that this beautiful woman he'd known such a short time seemed to feel his pain right along with him? "I'm so, so sorry."

"I keep hoping that someday my muse will return. Just need the right spark," he shrugged. "What about you? What did young Gigi want to grow up to be?"

"Promise not to laugh?"

Holden could hear the apprehension in her question, and he wished he had the magic cure to fix her confidence. It was a good thing her asshole husband was dead, or he'd be more than a little tempted to kick his ass.

"Of course."

"A book editor."

"Seriously?" He was taken aback by her answer. She had told him that she'd majored in literature in college, but it hadn't occurred to him that an interest in publishing would have been the motivating factor.

"Yup. I've always loved to read, but I've never really been good with words. I figured being an editor was the best way to basically read all day. I mean, I know they do more than that, but that was still young Georgia's logic."

"Why would you think I would laugh at that?"

"Because everyone I've ever told has laughed at that answer," she whispered, looking down into her almost empty mug.

"Well, I'm not laughing," he whispered back, tightening his grip around her. "Are you still interested in that?"

"Oh no. I still like to read, but I don't think I could do a job where I had to tell people their stuff wasn't good. I'm not mean enough. Is it bad that I'm thirty-four and don't know what I want to be when I grow up?"

"Only if it's bad that I'm thirty-nine and don't know either, sweetheart."

"I never thought that I'd enjoy baking as much as I am though. It's been so much fun to play with the recipes, even the ones I've messed up. Maybe someday I can have my own cake shop."

"I think that you can do anything you put your mind to."

Gigi twisted in his arms so she was facing him, pressing her lips to his. It might have been early December in Vermont, but every part of him was on fire. How could it not be with Gigi sitting in his lap. His erection surged, and he shifted underneath her, not wanting her to think this moment was about sex. He was enjoying being close to her, listening to her talk about her dreams. The flicker of candlelight danced across her face, showing off everything she was feeling. What Holden saw in her eyes made him feel like the luckiest man in the world.

"I don't think I've ever been as comfortable with another person as I am with you," she said softly.

Gigi's words hit Holden like a wrecking ball, overwhelming him. He knew what these feelings were, he'd been here before—he was falling. But everything was still new and different, like he was experiencing it all for the very first time. She was bringing him back to the world he'd known before, one that he'd thought was lost forever.

"For someone who thinks she's not very good with words, you certainly know what to say to get me going."

"It's easy with you."

She twisted in his arms again, this time positioning herself between his legs and pressing her back to his chest. Making sure she was fully covered by the blanket, he wrapped his whole body around her, engulfing her small frame in his. The soft mewls she made let him know that she was enjoying this moment as much as he was. They sat and simply watched the small snowflakes that began to fall, glittering in the moonlight.

"It's my first Vermont snowfall," she said, mesmerized by the fluffy white prisms that started sticking to the ground.

"Just one of many firsts for us," Holden said, thinking of all the other things he couldn't wait to experience with her. If she was this taken by a few snowflakes, he could only imagine what she would be like once the holidays drew closer, and he couldn't wait to be by her side for it.

"It's so pretty," Gigi commented, snuggling deeper into his arms.

"Just not quite as pretty as you," Holden whispered in her ear.

"Holden…" she cooed.

"I mean it, sweetheart," he said, placing a kiss just underneath her ear. "I know we haven't known each other that long, but you have brought more light into my life in that amount of time than if we were in Times Square. I feel alive for the first time since losing Hannah and the baby. You have no idea what you do to me, Gigi."

Spinning in his arms, Gigi looked him in the eye. There was so much emotion in hers, and he hoped she knew how much it was returned. "You have no idea what you do to me. No one has ever believed in me the way you do, Holden. Thank you for taking a chance on me."

"I will gladly take a chance on you, and your baked goods, over and over again," he told her, leaning in for a kiss. "Now, how about I get you home and warm you up. *Properly*..."

17

GIGI

"Boss ladies were looking for you," Roderick said, walking into the kitchen of the Busy Bean.

Gigi popped up from the small cake she was decorating for a special order they'd received and looked at him wide-eyed.

"I didn't do it!" she exclaimed, a response so automatic she wasn't quite sure where it came from.

Roderick stared at her for a moment, a puzzled look crossing his face. Gigi grinned awkwardly in return, trying not to look like she had a secret to hide, fearing that was exactly what she looked like right now. Had Roderick figured her out? Had Bradley found her?

"The dopey look on your face for the last week tells me otherwise, and I hope for your sake, it's your hottie landlord," he said, catching her off guard.

"Whatever could you mean?" she asked, trying to pass off some innocence, relieved to hear that's where he was taking this.

"Girl, I know the power of a smoldering roommate, and yours...he's got the part down pat. And it's hot. So if you haven't already, I recommend taking that for a ride."

Gigi opened her mouth to respond but stopped herself. Just what did you say to that? She couldn't deny the dopey smile part. Roderick was right—there had been one plastered to her face ever since that night in the gazebo. Gigi had been so nervous when Holden had used the word "date" that she had changed her outfit at least a half dozen times. But once they were cuddled up under those blankets, all her nerves had melted away—and all those walls she had put up seemed to melt away right along with them. The man saw through to the real her like no one she'd ever known. She'd spent so long putting on a face—the perfect daughter in high school, the fun-loving coed in college, the dutiful wife after marrying Bradley—that she had almost forgotten who the real Gigi was underneath it all.

The rhythm they had found themselves in prior to Thanksgiving—of doing their own thing during the day and meeting up in the kitchen in the late afternoon/early evening to play test kitchen—still seemed to be working. Although now their playing around in the kitchen also involved kisses and caresses, and they always seemed to end up cuddled on the couch. Holden was the perfect mix of sweet and affectionate. For as generous as he was with his kisses and all his attention, she never felt like he was pawing at her. His touch was thoughtful, intimate, and oh so sexy. He seemed to know just where to touch her to get her all worked up, as well as when she just needed some reassuring. Evenings with him were officially her new favorite thing.

A slight pang of guilt hit her, wondering if she should have told Holden the full truth that evening on the couch, or most certainly after their date. He deserved to know the truth—to know that she still feared Bradley showing up any moment and causing a scene. But every time they were together it was as if there was nothing else but them. The world outside melted away, and they were enclosed in their own little world. A world she knew she would have to rock at some point, she just wasn't sure when or how.

Throwing an exaggerated wink over her shoulder, she heard

Roderick let out a deep belly laugh as she walked through the kitchen door out into the café. Slipping around the counter, Gigi found Zara and Audrey sitting at the same table by the window where they'd been when she'd first met them. She felt like that evening was a lifetime ago and that a completely different person was standing here now than had walked through that door waiting for her tire to be fixed.

"Gigi, this sticky bun is incredible!" Zara said, holding her hand to her mouth to cover the bite she just took. Gigi blushed slightly, hoping that Zara took it as a reaction to the compliment, and not because she was thinking dirty thoughts about what those sticky buns had led to.

"Thanks! I had a lot of fun playing with the recipe," she responded, letting her mind wander back to the feel of Holden's mouth on her for the first time. Even though they had joked about it, Gigi hadn't made them at home since then. Maybe that was something she should do on her next day off.

"Please sit. We have a question for you," Audrey said, pointing to an empty chair at the table.

"The cakes have been such a success," Zara started. "We already have people asking if we're going to take orders for Christmas. I hope it's okay, I already said yes."

"Of course! I'm so excited people are liking them!"

"We'll keep it simple again, promise. That seemed to work well for Thanksgiving, plus it'll give you time to do your own holiday baking."

Gigi hadn't put any thought into holiday baking at home. She'd been so caught up in the whirlwind of her new feelings for Holden, and in having those feelings returned, that the fact that it was the Christmas season had barely registered. What did Holden do for Christmas? Would he want her to be a part of it? Was this holiday also another trigger?

"I haven't even gotten that far," she laughed, waving off the idea. She made a mental note to broach the subject of the holiday when she got home. *Let's just hope it goes better than the last time we had this conversation...*

"And not to add to your plate or anything," Audrey chimed in. "But we wanted to talk to you about maybe creating a signature item."

"A signature item?"

"I'm not thinking you need to invent the next croughnut or anything, but a new flavor of cupcake or something. One you can only get at the Busy Bean."

"Any old family, southern recipes?" Zara suggested.

Gigi laughed at the statement but quickly stopped herself. She'd kept everything really vague where her family history was concerned to anyone other than Holden—heck, she was still pretty vague with him—and now was not the time to reveal anything additional.

"No, no old family recipes. I don't exactly come from a long line of bakers," she answered.

"I get it. I don't think my own mother has ever cooked anything," Audrey told her.

"So...will you do it? You don't have to have the idea tomorrow. Just be thinking about what you could possibly come up with."

"Of course!" Gigi agreed, excited about the prospect. The idea of a new project for her and Holden in the kitchen sent a thrill through her. Just what kind of "trouble" would they be able to get up to now?

She sat and talked with Audrey and Zara for a little while longer before returning to the kitchen to put the finishing touches on the cake she'd been working on. When it was finally complete, she boxed it up, placed it in the fridge, and headed home, excited to tell Holden all about their new challenge.

Climbing the stairs to the loft, she could hear Holden's voice come and go as if he were on the phone. As she walked into the loft he came into view, reclining slightly in his office chair, laptop open in front of him, phone pressed to his ear.

"Arriving on the twenty-fourth works. We can take care of the tree and all that beforehand, so don't even worry about it," he said into the phone. Looking up at her as she stopped right next to him, he ran a hand softly up and down her thigh in greeting, sending shivers up her spine.

Twisting a bit to look at his laptop, Gigi saw an open Word document, but what really caught her attention was that today it wasn't blank. Had Holden actually written today? She turned back to look at him, her brow furrowed, but a smile tugging at her lips. The smile on his face told her that he knew what she was thinking, and that he couldn't get off the phone fast enough.

"I don't know, I haven't asked her yet," he told whomever he was speaking to. A wicked grin replaced his knowing smile, and he threw a mischievous wink her way, still rubbing her thigh. "But if you let me get off the phone, I can do just that, and then we can plan from there. Sound good?" He paused, muffled sounds coming from the other end of the line. "Okay, bye, Mom. Love you too."

Tapping the end button on his phone, he tossed it onto the desk and turned his attention fully to her.

"Hi." He hauled her into his lap, and she let out a little shriek before laughing. Capturing her laughter with kisses, Holden squeezed her tight.

"Hi back," she answered. "I take it that was your mom?"

"It was," he nodded.

"What did she want?"

"She was calling about Christmas, trying to figure out what the plan is."

"And what is the plan?" Gigi asked, trying to not make it seem like she was at the edge of her seat with curiosity. This conversation was already night and day compared to how the Thanksgiving one had gone, and it made her that much more anxious to know the answers. The idea of spending Christmas here with Holden was something she hadn't realized she wanted until now.

"Well, that depends on you," he said, his eyes full of emotion.

"Me?"

"Yes, you. GeorgiaGrace Hawthorne, will you spend Christmas with me?"

HOLDEN

Gigi's eyes went wide as Holden asked her the question that had been brewing in him for the last couple of days, making his heart skip a beat. *Oh fuck, was that the wrong question?*

"Really?" she asked in return, her voice just above a whisper.

"Yes, really," he told her. How could she think otherwise? "I want you to experience Christmas at Montgomery Manor in all its glory."

"You make it sound like it's a big to-do," she giggled.

"Oh, Christmas here, with my family, *is* a big to-do. Other than a few years when I was abroad and we couldn't make it back, I have spent every Christmas of my life in this house. And every year we would drive out to this little tree farm and pick out a tree, and then bring it home and decorate it. And by 'we,' I mean all five of us squeezed into my mom's station wagon. On Christmas Eve, dinner was really just a snackfest with all sorts of appetizers, dips, and cookies and such, and we'd sit by the fire while my dad and Uncle Field read *A Christmas Carol*. Christmas morning was a flurry of presents and laughter. Shortly after that, the men were kicked out so the ladies could make Christmas dinner. We'd usually end up outside kicking around a soccer ball. After dinner, there was either more reading or sometimes we would watch a movie."

"Sounds amazing!" Gigi gushed. "You must have some wonderful memories!"

"I do. What about you? What was Christmas like for the Shaws?"

"You know, I don't really have a lot of memories of Christmas as a little kid. I'm sure Santa came, but there weren't any special family traditions or anything. Our cook was given the day off, so we would go to the country club for Christmas dinner, usually with another family my parents were friends with or one of my dad's clients. After that, we all just came home and did our own thing," she sighed. "I love that you guys picked out your own tree! Ours just always appeared, set up and decorated while I was at school."

"You've never decorated a Christmas tree?"

"Nope. Even after I got married, Bradley was insistent that was something we hired people to do. The tree had to be perfect looking, like something out of a magazine, in case clients came over. I was always jealous of the trees I saw with handmade ornaments, or the ones you could buy at the mall and have your names put on them. I bought one for our tree the first Christmas after we were married and secretly put it on the tree in a spot I thought no one would see it. But the next day it was gone, and I never saw it again."

"I'm so sorry, sweetheart," he said, pulling her in close. His heart ached thinking about how she didn't have happy Christmas memories. Just one more thing to add to his list of things to take care of for her. "What do you say? Spend Christmas with me and my family?"

"Of course!" she exclaimed, throwing her arms around his neck and squeezing. He shifted in his chair, making sure she didn't fall out of his lap, squeezing her back just as tightly. "Christmas isn't a trigger for you like Thanksgiving?"

"It's not. I guess maybe because it was already a St. James-Montgomery family thing, and Thanksgiving was a Hannah thing. Don't get me wrong, it's been hard, but we won't have a repeat of the flying turkey," he promised. He hated that she was worried about that, even if she didn't voice the concern, but he loved that her first thought was of him and his feelings. She had one of the biggest hearts he'd ever known, and he was incredibly grateful to have worked his way into it. "My mom says that since the kitchen is yours now, that dinner is your call. She's all about helping but doesn't want to step on toes."

"I would love her help! I've never done it, and I have no idea even where to start."

"She'll be thrilled to hear that."

Gigi twisted toward the desk, eyeing the laptop. He'd wondered how long it would take for her to notice that. Prior to his mom's call, this had been the most productive afternoon he'd had in a long time. Probably years. The idea had struck him while he was out on his morning run, and by the time he'd finished his shower, he couldn't get up to the loft and the keyboard fast enough. It was as if the flood gates had been opened, spilling years of pent-up energy and words. It all flowed through him in a way that it never had before. The only difference now was the stunning creature currently occupying this chair with him.

"What's that?" she asked, nodding toward the screen.

"That, is almost seven thousand words," he told her, feeling pretty proud of himself.

"Holy cow! That's a lot!" she said, looking back at the screen and then returning her focus to him. "That is a lot, right?"

"Depends on the author, but generally speaking, yes. Seven thousand words in a day is a lot. For me, it's a shit-ton."

"Holden, that's amazing!" The joy that spread across her face tugged at his heart, making him even happier about the day he had.

"Well, for all I know they are shitty words, but at least they are words. Step in the right direction."

"So, your muse is back?"

"I think I have a new one." He wanted to tell her that she was the reason he was writing again, and that she was the inspiration for each and every one of those seven thousand words. But he also didn't want to come on too strong.

"Willing to share her?" she asked.

"Ummmm, threesomes aren't really my thing, sweetheart..." he joked.

She smacked his chest playfully with the back of her hand while sticking her tongue out at him, like she was a kid on the playground. "Not what I meant!"

"Why do you need her?"

"Zara and Audrey asked me to come up with a signature item for the Busy Bean," she answered with a heavy sigh. Holden watched as her shoulders slumped and her entire demeanor changed. "I don't even know where to begin."

"You said that once before, sweetheart, and you landed on your feet pretty quick. You've come a long way. Don't give up now."

"But I need something fun and clever. Something that will stand out!"

"Call Hunnie—I'm sure she has all sorts of weird and out-there ideas. Maybe that will spark something. And once you two have concocted some crazy cupcake, you and I will head to the kitchen and make them."

"You don't mind another kitchen project?"

"Mind? Sweetheart, I look forward to it. It's kind of our thing."

"You spoil me, you know that?" she asked, leaning in so their foreheads were touching.

Holden closed his eyes and inhaled her sweet smell and savored the feel of her body against his. He was the one who was spoiled, having someone like her just dropped in his lap. As crazy as it probably sounded to anyone else, he really was starting to believe that Hannah had sent him Gigi. How else could it have worked out so perfectly? She was everything he needed, and he hoped she was falling just as hard as he was.

"It's not spoiling you to give you what you deserve, sweetheart. And you deserve to be cherished and adored. I'm just grateful that I get to be the man in charge of that."

18

GIGI

"But my real question is, did he taste *your* sticky bun," Hunnie said, a teasing lilt to her voice.

"Hunnie!" Gigi exclaimed, quickly picking up her phone from the counter, turning off the speaker and placing it between her ear and shoulder. Her heart sped up as she looked around her to make sure she was still alone in the kitchen, trying not to make a mess with the last of the batter she was pouring into the cupcake liners.

"What? Had I realized that my creation was going to be the push you needed, I would have given it to you sooner," she said, completely ignoring Gigi's embarrassment. "I wonder if I could market it as a love potion?"

Gigi simply shook her head, laughing at her friend's reaction. This was not the road she had meant to go down when she called Hunnie to give her the sticky bun recipe and get her opinion on fun cupcake ideas. But like any conversation between girlfriends, they'd gotten sidetracked and even after almost thirty minutes of talking, hadn't found their way back.

Not that Gigi minded talking about Holden. He was her new

favorite subject after all. Just the thought of him made her all melty inside, and she found herself thinking about him a lot. But it wasn't just the sex—which for the first time in her life, she was *really* enjoying—it was everything about him. He was thoughtful, kind, and considerate in everything they did. They spent their evenings cuddled on the couch, reading or watching movies, and it didn't seem to matter to him whether or not they did more than snuggle. He was just as interested in her mind as he was her body. He was everything her husband hadn't been, and no part of her was taking a single second for granted.

She also loved having a girlfriend to talk to about all this. None of her friends in Atlanta would have ever gushed about men or sex this way, and it was incredibly refreshing to be able to talk about it with someone who was not uptight about the subject. College was probably the last time Gigi had taken part in a conversation like this, but even then, she wasn't sure if she'd ever met someone as laid-back and open as Hunnie was. The old Gigi would have written off this eccentric little woman and moved on without thought. New Gigi, however, couldn't imagine what she would have done if she hadn't stumbled across her that night at the festival.

"What would your tag line be? Drizzle a little of this on his muffin and he'll come running?" she commented, sliding the muffin tray into the oven and setting the timer.

"Men don't have muffins. You'd need to drizzle it on his churro, add in a few long licks, and coming will be exactly what he does..."

Gigi let out a snort so loud it seemed to reverberate off the cabinets. Sucking in a large gulp of air, she tried to catch her breath, but no matter what she did, she burst into giggles all over again.

"It wasn't *that* funny," Hunnie responded, still giggling herself.

Wiping away the tears that were forming in her eyes, Gigi looked up to see Holden appear in the kitchen, giving her a strange look. She held up a finger to indicate that she'd be just a moment, returning her attention to her conversation. She managed to stop laughing long enough to hang up with Hunnie, before she felt Holden come up behind her, wrapping his arms around her and nuzzling her neck. The giggles started up again as his beard tickled her. She was still amazed at how soft it was and had almost started to crave the feel of it on her skin.

"Do I dare ask what all the giggles were about?" he asked, his nose still buried in the crook of her neck.

"Just chatting with Hunnie. We were throwing around ideas for a signature cupcake," she told him, not wanting to go into too much detail. She had no idea how he would feel knowing that she talked about their relationship with Hunnie. Had he mentioned her to anyone? Based on their conversation the other day, his family knew she was in the picture as more than just a renter now, but just how much had he told them?

"What did you come up with?"

"Not a whole lot. She thinks I should create a uniquely southern cupcake, which is a great thought, but I have no idea what that really means," she said as she measured out the needed amounts of powdered sugar, butter, and cream into a mixing bowl for the frosting.

"What was your favorite dish from your favorite restaurant back in Atlanta?"

"That's easy. Shrimp and grits from Pittypat's Porch!"

"Not something that anyone would want in a cupcake," he commented, handing her the electric hand mixer from the cabinet.

Gigi scrunched her face in disgust. As much as she loved shrimp and grits, they were the opposite palate she was trying to cater to with the signature item. She wanted to help the Busy Bean, not put it out of business.

"Oh! But maybe an idea for Christmas?"

"Shrimp and grits?"

"Yeah. Maybe even give them a little Cajun flare for Caulfield? Would he like that?"

"He would love that," Holden told her, leaning back against the cabinets watching her work. She wiggled her hips a little, letting the skirt she was wearing dance against her legs. The blue knee-length skirt with white polka dots wasn't exactly winter in New England appropriate, but she'd woken up wanting to feel pretty and since she knew she wasn't leaving the house, she figured why not. The way Holden was staring at her in it, the idea seemed to be paying off.

"I'm really at a loss for what else to make. I mean, what do you cook for a legend?"

"For starters, in this house, he's not a legend. He's just an ornery old widower. Second, whatever you make is fine."

"I need to figure out something green. But not like a green vegetable. That's the wrong shade of green."

"Why the color green?"

"Seriously? Because of *At Midnight,*" she said, looking at him like he should know this. Caulfield Montgomery was his godfather. How was he unaware of the importance of this detail? "The color green is what he used to show the true hearts and motives of the characters."

"Come again?"

"Everyone who betrayed the family in some way had something green. D'artagnan had the custom leather in his car, Anaura had the jade necklace, Aiden had the green rabbit's foot, and Xander had green shading on his tattoo," she said, turning back to the frosting. "Cretia, the biggest betrayer of them all, had a green aura. And I quote, 'But not like the color of money. It was a pale, placid color, like the inside of a lime.'"

Holden stood then, giving her a stunned look, like he couldn't believe she'd just quoted his own godfather's words to him. She suddenly felt very self-conscious, unable to tell if he was impressed or thought she was potentially a little crazy. Maybe both.

"You really do know that book inside and out, huh?" he asked, thankfully sounding impressed rather than concerned.

"I told you, I wrote my capstone paper on it. It's my favorite book," she responded.

Holden just stared at her for a moment, before making a show of turning to walk out of the kitchen and into the living room. A moment later he returned, phone in hand, tapping away at it like he was sending a text.

"What are you doing?"

"That's it. I'm canceling Christmas. Both my father and Uncle Field are just going to adore you, and once you bust out knowledge like that about Caulfield's books, we'll never heard the end of it! Can't have my godfather stealing my girlfriend, now can I?" he told her, a sly grin on his face.

Gigi stopped mixing the frosting, and she felt her pulse start to race. Girlfriend? Did he just call her his girlfriend? Did he even realize what he just said?

"Girlfriend?"

HOLDEN

Holden hadn't actually meant to use that word out loud. Girlfriend had been the term he'd been using in his own head to think about Gigi ever since that night at the gazebo. But in his own mind was a very different place than actually voiced. Surprisingly, saying it out loud felt really good.

"Ummm, yeah," he admitted, feeling a little ridiculous. For as good as it felt to use that term, he was suddenly very aware that they hadn't had any kind of conversation about what they were. He knew it was something—neither of them were the type to only be in this for the "benefits"—but he probably should have initiated this conversation a little differently. "That's kinda what I've been referring to you as in my head. If you have a better term…"

"I like that one," she said, her eyes full of warmth.

"Good, so do I."

"But I can't make any promises to not run off with Caulfield Montgomery. A girl would be crazy to turn down a living legend like that!" she teased.

Holden lunged across the kitchen, earning a playful shriek from Gigi. Grabbing her around the waist, he lifted her slightly off the ground, spinning her around. The skirt she was wearing flared a bit as she wiggled and giggled in his arms. The sound of her laugh went straight to his dick, and it took all he had to not haul her to the bedroom right then and there. But he knew she had cupcakes baking, and he didn't dare put her at risk of burning something else.

Putting her back on the ground, he twirled her around so she was facing him, her eyes still filled with the giddiness of the moment. He loved seeing her this happy. In moments like these, it seemed like all was right with the world, and they were both exactly where they should be. Long gone were the ghosts of their pasts, and the only thing that existed was the two of them.

BEEEP!

"You, young lady, have been saved by the bell, it seems," he said to her, not letting the oven's timer ruin the moment the way it had the last time they were in this situation.

"It's nice to have the appliances on my side for once!" she commented. When she bent over to pull the pan out of the oven, the sight of her glorious ass was more than Holden could bear. His dick strained against his pants, and his hands itched to take hold of the perfection he knew was under that sky-blue fabric. Feeling a little impish, he took a step closer and lightly smacked her backside, earning another shriek.

"I probably deserved that, huh?" she said, returning his playful grin.

"And so, so much more," he told her, leaning in for a kiss. Her lips were sweet, like the frosting she had just been mixing, and Holden was more than willing to spend some time getting lost in her this afternoon.

"All teasing aside though," Gigi said, turning serious. "I don't want to mess up Christmas. Not just because my favorite author happens to be coming, but because this is your family. I'm going to be so embarrassed if I screw this up. What if I give everyone food poisoning?"

"Hey, hey now," he said, wrapping his arms around her. "None of that. Where's all that confidence you've found?"

"It's currently freaking out that I'm going to ruin the holidays with your parents!"

"Sweetheart, you have become a magician in the kitchen. Whatever you make is going to be spectacular. But do you want the real secret to winning over my dad and Uncle Field?"

"Yes!"

"As long as you have sweet tea and lemonade for them to make an Arnold Palmer, we'll have a house full of happy campers."

Gigi's eyes went wide, and her mouth flew open with surprise. Holden had no idea what he said that was so shocking, but whatever it was, it seemed to have sent Gigi into a tizzy.

"That's it! An Arnold Palmer cupcake! A sweet tea cake and lemonade frosting," she exclaimed. "That's the signature item!"

"That sounds delicious."

"You're a genius, Holden!" She launched herself at him, throwing her arms around his neck as if she hadn't seen him in months. Grabbing her by the waist, he picked her up and set her on the counter behind her. With her hair swept up, showing off her neck, glowing with excitement, she was too adorable for words. His pulse raced as he took her in, all sweet and innocent. She looked almost good enough to eat—and Holden really, really wanted a taste.

"It was your idea, sweetheart. I'm just here to taste test," he told her, moving in between her legs. He placed a kiss on her collarbone, feeling her shiver underneath him. When he repeated the motion on the opposite side, she moaned softly from the contact, shifting her hips closer to his.

"I need to frost the cupcakes," she said to him, breathless from his attention.

"Maybe I could frost your cupcakes," he countered, his voice gruff with desire.

Gigi's sharp inhale of breath was all the reaction he needed, and he wasted no time in pulling her shirt over her head and ridding her of her bra. Her beautiful breasts heaved from her deep breath, and Holden couldn't look away. Everything about her was stunning. Reaching behind him, he grabbed the bowl of frosting she'd been mixing and dipped a finger into it, scooping out a chunk of the sugary concoction. Slowly and deliberately, he ran his frosting-covered finger over the swell of her breasts, circling her nipple, like he was an artist and she was his canvas. The whimper that escaped her lips as he traced his way along her cleavage sent a whole new surge of lust through his body, amping him up and fueling his desire to pleasure the beauty in front of him.

Holden leaned in and kissed Gigi, softly at first but quickly turning up the heat. He was so fucking turned on and wanted nothing more than to have her writhing underneath him, screaming his name. He kissed his way along her jaw and down her neck, making his way toward the sweetness he knew was waiting for him a few inches south. When he reached his handiwork, he took a long, drawn out lick across her breasts. A loud moan came from Gigi, and she arched backward, pushing the stunning orbs closer to his face, trying to direct his attention. He didn't hesitate in giving her what she wanted, taking her now erect nipple in his mouth, swirling his tongue around the peak. She let out another moan, this one even louder than the last, as he worked his way from side to side, making sure not the smallest amount of frosting was left.

"Holden..." she groaned, as he returned to her mouth. His name sounded amazing coming from her. It didn't matter what they were doing, that sound made his heart squeeze. But hearing it in reaction to him making her feel so good she couldn't think to say anything else? That might be one of the best feelings in the world.

Grabbing on to her hips, he quickly found the zipper on her skirt and undid it. Taking the cue, she shimmied out of the garment until she was sitting there in just a thong. It was Holden's turn to groan as he ran his fingers under the lace sitting on her hips, wondering how mad she would be if he just ripped the panties right off of her.

"The frosting was sublime, sweetheart. And you know I love your cupcakes," he told her, continuing to kiss her. "But there is another part of you I have been dying for a taste of."

Gigi stilled for a moment before opening her eyes and staring into his. He could see the uncertainty in her eyes, wondering where he was going with this.

"I want nothing more than to devour your sticky bun."

19

GIGI

"You…you do?" Gigi stuttered, not sure what to make of his comment.

"I absolutely do," he told her, still looking intently into her eyes. She saw a fire there that told her he was not only serious but filled with desire. It sent sparks shooting through her to think that he wanted her this much. "And not just because I heard Hunnie say it earlier. I've wanted it ever since that first afternoon in my bedroom."

Sugar Honey Iced Tea!

"You heard that?" she squeaked, swallowing hard. A new wave of embarrassment flooded over her, and she closed her eyes, letting her head fall forward, hoping she could just magically vanish into thin air.

"Sweetheart, look at me," he said, taking her face in his hands. "You never, ever have anything to be embarrassed about with me, understand? *Never*."

Gigi nodded, still feeling slightly silly, but the look in his eyes was unchanged. The fire was still there, and the heat from his gaze was almost burning a hole in her. She wanted him so badly she could feel it in every ounce of her being.

"Good, then I have a taste test to get back to," he growled. He captured her lips with his, bringing her right back to the state she'd been in while he had finger-painted her with the frosting.

Kissing his way down her body, he paused for a moment, lavishing her breasts with attention all over again. Still sensitive from moments ago, she felt all-new sensations rush through her. How was it possible to feel this much pleasure? Every place he kissed her seemed to be filled with a thousand nerve endings, exploding with just the lightest touch. He let go of her breasts, his mouth making a popping sound, and continued his journey down her belly, until he reached the lacy hemline of her panties.

Butterflies swarmed her insides as he slipped his fingers under the sides of her thong and started to drag it down her hips. He was slow and careful, drawing out the moment. She didn't know if that was his way of telling her that he knew she was nervous or if it was because that was just the pace he wanted it, but either way, she was grateful. When he reached her ankles, Gigi gasped as he slowly spread her legs apart and methodically inched his way back up, this time with kisses on the inside of her legs. The softness of his beard against her thighs surprised her. It tickled, but not in a way that made her want to giggle. It was as if someone was running a feather along her skin, letting her know he was there, drawing all the attention to that spot.

His kisses went from light and sweet to open mouthed and purposeful the closer he got to her mound. She could already feel the anticipation building in her, her pulse racing as she tried to catch her breath, with each new touch of his lips. As much as she always wondered what the hype was about, the idea of letting a man do this to her had always scared her a bit. Holden was the only man she could have ever imagined allowing down this road —that was how much she trusted him.

Before she knew what was happening, Holden placed one of those searing open-mouth kisses directly on her sex. The sound that came from her mouth was one she didn't recognize, but so was the immense pleasure she was feeling. She heard Holden chuckle softly as she fell backwards onto her forearms and opened her legs wider, giving him access to whatever he wanted. He ran his tongue up and down her pussy in long, languid strokes, following with nibbling and sucking that was driving her out of her mind. She had never felt anything like it, and she never, ever wanted it to stop. Every movement of his tongue sent her further and further into space. He continued to lick and suck, carefully avoiding her clit, where she was dying for his touch. She writhed under his attention, trying to coax him into finding the bundle of nerves, but no matter what she did, he expertly avoided the area.

Just when she thought there was no way this could get any better, he inserted two fingers, finding the secret spot inside her, and his tongue flicked her clit. Gigi flew up, arching her back from the new, sudden contact, letting out a groan that made her glad the closest neighbors were miles away. Holden reached up with his free hand, grabbing hers, entwining their fingers. The tender gesture made her feel even more connected to him, and her heart squeezed. She felt so much for him, and not just because he was driving her crazy with his mouth, but didn't have the words to express any of it.

"Oh my…Oh my…I…" Gigi started to say, but was cut off by the all-consuming bliss that took over all her senses as Holden took her clit in his mouth and sucked. Hard.

Her orgasm crashed over her, sending her throttling through the air. Every inch of her felt like it was on fire, like fireworks detonating rapid-fire. Her hand found the back of Holden's head, running her fingers through his hair as he continued, never letting up as the pleasure rolled through her over and over again.

When her climax finally subsided, Holden placed a few more tender kisses on her mound before rising up off his knees and leaning over her body with his, kissing her passionately. She kissed him back harder than she had ever kissed anyone, and it still wasn't enough. She wanted nothing more than to wrap her entire being around this man and stay that way forever.

"That might be the best thing I've ever eaten in this kitchen," he whispered, just before nibbling her earlobe. Wrapping his arms around her, he stood back up, returning her to an upright position, but thankfully not letting go. She wasn't sure that any of her muscles were working enough to hold her in place. He just held her there, their foreheads resting against each other, catching their breath.

"Holden, can I tell you a secret?"

"Of course."

"No one has ever done that to me before."

"I know, sweetheart."

"Was it that obvious?" she asked, feeling the panic rush through her.

"No, sweetheart. But you thought cake was better than sex. It wasn't hard to deduce. It was just one more thing I knew I needed to fix."

The blush Gigi felt rise up the back of her neck was nothing compared to the swoon that rushed through her. There was so much to this man that he hid from the world. So much that she still needed to discover. Her feelings for him overwhelmed her—she was falling harder for Holden than she had ever fallen for anything else in her life, all combined. How was it possible to feel so much for one person? But right now, that wonderful feeling of being somewhere between like and love was not what was burning inside of her. It was something else entirely. Something a lot more…primal.

"Holden?"

"Yes, sweetheart?"

Without another word, Gigi locked her legs around his waist, pressing her core into the crotch of his jeans, and taking him in a devouring kiss. Finding the button of his jeans, she undid them in a hurry, and slipped her hands into his briefs, giving his cock a good, hard squeeze.

HOLDEN

The groan Holden let out at the feel of Gigi's hand on his cock vibrated through his whole body and probably could have been heard all the way at the Busy Bean. Something about the way she took charge in the moment, grabbing him like he was the last cupcake at a BBQ, made him even harder than he already was, which he really hadn't thought possible. Going down on her had been a truly erotic experience. Armed with the knowledge that he was the first, that no one else had ever given her this kind of bliss, was special enough. But seeing and feeling how she reacted to his touch and watching her come undone from his handiwork had been something else altogether. He loved how responsive she was and loved even more that it was because there was something special between them.

She continued to stroke his dick, changing up the speed of her strokes, her sex only inches away. He could feel her heat calling to him, and he wanted nothing more than to sink in there and fuck her until neither of them could move.

Wiggling out of his pants and briefs, trying not to break from the fevered kisses, Holden managed to step out of his discarded clothes and kick them off to the side. He reached for her breasts again, stroking and caressing them, wanting to make sure she was as turned on as he was. Up until now, all their sexy times, while driven by desire and attraction, had still had an element of softness to them. But not this moment. This moment was filled with nothing but lust and primal need. He was going to show Gigi just how frenzied sex could be.

Leaning back a couple of inches, he finally broke their kiss, whipping his T-shirt over his head. Gigi's eyes were wild, matching his own, and her lips were swollen from their making out. He loved this look on her face. Grabbing her ass, he lifted her off the counter, positioning himself right at her entrance.

"Hold on, sweetheart, it's gonna be a wild ride," he growled, just before he slid her down his shaft. She was hot, wet, and felt so fucking good that Holden needed a moment. Gigi shuddered in his arms, whimpering from the joining of their two bodies.

He started slow, wanting to make sure she had time to adjust to the position, but after a few strokes, Holden picked up the pace, driving harder and harder into her. The movement from his thrusts made her breasts bounce, and the sight captivated his attention. He wanted to lean down and take them in his mouth again, but there was no way to do that and maintain the pace he was on. It was like he was a crazed animal who couldn't control himself, still he knew exactly what he was doing, how hard he was fucking her, and just how much they were both enjoying it. Gigi's head was thrown back, her moans echoing throughout her body. He could feel her body react to his motions, to his own animalistic desires.

"You like that, sweetheart? You like when I fuck you like this?" he growled.

"Yes...don't stop..." she said. "Holden...I'm gonna..."

Holden felt her insides clamp down on him, gripping him for dear life as an orgasm rolled through her body. Flinging herself forward, her nails digging into his shoulder, Gigi screamed, spurring him to go faster, harder, never letting up. He felt every single thing she did and more. His skin was on fire, his heart was pounding a mile a minute, and nothing else seemed to exist around them in this moment. Just the two of them, joined together, giving in to their passion.

When her orgasm finally let up, Holden slowed down until he was all but at a halt, letting her catch her breath. His heart squeezed, taking her in, her post-orgasmic state forming a blissed out look on her face. He pressed his lips to her, as if he could somehow share that bliss just through the contact of their lips. But that wasn't enough. He needed his own release and couldn't help but wonder if he could get her to another.

When he glided all the way out of her, Gigi whimpered in disappointment as he lowered her to the ground.

"Don't worry, sweetheart, we're not done," he said, spinning her around and bending her over the counter. "I just want to see this glorious ass of yours as I fuck you." He gave her backside a swat before driving back into her, letting out another groan.

"Yes!" Gigi called out. It was a reaction neither of them were expecting from her, but one that sent lightning through his veins nonetheless. *Alright, my sweet southern belle likes it a little rough sometimes...*

Gigi moved her hips backwards, meeting him thrust for thrust as he picked up the pace again. He was a man on a mission, wanting her to crest that mountain one more time. He didn't have the words to express how he felt about her, but he hoped that his actions now, in giving all of himself to her like this, showed her just what she meant to him. Just how much she had changed his world for the better, and how he had no idea what he'd do without her. He had a different outlook on the world now, and it was all because of her.

Feeling his own climax start to build, he reached around her and found her clit. Gigi mewled as soon as he made contact with the little bundle of nerves, crying out as he started to circle it with his finger. She was so incredibly responsive to his touch, which only served to fuel his own orgasm. A few strokes later, Gigi gripped onto the counter as she exploded again. Her pussy clamped down on Holden's cock right as his own release overtook him. She milked him for all he was worth, their bodies writhing together as they both came.

A long moment passed before either one of them could move, the room filled with nothing but the sounds of their breathing. When Holden finally felt like he had the strength, he stepped back from the counter, hauling Gigi into his arms. He picked her up and carried her up the stairs.

"Where are we going?" she asked, her eyes closed, snuggling against his chest.

"I think after that ride, what you need is a bubble bath," he said, turning into his bathroom. "A little roughness calls for a little softness in return."

He set her down on the vanity and turned on the hot water spigot on the clawfoot tub. Turning back to her, he was confused by the look on her face. She was looking at him like she was trying to work out a puzzle, or like what he had just said had been in a language she didn't understand.

"Are you going to get in with me?" she asked.

"If you would like me to."

She nodded. "I trust you, Holden. I feel safe with you. I…I more than like you."

"You 'more than like' me?" he asked, halfway teasing, halfway curious what that was supposed to mean.

"There isn't a word for that step in between like and that other L word. More than like was the best I could come up with," she responded, looking a little sheepish.

"I more than like you too, sweetheart. A lot."

20

GIGI

With only a few days left until Christmas, Gigi seemed to have lost track of whether she was coming or going. The Busy Bean was the busiest she'd ever seen, with the whole town of Colebury seeming to be in and out of the café as they were doing their holiday prep. The peppermint-bark cupcakes she'd created on a whim had been a big hit, both the test batches she'd dropped off at Speakeasy and the Gin Mill and at the Busy Bean as well. So much so, she now had special orders for them for the holiday seemingly coming out of her eyeballs. But the cupcake, which had either white or dark chocolate cake with chunks of peppermint candies mixed in, a chocolate mousse frosting, and was topped with a decent-sized hunk of the peppermint bark, was so much fun to make that the task didn't seem quite as daunting as it would have only months ago.

Today, however, was not about baking. Holden had made her mark off the entire day, telling her they had plans. Not that she had any idea where they were going. He'd been all kinds of secretive the last few days, telling her it was a surprise and that all she needed to do was be ready to go by two o'clock, and to wear warm clothes. Every time she tried to figure out what he could possibly have up his sleeve, her whole body thrummed with excitement. She had tried to coax it out of him that morning in his bed, peppering his chest with kisses, as she had recently discovered he liked, but he held strong and didn't crack even in the slightest.

"You're about to explode over there with anticipation, aren't you?" he asked, after they'd been driving for about forty-five minutes.

"Yes!" she told him. It had been what felt like forever since they'd seen anything other than trees and farmland, but Gigi had learned that Vermont was just like that, and it didn't mean they were lost. She trusted that Holden knew where he was taking her —she just wished they would hurry up and get there.

"Good, because we're here."

Gigi sat up in her seat, looking around to see if there were any signs of life, but still nothing. Until a second later, when a large sign reading "Aurora Christmas Tree Farm" came into view. A few hundred feet past the sign, they pulled into a parking lot that was streaming with people and families, some carrying trees, wreaths, and other assorted Christmas décor, while others milled about and chatted.

"A Christmas tree farm?" Gigi asked, her excitement boiling over. She knew she must sound like a little kid, but she couldn't help it. "Are we going to pick out a Christmas tree?"

"Sure are, sweetheart," he said, parking the truck and hopping out. When he came around and opened her door, he looked at her like she was the only woman on earth. It sent a ripple of emotion through her, loving the way he made her feel with just a look. "You said you don't have a lot of happy Christmas memories. That changes today."

Gigi bounded out of the door so fast, Holden had to take a step back to not lose his balance. She didn't have the slightest idea how this was done, but that wasn't going to stop her from enjoying every moment of this day. She rushed toward the area where most of the people seemed to be heading, with Holden hot on her heels, snow crunching under their feet as she found her way to the grove of pine trees.

"Okay, stupid question," she said, stopping in the middle of a row of trees. "What makes a good tree?"

There were fewer people around now that they were out among the spread of pines. It amazed her how each tree could look so similar and yet so different. Looking between them all, she had so many questions about this process and couldn't even begin to form them all.

"You just kinda pick one," Holden said with a shrug.

"So, we just walk up and down the rows until we see one we can't live without?"

Holden chuckled, grabbing her hand and pulling her into him. "Pretty much, sweetheart. Christmas trees are kinda like love in that sense—when you know, you know."

"I thought I knew once," she said, looking down at her feet, her joy over this experience fading slightly to the pain of thinking of Bradley and her sham of a marriage. "But I was wrong. It wasn't real. I chose the wrong tree."

Holden squeezed his arms tighter around her, drawing her into the warmth of his chest. She inhaled his spicy scent, finding comfort in it as well as his embrace. A brief wave of guilt hit her, reminding her that she still needed to let him in on the rest of her secret. Sucking in a deep breath, she tried to find the words now, but couldn't. His arms around her left her feeling safe, like everything she had left behind in Atlanta wasn't real. The thought slipped from her mind just as Holden rested his head on top of hers, allowing her a moment to deal with her emotions.

"That tree had no idea what it missed out on, in my opinion," he said, still holding her tight against him. She could feel his chest rumble as he spoke and couldn't help but smile at the vibrations. "Today's tree, however, will be so overjoyed to have been chosen by you, that it won't have the ability to do anything other than stand proud and try to make you happy every day."

"Is that so?" she asked, lifting her head to look him in the eyes.

"Absolutely." He took a step back, releasing her, but almost immediately took her hand in his and started to lead her down the row. "Now, traditionally the tree goes in the living room, right by the fireplace. We've also put it in front of the bow windows before. So, picture that space in your head and the shape of the tree you can see there."

Gigi looked around at the different trees, trying to place each one in front of the large window. She liked the idea that you'd be able to see the tree as you drive up to the house, like it was greeting you from inside. She squeezed Holden's hand as they walked along, each tree they passed not quite right. When they got to the end of the row they were on, they made a little U-turn into the next one, continuing their stroll. After about twenty minutes of walking, she was starting to wonder if maybe she was being too picky, if she'd gotten too far into her own head thanks to the love metaphor, since every one they saw had something "wrong" with it. They were all either too tall, or too skinny, too robust, or missing a patch. *So much for knowing it when I see it...*

The sun was starting to set, and a shiver ran through her from the cold. It was only going to get colder as the sun disappeared, and Gigi started to wonder if she needed to give up and just let Holden pick one.

"Cold, sweetheart?" Holden asked as she shivered again.

"A little," she replied sheepishly. She hated admitting to her failure, but she was really starting to not see any more options.

"Come here." Coming up behind her and drawing her in close, he wrapped himself around her, letting his body heat engulf her. His hard chest felt so good against her that she let herself get lost in it for a moment, leaning her head back on his shoulder. Closing her eyes, she took in a deep breath.

When she opened them again, she was stunned at what she saw. The perfect tree was standing right in front of them.

"Holden, that's it. It's perfect!" she said, unable to take her eyes off it. The evergreen was shorter than most of the ones that surrounded it and almost pear shaped, with its wide base and narrow top. Gigi couldn't exactly put her finger on the reason, but this was *the* tree.

"Yeah?" he asked. "Then it's yours." Holding up the bow saw he'd been carrying, a childlike smile crossed his face, and Gigi could have sworn she saw his eyes sparkle. Crouching underneath the tree, he sawed away at it, until the tree fell, hitting the ground with a loud thud.

"Alright, sweetheart, let's get this bad boy loaded into the truck and home so we can get it decorated."

HOLDEN

Out of the corner of his eye, Holden could see the joy written all over Gigi's face. She hadn't stopped smiling, or bouncing up and down, since they'd gotten the tree loaded into the truck back at the tree farm. When he'd asked his parents if they minded if he did this with her, wanting to make this first Christmas without her husband a happy one, he'd known it would mean a lot to her. He just hadn't realized that it would also mean so much to him.

Holding her this afternoon while she mourned had been an emotional moment for both of them. His marriage might have been a lot happier than hers, but their spouses were both just as gone, the both of them navigating the mess of moving on. Having her to walk through all of this with him had been exactly what he needed.

Taking a brief detour, he did a loop through Colebury green so she could get the full experience of seeing it all lit up. She ooohed and ahhhed, taking in the massive tree that stood directly in the middle of the square, covered in a myriad of colored and white twinkle lights. Large green, red, blue, and white ball-shaped ornaments were sporadically placed on the branches, adding to the flair, with a sparkly gold star at the very top which glittered under the flood lights cast on it. The front lawn of the town hall was aglow with a winter scene, complete with spiraled lights forming trees, and reindeer formed from twinkle lights. The Catholic Church next door had the requisite nativity scene out front, as well as a large wreath hanging on the side of the building.

When they pulled into the drive, Gigi bounded out of the truck, more energy flowing out of her than a small child with a new toy.

"How do we get it inside?" she asked, opening the tailgate.

"I'll handle that part, if you'll go make the hot chocolate," he told her, kissing her softly. He was pretty sure he would never tire of her kisses, and he could only hope that she felt the same. She nodded gleefully and skipped into the house.

Holden couldn't help but sing "Fat Bottomed Girls" by Queen as he maneuvered the evergreen that Gigi had picked out into the house. It took some doing, but he managed to make it through the front door and into the stand with no major damage to the tree's shape and minimal pine needle loss. Taking a look at it again, he silently laughed to himself that this was the one she picked. He had no idea why she felt so taken with this one, but it wasn't lost on him that she'd picked out a tree that had quite the set of hips, so to speak, and that her own hips were one of his favorite things about her. Not that he would ever admit to any of this out loud.

"Here you go," Gigi said, coming up behind him and handing him a mug. "Careful—it's hot."

"Ready for this?" he asked.

"You have no idea," she beamed.

"The St. Jameses and the Montgomerys are strictly white twinkle light people. None of that colored light nonsense," he said, in mock sternness, holding up a string of lights. "But other than that, it's free rein. I'll do the lights, if you want to start picking out ornaments. The standard ball ornaments and such are in that box, and the family ones are in there. Have at it."

Gigi went straight for the family ornament box, just as Holden would have guessed. Based on everything she'd told him, she'd had enough of generic decorations in this lifetime, and she wanted this tree to have heart. She pulled out a bunch, slowly unwrapping and admiring each one before laying them out on the coffee table. Once he was finished adorning the tree with the lights, she handed him a bright red ball and set to work on finding the perfect spot for everything she'd unwrapped.

"What's this one from?" she asked, holding up a pine cone with red glitter all over it.

"*That* is from sometime in preschool. I'm not even sure how the thing still has glitter on it. But there is no way my mom would have ever thrown it out. I'm not sure she actually understands the concept of throwing things out."

"That's so sweet though." She unwrapped a small, star-shaped frame ornament, covering her mouth to stifle a laugh as she looked at the picture inside. He didn't even need her to hold it up to know what it was, but he let her continue anyway. "Is this you?"

"Seventh grade," he said, owning up to the insanely embarrassing photo. "Braces, acne, and spiked hair. I mean, it's every thirteen-year-old boy's dream to look that cool!" Gigi laughed as he took the ornament from her and held it up to his face so she could see the comparison. "I'm sure that had Lexi Reynolds only known that this kid would turn into this stud, she never ever would have turned me down for the dance that year."

Taking the ornament out of his hand, Gigi stood on her tiptoes, pressing her lips to his. She tasted like the hot chocolate they'd been sipping on, making him want to devour her.

"That stud is mine now, so Lexi Reynolds can just back off!" she joked, before finding an opening on the tree for it.

"I am sure she is just as unconcerned about me now as she was back then. What about you? Who was your first crush?"

"Archie Porter," she said without hesitation. "He was *soooo* cool."

"And did Archie know that you existed?"

"Oh, absolutely. Our mothers lunched together. We 'dated' for three years," she said, using her fingers to make air quotes around dated.

"Dated?" he questioned, repeating her gesture.

"He broke my heart just before Homecoming in the eleventh grade. Said he just didn't see us working long-term. Sophomore year of college I found out he was dating the kicker of the football team at Tennessee. They're married now and have the cutest cocker spaniel."

"I can't compete with that story," he laughed, placing another ornament on the tree.

"I didn't realize we were competing," she laughed in return. "Here, do you want to put this one there?" She handed him a small wad of white tissue paper, opened up to display two small figures molded together, both wearing matching red Christmas pajamas. His and Hannah's names were written on each corresponding figure, with 'Our First Christmas' written underneath it. Holden felt the tears prick at the corner of his eyes as he stared at it, not sure what to do.

"You don't think it's weird?"

"No, why would it be? She's a part of your life, a part of you, Holden. I know you miss her, and that you'll always love her." Gigi paused, letting her words sink in. He loved that she was so understanding and that she wasn't threatened by his love for his late wife. She was right—Hannah was a part of him and always would be. Stepping in closer to him, she continued, "I want it on our tree. I think it belongs there." He nodded, his heart squeezing all over again.

They continued like this for another couple of hours, exchanging stories and loading the tree up with everything they could. When they finally didn't have anything left to hang, Holden went and turned off the lights in the living room. The glow of the fire was the only thing helping him to find his way over to the plug so that he could light their tree.

"Ready?" he asked, peeking around the robust bottom to see Gigi.

"Yes! Just plug it in already!"

Doing as she asked, he jammed the plug into the socket, and the tree came to life. The bright white lights illuminated the room, reflecting off the balls and the keepsake ornaments that adorned the branches. However, even all those lights were nothing compared to the look on Gigi's face as she admired their handiwork.

"What do you think, sweetheart?" he asked, wrapping his arms around her waist and pulling her into him so her back was against his chest.

"It's perfect," she whispered.

"I think it's missing something," he told her.

"What? We put everything on there. What could it possibly be missing?" Her voice sounded panicked, and he could feel her tense up in his arms. He gave her a squeeze before letting her go and reaching over to the couch. Digging in between the cushions, he pulled out the small flat box he'd shoved in there before they had left earlier.

"Here," he replied, handing her the box.

"Holden," she said, her panic turning to another emotion he couldn't quite place.

"Open it."

She slipped her finger underneath the red ribbon that surrounded the box, letting it fall to the ground. Opening it up, she found a brightly colored cupcake ornament, her name written on the bright blue cupcake liner. She gasped, covering her mouth with her hand as she took it in. Holden's heart stopped, waiting for her to say something, hoping that he'd done the right thing.

"This is our tree, so it needed a little Gigi on it. I thought nothing was better than a cupcake for Colebury's cupcake queen."

"Holden…" she choked out, looking up at him with tears in her eyes. "I…I…I…"

"I know, sweetheart, I know."

Throwing her arms around him, she crushed their mouths together. She still tasted like chocolate, but now, she also tasted like something else. Like all the happiness in the world. He felt like he could burst from all the love radiating through him right now, making it seem like all was right with the world. With Gigi in his arms, there wasn't anything else he could ever want.

21

HOLDEN

This was the kind of moment when Holden knew he should be nervous. His parents and godfather were due to arrive any time now, but the only thing he felt was a sense of excitement. Just like a little kid on Christmas Eve waiting on Santa, he couldn't wait for them to arrive and to meet Gigi. The first time he'd done the meet-the-parents thing had been over a scheduled dinner when Hannah's parents had come to visit Dartmouth—and he'd been scared out of his mind. He'd had no idea what to expect since every time he'd asked Hannah what they were like she'd simply respond, "They're parents." But now, his insides were humming with anticipation.

Gigi, on the other hand, seemed to be distressed enough for the entire state of Vermont.

She'd spent most of the morning rushing around the kitchen, trying to make sure that everything was beyond perfect. The buffet in the dining room was covered in more food than Holden had seen in there in maybe his whole life. Crab cakes, buffalo chicken sliders, chicken parmesan sliders, deviled eggs, sun-dried tomato pinwheels, and mini quiches were just some of the finger foods she'd already laid out, while he knew there was still more to be cooked or assembled. Not to mention the four types of cookies and two types of cupcakes she'd made. For a woman who had almost burned down a building a couple of months ago, she was certainly kicking ass and taking names now.

The crunch of the gravel pulled Holden's attention away from all the incredible smells wafting out of the dining room and toward the drive just in time to see his dad park their SUV. Running outside to greet them, he was a little taken aback when his godfather marched right past him and into the house.

"Hello to you too, old man," Holden called after him.

"Yeah, yeah," the tall, wire-thin man called back without even bothering to turn around. His salt and pepper hair was a little longer than Holden was used to, but at least from the back it seemed to suit him. "I want to meet this southern beauty who managed to remove your head from your ass."

Holden looked to his parents, both of whom shrugged in response. Everyone had always told him that he was the spitting image of his father, a fact that he'd always taken pride in, since Heathcliff was usually regarded as a good-looking man. These days his long beard disguised most of the resemblance, but he knew that if he were to shave, it would be like looking at his father in the mirror. Except for the eyes. The piercing blue eyes were the only part of his mother that he'd inherited, her fair hair and skin losing the genetics battle to his father's dark ones.

"He's been like this the whole drive up," his mother said. "You know how he gets."

"How are you, son?" his dad asked, embracing him. The contact felt good, and Holden wondered if it had always felt like this and he just hadn't realized it, or if this was one more thing the magic of Gigi had changed.

"I'm good. Although maybe a little worried about Gigi being left alone with him. She was already nervous enough about all this."

"Well then, let's go save her," his mom suggested.

Holden and his father grabbed their suitcases, and he gestured for them to lead the way. The three of them made their way inside just in time to find Gigi standing in the living room, wide-eyed and slack-jawed in front of Caulfield, frozen in place, a tray of mugs in hand.

"I should take that before you drop it," Holden said, rushing over to her. She managed to hand him the tray, and he stole a quick kiss from her, not caring in the slightest that they were on display for his family.

"Stop hoggin' the pretty girl," his godfather said, shooing him out of the way. "Young lady, I'm Caulfield Montgomery. It is a pleasure to make your acquaintance."

"GeorgiaGrace Elyse Hawthorne, née Shaw, as in Shaw Investments, not Shaw flooring, that's a whole other set of Shaws..." Gigi rambled. The words tumbled out of her mouth so fast, in such a thick southern accent, that it caught even Holden off guard. "And the honor is mine, Mr. Montgomery."

"Oh my dear, Mr. Montgomery was my father. You may call me Caulfield. Or even just Field like this one does." He gestured to Holden with his thumb, a large smile taking over his face.

"And these are my parents, Heathcliff and Catherine."

"It's a pleasure to meet you both as well. I made hot chocolate," she said, gesturing to the tray he'd taken from her and set on the table. He could tell she was still nervous, so he walked over to her, taking her hand, hoping that it would be of some comfort. She let out a small sigh while giving his hand a squeeze, and he knew he'd made the right call.

"So, Holden tells us that you've found a love for baking?" Catherine said, grabbing a mug and sitting in one of the chairs by the fire.

"Yes. I kinda fell into it, actually. I took a class years ago on cake decorating, but skipped the learning to bake part," she answered, as she and everyone else followed Catherine's lead in sitting down. "I had a bit of a rough start, but I think I'm doing pretty well now. I hope y'all don't mind, but I have a couple of new cupcake flavors that I need opinions on, so I figured I could try them out on you."

"What did you end up making other than the Arnold Palmer ones?" Holden asked.

"You made an Arnold Palmer cupcake?!" Caulfield exclaimed, pushing up out of the chair he'd just sat in and hurrying into the dining room.

"I made those, plus an espresso bean cupcake—so think a chocolate cake with espresso mixed in, with a mocha frosting, and chocolate sprinkles and a chocolate covered espresso bean. I thought since it's a coffee shop, that maybe a coffee inspired item would be more appropriate."

"Heath! You gotta try this thing, man," Caulfield called out.

"On my way!"

An awkward silence fell over them as Heathcliff joined his best friend in the dining room, and Holden searched for something to say. Every time he opened his mouth to say something though, he stopped himself, not wanting to say the wrong thing. He wanted to put Gigi at ease, to make her feel like part of the family. One look at her and he could tell what she was thinking. That she wasn't good enough and that she was ruining his family holiday. *Think of something, dumbass. Don't just let her sit here and think she did something wrong...*

"Why's it so quiet in here?" Caulfield asked, walking back into the room with a plate full of food. "Catherine, bust out the photos!"

"Photos?" Holden asked, looking between his parents and Caulfield, all of whom suddenly had very guilty looking grins on their faces.

"Oh, good idea!" Catherine said, reaching for her tote bag. As soon as Holden saw the spine of the mint-green photo album, he knew exactly where this was going.

"Oh no, put that away!"

"What is it?" Gigi asked.

"Holden's greatest hits!" Heath said, coming out of the dining room with plates of food for himself and his wife.

"No, no! The greatest hits album has no place seeing the light of day on Christmas!"

"I'm confused," Gigi said, looking at him like his whole family was speaking in Russian.

"You see, Gigi, Holden is an only child, with parents and godparents who are only children," Heathcliff explained. "So we have albums upon albums of photos of him. At one point in high school, his Aunt Viv thought it would be a good idea to pick out the best of the best photos and put them all in one album for easier viewing."

"And when we say best of the best, naturally, we mean the most embarrassing," Caulfield added on.

"Join me on the couch. We can start from the beginning."

"Mom, I really don't think that's necessary," Holden said. But it was as if he was the only one in the room listening, because Gigi moved about as fast as he'd ever seen. "Gigi, really, you don't have to."

"Oh, but I want to!" The smile she gave him was mischievous and full of joy, making his heart squeeze. He loved seeing the light shine in her eyes like that, and if it meant he'd have to sit through his parents showing off every stupid thing he'd done as a child, well then, so be it. *Better get cozy…*

"Holden was quite the nudist when he was younger. But the best was when he was about four, we were out shopping for Christmas. Viv had gone off to do something, I don't remember what. Anyway, I had to use the bathroom, and like any mother with a small child, I took him with me. So there I was, sitting on the toilet, trying to pee as fast as I could, and there was someone in the stall next to us who was…well, this poor lady had eaten something that hadn't quite agreed with her. If that's not embarrassing enough, having that kind of moment in the mall restroom, then Holden here drops to the floor, halfway slides under the stall, looks up at the lady and goes 'I smell you!' I wanted to die! I pulled up my pants as fast as I could but wasn't fast enough, because Holden shimmied his way out of the stall completely and took off! Along the way, he decided to strip…so I'm running through the mall, trying to find my child, left with a Hansel and Gretel type trail of his clothing. Viv and I finally found him on a rocking horse in the little tot lot area, naked as the day he was born! Luckily, Viv had a camera in her pocketbook, and we got this photo."

The whole group burst into laughter as Catherine finished her story. Even Holden couldn't help but let out a chuckle and shake his head as his mother looked at him proudly. It was not the worst story she could have shared. But the look of happiness and ease on Gigi's face would be worth every second of mortification.

"Wait…wait…" Gigi managed to say, trying to catch her breath from laughing. "The kid stripping in the mall, that was in *A Murder of Crows*! Raewyn watches the two women chase a naked toddler through the food court! That was based on you?"

GIGI

Caulfield stopped, his second Arnold Palmer cupcake halfway to his mouth, and stared at Gigi. She froze under his gaze, suddenly worried she'd said the wrong thing. *It was Raewyn, in A Murder of Crows, right?* Yes, she was sure of it. She knew his books like the back of her hand. That particular story was toward the bottom of the list when she ranked his catalog, but it had still been written by him, which meant it was better than most other books out there. At least in her opinion.

"Well, color me impressed. This beauty knows her books."

"I told you she was a fan," Holden said. Gigi couldn't help but feel a bit shy as Holden shared this fact. Caulfield Montgomery probably met fans everywhere he went. He didn't need to be bombarded with yet another one in his own living room on Christmas Eve.

"No, you told me she had read my stuff. You didn't tell me she could quote my own work back to me. Tell me darlin', which one is your favorite?"

"Oh, hands down *At Midnight*. I have lost count how many times I've read it. And each time, even though I know it's coming, I feel betrayed by Cretia. Ellis trusted her so blindly, and in the end, she was just a pawn in Cretia's game." She felt as though she were rambling and hoped to God that the words coming out of her mouth made sense. Holden reached over and took her hand, giving it a light squeeze. The contact felt good, natural, helping ease some of the anxiety rushing through her. Having him close like this made the moment feel as if she were a part of this family, and sitting adjacent to her favorite author was a regular occurrence.

Caulfield threw his hands up in the air, like he was signifying that there was nothing left to say after that statement. "Young lady has excellent taste in books, I vote we keep her! Now, would you like to know which scene in *At Midnight* was inspired by this one right here?" he asked with a nod toward Holden.

"Oh no! I draw the line at that story!" Holden said as his father burst into another fit of laughter.

"Is there a Holden anecdote in every book?"

"Sure is! Well, I take that back, he's not in *Convocation of Eagles*, simply because he wasn't born yet. But do you remember the café scene in *On Parade*? The baby boy that the waitress kept calling a girl? That was him."

"So what in *At Midnight* is Holden?" Gigi asked, her curiosity gnawing at her.

"Don't you dare!" Holden said sternly, pointing to his godfather.

"Oh honey, just tell her. It's not that bad," Catherine said.

Gigi looked at Holden, who was simply shaking his head in

disbelief. She loved seeing this side of him—so at ease and so full of life. His family certainly brought out the best in him.

"Fine, but I'm telling the story!" he said. Caulfield motioned for him to continue, and Holden sucked in a long, deep breath, taking his time to exhale. "So, you know the scene where Godwin asks Xander for a big Band-Aid? Well, I might have had a similar experience."

"Hold on...you..." Gigi stumbled on the words, trying to wrap her mind around what the always sexy, uber broody Holden was trying to tell her. "You nicked yourself manscaping?"

Holden groaned, launching himself against the back of the couch, head thrown back as if he were trying to avoid looking at her. She squeezed his hand, just as he had done for her a moment ago. She wanted to remind him they were in this together, and that she would be here for him no matter what. Even if she did learn all his embarrassing secrets in one sitting. Goodness knows she had plenty of her own.

"He's leaving out the good bits!" Caulfield cackled. "He was a good bit younger than I made Godwin—so twelve, thirteen, somewhere in that range—and he'd read an article in Playboy or something that girls liked that kind of thing. Not that I have any idea who he thought was going to be seeing it. So he was upstairs in the bathroom, trying to give the boys a haircut, and sliced himself open! He hollered bloody murder, which I don't blame him for, because that had to have hurt. So Heath and I go running up there, to find him standing in the bathroom, cupping his balls, hands all bloody."

"I freaked out, thinking something was really wrong," Heath said, picking up where his best friend left off. "And called for Catherine to call 911. So she comes rushing upstairs to ask why, sees the scene, and about faints. That's when Holden decided to fess up about what he was up to and where all the blood came from."

"I quietly excused myself at that point," Catherine added in. "Best let the men handle that."

"This was not a story I ever intended for you to hear," Holden murmured, still staring at the ceiling.

"Would you feel better if I shared something?" Gigi asked, wanting to take some of the pressure off Holden. As much as she was enjoying hearing these stories about him, she wanted this occasion to be a good one for him too. For him to look back on this Christmas and smile. This was already the best one of her life, and she knew it was only getting started.

He sat up, his eyes meeting hers. There was a warmth in them that was new, but still as comforting as ever. She felt her insides melt under his gaze, and she had to resist the urge to snuggle into him, kissing him until they were both blue in the face. The connection between them was so strong, making her feel like they had been celebrating the holiday like this their whole lives, rather than only a few hours. A smile tugged at one corner of his mouth, his eyes still burrowing into hers, letting her know that he was feeling it too.

"Well," she started up again, trying to figure out which story to go with that could rival the one that Holden had just shared. "I was one of the first girls in my little friend group to get boobs. Which I know sounds cool, but really, it was just awkward, because I had a bra and no one else did. The summer I was twelve, we had a sleepover at the country club. We did it every year. Set up tents by the pool, swam at night—it was a lot of fun. Since we basically spent all night in our swimsuits, my clothes were left in my duffel in my tent. One of the boys, on a dare or something, snuck in at one point and stole my bra. I had no idea until the next morning, when we woke up and went to get dressed and I couldn't find it. Then we heard a whole bunch of laughter and went outside—to find my training bra flying high right in between the American flag and the Georgia state flag. So of course, then everyone knew it was mine, because when the head lifeguard finally got it down from there, he asked out loud who it belonged to and I had to go claim it."

"Oh sweetheart," Holden said, hauling her into his side and

wrapping an arm around her as he laughed. As much as she hated telling that story, it didn't seem so bad confessing it to Holden and his family. "I will never complain about the manscaping story ever again. At least the only people who witnessed it were these guys. And I promise to never put it in a book." He looked pointedly over to his right, where Caulfield was busy savoring his third cupcake.

"You have to write one first, kid," the older man lobbed back.

"I have about 50K sitting on the laptop upstairs if you want to take a look at it, old man," Holden responded, not even skipping a beat.

Pride swelled inside Gigi as she watched Holden watch his family's reactions to his news. The look on everyone's faces told Gigi that they had no idea that he'd started writing again, and for a moment, she was unsure if she should say anything. She had no idea what his book was about, but she knew by the change in his attitude and demeanor that finally having that outlet again meant a lot to him, and by extension her. She couldn't wait until she could read it.

"You're not kidding," Heath finally said.

"Not kidding."

"He's been up in that loft plugging away for about two weeks now," Gigi added in. "He won't tell me what it's about, but I'm sure it's amazing."

Without a word, Caulfield popped up from his seat, shoving the rest of the cupcake in his mouth, and walked over to Gigi, holding out his hand as if to shake hers. Sliding her hand into his, she looked around at everyone else, trying to figure out what was going on. Each member of the family shook their head and shrugged, just as confused as she was.

"I don't know what magic it is you possess, Miss Georgia, but between the best damn cupcakes I've ever eaten and the fact that he's writing again, it must be something special. Welcome to the family."

22

HOLDEN

Much to Holden's displeasure, the greatest hits album did not make an exit after the first round of stories. His mother made sure that Gigi saw every last photo that she had in there, and gladly told her the story behind anything she asked about. For as embarrassed as he was though, no part of him would change how the afternoon played out. Watching as they initiated Gigi into the family made him happier than he'd thought he could be ever again. He'd known as soon as she mentioned her love of reading that his dad and godfather would be taken with her, and his mother was just one of those people who seemed to like everyone, but actually seeing it all unfold in front of him was something else.

"Storytime!" Caulfield announced, emerging from the loft, where he had spent the last couple of hours. He'd made a beeline up there shortly after they had finished looking at the photos, insisting he be left alone to "properly immerse" himself in the manuscript Holden had been fiddling with for the last couple of weeks. A pit formed in his stomach, waiting for his godfather—a man he admired on many levels, but especially as a talented storyteller—to say something, anything, about what he'd just read. Instead, Caulfield turned to him and said, "I didn't see *A Christmas Carol* up there, so I assume you brought it down?"

"I did," Holden responded, still waiting for more.

"Perfect! Then grab your girl and cuddle up!"

As everyone settled themselves into their chosen spot, Holden did as he was told, taking Gigi's hand and pulling her onto the couch with him. He burrowed himself into the corner, making sure he was comfortable, before she settled in between his legs, resting her head against his chest and wrapping his arms around her. The sun had mostly set, but there was still a little sliver of light coming through the big bow window, that mixed with the light on the tree and the glow of the fire gave the room a cozy feel perfect for the occasion.

"'Marley was dead: to begin with. There is no doubt whatever about that,'" Caulfield began, his voice lowered and serious sounding, like he was narrating a documentary. The words were familiar, as was the older man's tone, but something about this moment held a new importance to him.

"I can't remember the last time I actually read the real Dickens version of this story," Gigi whispered to him. "I don't think we even read it during the Dickens elective I took in college."

"When it comes to British Victorian era authors, in this house we prefer the Brontë sisters, for obvious reasons," he replied, taking a moment to inhale her sweet scent. She smelled of cupcakes and frosting, and it flooded his senses, sending a thrill up his spine. Add in the comforting feel of her soft body against his, and he was pretty sure this moment couldn't get any better. "But good ol' Chuck makes an appearance every Christmas Eve. Give it a couple of years, and you'll be able to recite this story, just like the rest of us."

Holden hadn't realized what he said until he felt Gigi tense in his arms. The movement was slight, and disappeared almost instantly, but he knew her and her body well enough now to have noticed the subtle movement. Instead of backtracking on his words though, he tightened his arms around her, placing a soft kiss on her hair and letting the words settle. He had no idea if the rest of the family heard his little slip or not, but he didn't care. She was his, and that was all that mattered.

Caulfield and Heathcliff traded on and off reading the tale, even forcing Holden to take on the chapter surrounding the ghost of Christmas present. He did his best to rival the other two with his own narration, however when he got to the part of Tiny Tim, his impression seemed to be lacking. Gigi giggled incessantly at the voice he chose, making him say lines over and over again, only spurring her laughter more.

When the story finally came to an end, and Tiny Tim had uttered his infamous "God bless us, everyone," the whole family was exhausted. The day had been filled with so much love and laughter—not to mention all the food—and Holden felt like he could just burst. More than anything though, he hoped that Gigi felt the same way.

"I think your mom is asleep," Gigi said, twisting in his arms to face him.

He looked over in time to see his dad lift his mother out of her chair, giving them a wink before taking her upstairs. It amazed him still that after forty-some years of marriage, their love was still so strong. Had he been asked six months ago, without a doubt he would have said he was jealous that they had each other to depend on, to grow old with. But now, his outlook had changed, and for the first time in what felt like forever, he thought he might just have that too.

"You two kids behave now," Caulfield said, following his friends toward the stairs. "Don't stay up all night or Santa won't come."

Gigi's giggle lit him up inside as they watched Caulfield disappear up the stairs. Once he was out of view, she snuggled deeper into his chest, like she was trying to burrow herself into him. Closing his eyes, Holden sighed, holding her close to him. He still couldn't believe how happy he felt.

"Holden?" Gigi said, after a long moment of silence. Her voice was so soft and quiet, but it had almost sounded like his name left her lips like a question.

"Yes, sweetheart?"

"This is the best Christmas I've ever had."

"It's just getting started, sweetheart. Santa still needs to come visit."

"I already got what I wanted. Besides, what I asked him for doesn't really fit under the tree," she said coyly. "I know because I watched said gift cut down said tree."

Holden opened his mouth to respond but couldn't find the right words. He didn't want to sound trite or rehearsed—he simply wanted her to know that she was easily the best gift he'd ever received and that he didn't take it for granted. They'd both had a hard road getting to this point, but maybe their finding each other made it all worth it.

"Well, Santa came a little early and wanted me to give you this," he said, finally finding his words. He reached into the couch, just as he had the other night, and pulled out an almost identical box.

Gigi sat up and spun around, still in his lap, wrapping her legs around his torso. She took the box from him, her eyes wide with confusion. His pulse started to race as he watched her undo the ribbon. He'd been nervous when he'd given her the cupcake after decorating the tree, but this one made him almost feel panicky. If all went as it should, this was going to take things to a new level, one he hoped she wanted just as much as he did.

Opening the lid, she carefully peeled back red tissue paper to display two small, molded figures sitting cross-legged, staring into a roaring fireplace, each one wearing a red shirt with pajama bottoms that were white with blue snowflakes. The blonde female figure had "Gigi" written on her back, while the dark-haired male figure next to her read "Holden." Along the mantel of the fireplace, in simple black letters, were the words "Our First Christmas."

A sob escaped from Gigi, and Holden's heart lurched. Had he done something wrong? Was this the wrong gift? *It's too soon, you've only known each other a couple of months, been together less than that. Nice job, dumbass...*

Covering her sobs with her hand, she looked up at him, tears spilling from her eyes. Holden expected to see sadness, or even fear, but the only thing he saw was the same emotion he was feeling.

Love.

"I hope it's not too presumptuous of me," he started. "But I thought the occasion needed to be properly marked and celebrated. I know that Christmas hasn't always been a happy time for you, but that changes now, Gigi."

"Can I put it on the tree?" she asked, swiping at her tears.

"Of course, that's why I gave it to you. And I promise, it will still be there tomorrow."

She leapt off the couch in a single movement, nearly knocking him over in the process, and pranced over to the tree, searching for the exact perfect place for it. When she finally found a spot, she pushed up to her tiptoes, trying to reach.

"Don't hurt yourself, sweetheart," Holden laughed, getting off the couch. "Let me help."

Before she could argue, he grabbed her luscious hips and picked her up, giving her access to where she had been trying to reach. When she got their ornament secured to the branch, he slowly lowered her back to the ground, spinning her in his arms. She looked so beautiful in the glow of the twinkle lights, he couldn't help but cup her face and capture her mouth in his. They stood there, wrapped in each other, kissing—soft, slow, and without agenda—for what felt like hours. Holden could feel all the blood rush to his groin every time Gigi would whimper. For as much as he wanted to take her right here, he wanted to simply love on her even more.

Finally breaking apart, their lips swollen from their efforts and Gigi's cheeks slightly pink from his beard, Holden felt like he was the king of the world. Right here, right now, he was sure that things did not get better than this.

"I know I said that I already got what I wanted. But I do have one more Christmas wish," Gigi said, an impish smile tugging on her pretty pink lips.

"Anything, sweetheart."

"Take me upstairs and unwrap me?"

GIGI

Gigi wasn't really concerned that her "wish" would go ungranted. She knew full well that Holden would not only take her up on said wish, but that he would make sure that she was left singing afterwards. What she had not expected was to be picked up and tossed over his shoulder like a sack of potatoes, much like when he rescued her from the fire she'd started.

"Holden, put me down!" she whisper shouted, lightly hitting his back with her fists. The giggles that escaped betrayed her mock seriousness and earned her a swat on the butt from him.

"Shhhh, don't want to wake my parents," he said as he slipped into his room and closed the door.

"I've never done it with parents in the house," she said, hoping the admission didn't make her sound stupid. "I guess that lands me on the nice list..."

"I can promise you, sweetheart, you are most certainly on *my* naughty list."

Gigi licked her lips in anticipation as Holden stalked closer to her, a look in his eyes like he wanted to eat her alive. She felt a chill run down her spine, causing her to shiver with excitement. She wanted him more than she could say—tonight in this bedroom, and for years to come. How could she have ever thought that what she had before was love? That hadn't even begun to scratch the surface of what she and Holden had. What was between them was the most powerful thing she'd ever experienced, and she wanted to spend the rest of her life exploring these feelings with him.

In a flash, they were in each other's arms, mouths melded together, hands everywhere as they worked on ridding themselves of their clothes. As the last article of clothing hit the floor, Holden grabbed ahold of her ass, picking her up and taking her over to the bed. He laid her down gently, looming over her like a villain, but she wasn't afraid. Not of him, not of how she felt, not of anything. She reached up and ran her hand along his jaw, feeling the softness of his beard in between her fingers. The softness of it still amazed her, as did just how much she enjoyed the feel of it against her skin. Lowering himself, he kissed her again, this time slow and sweet, like he was memorizing her mouth. His kisses only served to fuel her desire even more, feeling her whole body come alive.

Holden started to kiss his way down her body, lavishing all the sensitive spots he'd come to know that turned her on. Gigi felt her nipples contract as he reached the swell of her breasts, his open-mouth kisses leaving a trail of heat as he went. The need pulsing through her caused her to arch her back, trying to find his mouth with her breast, but he swerved just in time to continue to tease his way across her chest. He looked up at her, a sly smile on his face. Even in the dark she could see his piercing blue eyes drinking her in, and she could feel herself growing wetter by the second just from the stare.

"No rushing tonight, sweetheart," he told her, his voice rough with desire. "Tonight, I'm going to make love to you like you've never experienced before."

Another shiver ran through her body. This was already more intense than anything else she'd experienced, and he'd barely touched her. How could it get any more erotic?

A heartbeat later, he answered her unspoken question, dipping his hand into her sex and slowly stroking her. She let out a whimper, trying to keep quiet and not disturb anyone else in the house, but the more and more he played with her, the harder it became. Up and down her folds he went, each time missing the bundle of nerves calling his name by such a small margin that she knew it was calculated on his part. Her heart was pounding in her chest, and her senses were on overload. He knew every inch of her and was playing her like a violin. Just when she thought she was going to burst, he slipped two fingers inside her while simultaneously finding her clit with his thumb. Grabbing onto the bedspread and arching her back, she opened her mouth to react, but her moan was captured by Holden's mouth crashing against hers. Everything about what he was doing was driving her crazy. She could feel her orgasm starting to build as he kissed her furiously, his hand never letting up on its pursuit. Shifting slightly, Holden adjusted the angle of his wrist, finding a new spot inside her. That was all she needed.

A moment later, fireworks seemed to burst from underneath her skin as her climax took over. Wave after wave of pleasure crashed over her, causing her to almost cry out again. She had no idea what it was—the holiday, the thrill of knowing that his parents were down the hall, or all the new, next-level feelings they were starting to admit to each other—but this wasn't like all the other amazing orgasms Holden had given her. This one was different. There was more power to it, like it had been building inside her for years, just waiting for the right time to surface.

When she finally came down from her newfound high, she was greeted with another set of long, drawn-out kisses from Holden. They had done this in what had seemed like every way possible, yet somehow, he still had tricks up his sleeve.

"You are exquisite, Gigi," he said, placing his forehead against hers. "I hope you know that. I hope you know how special you are. Not only to me, but in general. Because you are so fucking special."

"So are you, Holden," she said, fighting back tears. She had no idea what she had done to deserve him, but she was so incredibly thankful nonetheless. He'd taken so many years of her feeling worthless, like she was nothing but a screwup, and made them all disappear in weeks. "Make love to me, please."

Without another word, he wrapped his arm around her, and rolled them over so he was lying on his back. Taking his cue, she straddled him, placing herself right at the tip of his dick. Slowly, she lowered herself down on him, taking him in, inch by glorious inch. She could feel herself adjust to his size, enjoying the moment. He felt so good inside her, like nothing else she'd ever felt. Following his pace from earlier, she leisurely moved her hips, finding a simple rhythm, drawing out the moment. Holden moved his hips underneath her, his movements complementing hers. Neither of them was in a hurry, wanting to feel and experience everything this moment had to give them. He reached up, cupping her breasts in his big hands, playing with the taut peaks of her nipples. A soft, barely audible whimper escaped from her. Everything he was doing to her was magic. He made her feel so beautiful, like she was the only woman on the planet.

Wrapping his arms around her waist, Holden sat up, never disconnecting their bodies. Placing his forehead against hers, he drew in a deep breath, holding it for a moment, before letting it go as if he were trying to inhale the moment. Gigi could hear their hearts beating in time with one another's, falling in sync with their breathing. Clutching onto him harder, she felt tears start to sting her eyes. She had no idea where they were coming from, or what exactly she was feeling, but it was so overwhelming that she couldn't stop them from falling. She wanted to tell him how she felt—wanted to use those three little words that she thought she'd never say again. But she didn't want him to think it was just something she said in the heat of the moment.

"Forget Christmas, you're the best gift I've ever been given. Period," he said, breaking the silence. She could hear the truth in his words and feel it in his touch as he started rocking them back and forth, giving them the friction both their bodies were craving. His thrusts were deliberate and unhurried, full of passion and meaning. She heard everything he was telling her with his body loud and clear.

Gigi could feel another orgasm start to build inside her. If he kept up these movements, hitting her in all the right spots, she knew she wouldn't last long.

"Holden..."

"Come with me, sweetheart. I want to be holding you when you fall apart."

His words were enough to push her over the edge. Her whole body shook, the powerful climax taking over her, sending her even higher than she was before. Holden pulled her impossibly closer, still thrusting, in search of his own release. A few more strokes and he found it, letting out a muffled groan.

They stayed like that for a moment, clinging to each other, letting the sounds of their heartbeats drown everything out again, before climbing under the covers. Gigi instinctively snuggled into Holden as if they'd been sleeping this way their whole life. Her entire body was exhausted from their lovemaking, but there was still one thing she needed to say.

"Merry Christmas, Holden," she whispered into the darkness.

"Merry Christmas, Gigi."

23

GIGI

The warmth of the sun shining in from the window next to the bed felt good on Gigi's face as she slowly drifted awake. Reaching over for Holden, she was startled a little to not find him there. Had he gone to the bathroom? She looked over to the bedside clock—seven fifty-five.

"Oh for heaven's sake!" she muttered out loud.

She had planned to be up early, wanting to make sure she had breakfast ready for the family as each one wandered downstairs. At least the sticky buns just needed to be put into the oven. But where was Holden? Why hadn't he woken her up?

She pranced around in a tizzy, trying to find a pair of sweats or something—anything other than the clothes she'd been wearing last night—to put on to head downstairs. But there was nothing but her discarded outfit. All her clothing was in her room, down the hall. Finally settling on a pair of Holden's sweatpants and an old T-shirt, she hoped that she had cinched the pants tight enough that they wouldn't fall down. At least if they did, the shirt she was wearing was long enough that she was more than covered.

The moment she opened the door, the sound of laughter

wafted up the stairs. She could hear the rumble of Holden's voice chiding his godfather about something he'd said, as Heathcliff and Catherine egged them both on. Her heart sank, the realization hitting her that she was the last one awake, and they were all downstairs without the yummy breakfast she had planned on serving. Rushing down the stairs as fast as her legs would carry her, she got her foot caught in the too-long pants, nearly causing her to slip on the last stair and faceplant into the hardwood floor.

"Whoa," Holden said, rushing over to catch her as she tried to steady herself with the railing. "Today is not the day to try new stunts. What's the matter? Why do you look so upset?"

"I overslept! I don't know where my phone is, so I didn't hear my alarm, and so now breakfast is going to be late..." she rambled, feeling the rush of anxiety start to grow within her.

Holden reached into his back pocket and produced her phone, holding it up and waving it in front of her. "You didn't oversleep. You slept in. There is a difference, I promise. You deserve a quiet, relaxed Christmas morning. I already took care of breakfast."

Gigi looked over to the rest of the family, who was sitting around the tree, sticky buns in front of them and coffee cups in hand. Her insides warmed as she took in the scene, armed with the knowledge of what Holden had done. For what felt like the millionth time, she wondered what she had done to deserve him and said the biggest silent thank you she could.

"You spoil me," she said.

"I told you, it's not spoiling you to give you what you deserve."

"Hurry up, you two!" Caulfield called out. "Santa came!"

"He does know Santa isn't real, right?" Gigi asked with a giggle.

"GeorgiaGrace, you take that back right now!" Holden said, his hand flying to his chest in mock indignation. "Life is too short to not believe in Santa. Is that understood, young lady?"

"Yes sir!" she nodded, holding back another laugh at the knowing look he was giving her.

"Gigi, we color code gifts, that way we know what belongs to who," Catherine explained as she and Holden walked over and sat on the couch. "Heath is the snowflakes, Caulfield is the Santas, Holden has elves, and yours is the ornaments."

"So, the Frankenstein, mismatched paper ones are yours then?"

"I've been wrapping her gifts like that for over forty years. Why waste the paper scrap when it's still perfectly good?" Heath commented.

Catherine rolled her eyes, but then immediately blew her husband a kiss. Gigi loved the way the two of them didn't shy away from being affectionate with each other, even after more than four decades together. It must have been where Holden got it from. Glancing over at the pile of gifts, she was taken aback by the size of the items that were wrapped in her designated paper.

"Y'all didn't need to get me anything!"

"Oh honey, of course we did! That's what family does," Catherine said.

Family.

Gigi's heart skipped a beat at the word. She'd spent so much of her life wanting a family like the ones she'd seen on TV, and now here she was, celebrating Christmas with one. It was almost too much. She sat there, trying to collect her thoughts, taking in the flurry of unwrapping gifts. Catherine nearly came out of her chair in excitement over some bubble bath, in a scent that had been discontinued years ago, while Heath and Caulfield laughed uncontrollably when they discovered they both had bought the other tickets to see some folk singer they really liked in concert. The whole scene was like something out of a made-for-TV movie.

"This one is from the whole family," Holden said, appearing at her side, carrying a large box covered in ornament paper.

Carefully, she ripped away the paper, unsure of what to expect. Everyone else's gifts so far were much smaller in size, leaving her a little apprehensive. A quick tug at the paper revealed a picture of a bright teal stand mixer, just like the one she'd secretly been looking at online.

"Oh my God," she gasped. "No, no, it's too much!"

"Nonsense!" Heath said. "Holden tells us that you're baking up a storm! If that's so, you need one of those things!"

"I don't know what to say."

"You can start by keeping us well stocked in these sticky buns," Caulfield commented.

Gigi glanced at Holden out of the side of her eyes, watching as he bit back a knowing smile. The look on his face was priceless—all furtive and flirty. She could tell he wanted to make some kind of innuendo but was still trying to respect the sanctity that was Christmas morning.

"Well, I didn't know about the color code rule, but the little box with the butcher paper on it is for you," she told him, trying to get his mind out of the gutter. Grabbing it, he tore into it, removing the paper in a single rip.

"Noise cancelling headphones? Talk about too much, Gigi."

"It's so you can concentrate on your writing if I'm in the house baking. That way you don't have to listen to Taylor and me duet all the time."

"I love your singing, but I'm sure these will come to good use," he said, giving her a kiss. Picking up a rectangular box, he handed it to her. "This is from me."

"But the ornament…"

"Was extra. This is my real gift to you."

She removed the paper, lifting the lid on the white box emblazoned with "Haley Made," and pulled the glittery tissue paper back, unveiling a stunning brown leather-bound journal. The front was embossed with "Recipes from the kitchen of Gigi Hawthorne" curved over a hand-painted image of a cupcake sitting in front of a snowcapped mountainscape.

"Holden, it's beautiful!" she said, fighting back more tears.

"Believe it or not, that was made right here in Colebury. Haley used to work at the Busy Bean, but now has an online store where she makes custom leather goods. I figured you needed a place to keep all those recipes you were developing."

The box slipped from her lap as she launched herself into Holden's arms, clinging to him for dear life. The tears she had been fighting back earlier seemed to have won the battle and were now streaming down her cheeks, but she didn't care. She was too overwhelmed by the thought and care he put into the gift. No one had ever given her anything as personal as Holden had, and it was more happiness than she could handle. The three little words she had held back last night were bubbling up to the surface again. She finally let go of him after a long moment and turned to watch everyone else open their remaining gifts but snuck a glance at her new notebook every couple of minutes.

When the last of the gifts had been opened, and they had cleared away all of the ripped paper and bows, Gigi let out a massive sigh. The morning had been absolutely perfect. Now, she needed to get to work on making sure their Christmas dinner was just as amazing.

"I should get started on dinner," she said. Standing up from the couch and stretching, she realized she was still in Holden's too-big-for-her clothes and immediately felt self-conscious. His family hadn't batted an eye at any of the outward displays of affection between them, so maybe the lack of her own clothes wasn't an issue in their minds.

"Would you like help?" Catherine asked. "I don't want to step on toes."

"I'd love it," Gigi said, meaning it wholeheartedly. Catherine struck her as the kind of woman who knew all sorts of secrets about cooking, something that Gigi was still lacking herself. Gigi also really liked the idea of some alone time with her, to get to know her better, without the men ragging each other about something in the background.

Holden grabbed her around the waist, tugging her into his lap and placing a sloppy wet kiss on her cheek, before leaning into her ear and whispering, "Before you go, I just wanted to let you know how fucking sexy you look in my sweats. I think we need to make that a regular thing."

"For you…anything."

HOLDEN

"Heath, you mind if I steal the boy for some one-on-one time in the loft?" Caulfield asked after they'd all showered and gotten dressed.

"Go for it. Keep you two out of my hair while I start this book," Heathcliff responded, holding up the new autobiography he'd unwrapped that morning.

"We'll take the long way. Best not to disturb the pretty ladies in the kitchen."

"Lead the way, old man," Holden responded, gesturing toward the stairs.

Making their way down the hall and past the bedrooms, Holden couldn't hold back a smile as he listened to the voices of Gigi and his mother waft up from the kitchen. The two were talking and laughing like old friends, just as he had hoped they would. Truth be told, Gigi had so seamlessly slipped into his family—along with the rest of his life—it was hard to believe that three months ago she hadn't been a part of his life. That three months ago he was alone in this big house, an empty shell of a human being, just tolerating life. Now, he woke up each morning happier than the last, and he was actually passionately writing again.

"So…your muse is back," Caulfield commented as he sat down in the leather desk chair. "Or should I say, she's taken on a new form. Perhaps one that is blonde and southern?"

Holden smirked, unable to deny the accusation. He collapsed into the old couch that was up against one of the walls, sighing as he tried to formulate the perfect response.

"I can't deny that certainly something has changed."

"Something has changed? That's what you're going with? Three months ago you were walking around like a zombie. You had all the personality of a stale ham sandwich."

"Wow, that's an analogy."

"Do you have a better way to describe yourself?" Caulfield asked, looking at him scoldingly. Holden shook his head and raised his hands in surrender—he knew when to shut up. This was one of those moments. "The Holden I have seen since I got here is the Holden I helped raise. You're the little boy who loved to laugh and joke around. The teenager who would go toe-to-toe with his dad and me, jab after jab, taking it as well as he dished it out. The man who loves with his whole heart and isn't afraid to show it. The author who has wild ideas inside his head, whose words bring to life a world that readers are never going to want to leave."

"So you did like it?" Holden asked, unable to hold back the question. His curiosity had been gnawing at him since Caulfield had emerged from the loft yesterday afternoon. He was dying to know what the man thought of his manuscript.

"It's rough, but so is every first draft," he said. "You have the makings of a fantastic ghost story. Where'd the idea come from?"

"Gigi," Holden sighed, thinking about the moment the idea had come to him. "She showed me her old, tattered copy of *At Midnight*, and it has all these notes in the margins. You know she wrote her senior paper in college about that book. About the use of the color green in it. She had all these passages underlined in it, every time you mention the color. She was so, so sure that it was Anaura. That it was all somehow tied to the necklace, and it got me thinking." The idea of writing something similar to Caulfield's work had never interested him until now. He knew it would have to be different enough to stand on its own, but for the first time in a long time he was confident that he could do it.

"Smart girl."

"She's brilliant. She doesn't think so, because that asshole she was married to spent years tearing her down, but she really is brilliant. She'd never baked anything in her life prior to arriving in Vermont, and now she's making her own recipes. She's shy and sweet, but man, the fire inside her is something else."

"Though she be but little, she is fierce," Caulfield quoted. "Does she know that you love her?"

Love? Was the old man crazy? He liked Gigi…he more than liked her, just as they had expressed the other day. But love? No, it was too soon.

"And just what makes you think—"

"I have ears, boy, and a bedroom right next to yours," Caulfield chided, cutting him off.

Oh shit, so much for being quiet…

"And more than that, I have eyes. I see the way you look at her. The way you watch her when she doesn't know you're looking. It's the same way I looked at your Aunt Viv. The way your dad does your mom."

Holden leaned forward on the couch, letting Caulfield's words settle around him. He loved Gigi. He wanted a future with her. One filled with cupcakes, sticky buns, and whatever else she created. A future full of reading by the fire, of nights snuggled up watching movies, of sitting out in the gazebo watching the snow fall. He wanted her to help him come up with story ideas and travel the country with him as he put those stories into people's hands. He wanted to explore the idea of a family with her.

Sucking in a deep breath, he looked up at his godfather, who was patiently waiting for him to arrive at the same realization he had. "She's my future, Uncle Field. No doubt about it. I love her."

"Then, at some point, you'll be needing this," he said, reaching into his pocket and pulling out a small, blue, hinged box and handing it to Holden. Holden took it, flipping it open, a stunned expression taking over his face as his godmother's ring stared back at him. "I'm not saying now. You'll know the right time. You did before, you will again. But I want you to have that for when the moment makes itself known."

"Uncle Field..."

"Hey, boys! Dinner!" Holden's mother's voice called up the stairs.

Without a word, Caulfield stood up, patted Holden on the shoulder, and turned to head down for dinner. Holden just continued to sit there, staring at the pear-shaped sapphire that his godmother had worn for more than thirty years. He couldn't believe that Caulfield had kept it all these years, as if he were just waiting for the universe to tell him what to do with it.

Gigi greeted him at the bottom of the stairs, sliding a large platter of ham off the counter. She looked radiant in a 1950s style red dress, her blonde hair loose and flowing. If it weren't for the rest of his family in the next room, he'd be hauling her into his arms and showing her just how much he appreciated that dress right here, right now.

He silently took the platter from her and followed her into the dining room, where everyone was already sitting in their seats.

"What this?" Gigi asked, looking around at the rest of the group. Holden spun around to see her holding a little black box with just a red ribbon tied around it.

His parents looked at him, then smiled back at her, like they were in on the secret but not going to say a word. Turning to Holden, she gave him a questioning look, but the only thing he could do was shrug. He had no idea what was going on or where that had come from.

Holden walked up behind her and watched as she removed the lid. He heard her breath falter, and her hand raced to her chest as she stared at the pendant. The jade lotus flower was small, maybe the size of a silver dollar, and attached to a corded black necklace. The simple etching on it reflected the light making it seem like it glowed. He knew this necklace just as well as he knew the ring he'd just tucked into his sock drawer, and for much the same reason. But also, a much, much bigger one.

"This is just like the one Anaura wore in *At Midnight*," she muttered, unable to take her eyes off of it.

"That *is* the one that Anaura wore," Caulfield corrected her. "Or well, I should say that's the one that hers is based off of. I bought that for Viv in Chinatown while we were on a book tour in San Francisco. She wore it the whole rest of the tour, and every city we were in, someone had a comment for us about what it meant. That's where the idea for using the color green came from."

"I can't accept this, Caulfield. It's way too much. You guys already got me the mixer. I can't take this too."

"You can, and you will, darlin'. I want you to have it, and Viv would want you to have it," the older gentleman said. Holden's heart squeezed, thinking about just what Caulfield was saying with this gesture. Gigi was it for him, and his whole family knew it. "I hope that it brings you two as much peace and prosperity as it did Viv and me."

24

GIGI

Gigi placed the last of the cupcakes she'd made into the display case at the Busy Bean, feeling more than a little proud of herself for how they turned out. The standard vanilla and chocolate ones featured little fondant champagne bottles, complete with matching flute embellishments. They almost looked too cute to eat. Almost.

Thankfully, they tasted as good as they looked. Or so customers had been telling her all morning. Everyone had been thrilled with their Christmas orders, especially the peppermint-bark cupcakes, and she'd even gotten an inquiry as to whether or not she would be interested in making a batch for a birthday party coming up. She'd been so stunned by the question that she had kind of stumbled through the answer, telling the lady to inquire with Zara about the order.

A small letter sign on the counter encouraged everyone to try both the new Arnold Palmer and the Dark Horse Mochaccino cupcakes and then vote on their favorites. Both had gone over so well with Holden's family, she'd been left unable to decide which to pitch to Zara and Audrey. Hoping the staff at either Speakeasy or the Gin Mill would help settle it, she'd brought some over there as well. However, both flavors had received rave results there too, so she'd opted to let Zara and Audrey decide. The two of them didn't want to have to choose either, so they opted to put it up to the customers to vote. Whichever one had the most votes come the end of January would be the Busy Bean's new signature item.

"Are those the peppermint ones?" Kirk asked her, interrupting her thoughts. "What's-her-face…uh, Lily, over at Speakeasy called earlier and asked if we had more."

"Really?" Gigi asked, surprised by the request. She had made one small batch of the peppermint ones, just to use up the last of the peppermint bark from Christmas. Catherine had suggested she make those a seasonal item, only available during the holidays, while the two had been cooking dinner, and Gigi loved the idea. So, after these were gone, that was it until next year.

"Why would I make that up?"

Gigi rolled her eyes at Kirk's dryness, but still couldn't help but find it somewhat amusing. He might be a strange dude, but you couldn't help but end up with a bit of a soft spot for him.

"I'll call over there on my way home and let her know that these are the last ones until next Christmas."

"Rushing off for some big New Year's Eve plans?" he asked.

It took her a split second to realize that he'd actually asked her a personal question. Had she entered the Twilight Zone? "Sorta," she said after a moment, a big grin taking over her face. "We're spending the night in."

"That doesn't sound very exciting."

"Someday, Kirk, you too may understand why a night on the couch can be very, very exciting," Roderick added in, appearing from the kitchen. He waggled his eyebrows knowingly at Gigi, and she stifled a giggle.

"Kirk, it's very exciting when you've spent every other New Year's Eve of your life having to get dressed up and go out," she told him, pulling off her apron. Turning to Roderick, she added in, "and for other reasons."

"That's my girl!" Roderick responded, giving her a high five.

"So, that said…I'm outta here!"

Gigi grabbed her stuff and hopped into her car, making sure to return Lily's call about the cupcakes. Smiling to herself, she made the short drive home, thinking about just how far she had come in the last couple of months. She'd left Atlanta broken—just another socialite with no skill or talent, save for a pretty smile, unsure where to even start in trying to find herself. But now, she had a job that not only was she good at, but that she loved. The strong, independent woman she set out to be had taken on a different form than she had imagined, but it was one that she was thrilled with. She finally felt like she knew who the real Gigi was.

Pulling up the drive and putting her Jeep in park, she noticed that the curtains on the bow windows were drawn. In the months that she'd lived here, she couldn't recall a time that the curtains were closed, ever. Holden had told her that he had a surprise for her, so whatever he was up to must have been super-secret enough to warrant this kind of privacy. At least in his mind. She laughed out loud as she opened the door, walking inside.

"What's all this?" she asked, taking in the living room. Holden had rearranged all the furniture, moving most of it back against the far wall, opening up the room even more. The only thing that wasn't up against the wall was the couch, which was now in front of the Christmas tree with the fireplace to the left of it. In front of the couch was a mattress, all made up with pillows and blankets, and a large projector screen.

"*This* is our New Year's plans," he said, wrapping his arms around her. She let out a small sigh as she let the warmth of his body and his comforting smell engulf her. "You, me, the roaring fire, and whatever movies your heart desires."

Sucking in a deep breath, she let out a long, happy sigh, wishing she could just melt into him. After his family had left the other day and he'd asked her what, if anything, she wanted to do to ring in the new year, she wasn't sure he'd fully understood her when she'd told him "nothing." But in true Holden fashion, he'd known the perfect solution.

"Just let me run upstairs and change," she said, giving him a quick kiss, before taking off for what had unofficially become "their" bedroom. They hadn't actually discussed it, but she hadn't slept in her own room in weeks, something she was more than okay with. She threw her clothes off, not bothering to pick them up off the floor, and found the same pair of Holden's sweatpants that she'd worn on Christmas. They were so big on her that she still felt funny in them, but the reaction he'd had to seeing them on her was worth the little bit of ridiculousness she felt.

"Fuck..." he exhaled as she came back down the stairs. The moment her feet hit the floor, Holden hauled her into his arms, kissing her hard. She kissed him back, just as passionately, unable to get enough of this man. Everything about him made her fall further and further, and she just couldn't believe that she thought she'd known love prior to him. In one swift movement, he lowered his hands to her ass and picked her up, her legs effortlessly wrapping around him. Walking them over to the mattress, he laid her down, never letting up on his kisses.

"I can't get over how incredibly sexy you are in my sweatpants," he growled, coming up for air.

"They're really comfy. I may never give them back," she teased, sticking her tongue out at him. He caught it with his lips, swiping his own against it and sending a shiver down her spine.

"If it means I get to see you in them all the time, you can have them."

"Thank you," she said softly. "For all this. You have no idea what it means to me."

"Gigi, for you I'd do anything. You deserve it."

"You keep saying that, and I'm not so sure I do. But I'm glad you think so. No one has ever believed in me the way you do," she said, sniffling. She could feel the tears forming in the corner of her eyes, and she knew there was nothing she could do to stop them. She didn't want to stop them. What she wanted was to be able to let Holden know just what she felt about him.

"Gigi..."

"Let me finish, please," she said through another sniffle. "When I arrived here, I didn't know which way was up. All I knew was that I needed to figure out how to stand on my own two feet. I needed to find out who I was and to make a whole new life for myself. I have no idea what possessed me to tell Zara and Audrey that I could be the cake lady, but something did. I was in so far over my head. Then I almost burned down the carriage house, and I was sure that I would never succeed. But you believed in me. You helped me figure this all out. I don't know what I ever did to deserve you or what angel brought you into my life, but you are more than I ever could have hoped for."

"I'm pretty sure that angel's name is Hannah," he replied softly. "Pretty sure she knew that you were exactly what I needed as well. To remove my own head from my ass and start living again. Gigi, you are smart, and talented, and so full of life. I might have given you a little push, but you did this all on your own. You're the one who figured it all out in the kitchen. The one who is making up her own recipes. I was just there to eat them. I hate that you had to go through what you did with Bradley to get here, and if I could go back in time and kill him myself for hurting you, I would. But he's gone, so all I can do is promise you that you won't hurt like that ever again."

The mention of Bradley made Gigi's gut clench. A pang of guilt hit her. She knew she needed to tell Holden the truth—that Bradley was still alive. She'd barely thought about him in weeks—she wouldn't let herself think about him—and to her he really was dead and gone. But that didn't change the fact that he was somewhere in Atlanta, potentially looking for her. She wasn't going to worry about that now though. She'd tell Holden tomorrow. Now, she was just going to focus on how she felt about the sexy, tattoo-covered, bearded man curled up with her in front of the fire.

"Holden, I…" she started, trying find the courage to actually say the words. "I…"

"I love you, Gigi."

HOLDEN

The words leapt off his tongue and out of his mouth before he'd even realized it. He'd been holding back those words for almost a week now, and it felt good to put them out there. The look on Gigi's face though, was even better.

"I love you, Holden," she said, her eyes overflowing with emotion.

He pulled her into him, closing the already almost imperceivable gap, but it still wasn't close enough. He loved this woman more than he could put into words, and he wasn't sure that he would ever get enough of her. Her smile, her laugh, her spirit. He loved all of her.

"When I showed up at the Busy Bean that day, and Kirk said that he'd told you about the empty apartment over the carriage house, I could have strangled him. Now I think I owe him a thank you."

"Which reminds me, I don't think I've ever actually paid you."

Holden let out a deep belly laugh at her comment. That was where her head went? He kissed her softly, unable to resist just how cute she was. A confused look crossed her face, and he couldn't help but laugh again.

"Gigi, you're not paying me rent. Absolutely not."

"But…"

"But nothing. I don't need the money. I've never needed it. I told you, my contract with Chelsea was enough to live a lifetime on. You stopped being a tenant a long time ago."

"I need to do something to contribute to the household."

"You already do. You fill this house with happiness, laughter, and most importantly, love. Not to mention cupcakes and sticky buns. Your love is all I need."

"Yours is all I need too," she returned.

They lay there in silence for a while, wrapped around each other, simply enjoying the moment. Holden couldn't have asked for a more perfect moment to tell her how he was feeling, and hearing her return those same three little words made him feel like he was overflowing. He let his mind wander, wondering what their future would hold—the recipes she would create, story ideas he would have, places they would travel.

"Can I ask you something?" she whispered, breaking the silence.

"Anything, always."

"Are you interested in more kids? Or would it be too painful after losing your daughter?"

Her question made him pause, a new set of emotions washing over him. Just as her mentioning Hannah the night they decorated the tree had endeared her to him, so did this. She was so thoughtful, always considering him and what might be a trigger for him. How was it that anyone could have ever treated someone so caring so poorly? But just like that night, the thought of losing his family didn't feel like salt in a wound, but a long-ago memory. He no longer felt like moving on was a betrayal to his girls, but what they would have wanted for him.

"I would love to have a family with you. If that's something you want."

Gigi nodded silently, looking up into his eyes. A small smile tugged at one corner of her mouth, and it was as if her entire face lit up.

"Very, very much. I haven't let myself want it in a very long time. A baby needs love and safety, and I didn't have that in that house. But I do here. This..." she paused, taking a deep breath. "With you...a family is something I'd at least like to explore."

Holden loved everything about what she had just said. She was his future. He knew that without a doubt. But hearing her say that she wanted one too—complete with a family—was everything he could ever ask for.

Rolling them over so that she was underneath him, he gave her a sly grin. He rolled his hips against hers, letting her know exactly what he was thinking. "We could start now…" he growled, just before capturing her lips in his.

Gigi giggled into the kiss. "I meant someday. We have a lot to figure out before then."

"As long as you're the one I'm figuring it out with, then I'm on board."

"You're just full of all sorts of good lines tonight, aren't you?" she teased.

"Beauty of falling for a writer. We're good with our words."

"Not the only thing you're good with," she said, wiggling her eyebrows knowingly.

"Is that so?" he asked, as he started to tickle her sides. Gigi let out a squeal, followed by bursts of laughter, squirming from side to side. His fingers danced across her skin lightly, finding all the spots where he knew she was ticklish.

A low beeping coming from his phone cut through the air, interrupting his efforts. Grabbing it off the couch, he cleared the alarm he'd set earlier and pushed himself up to his feet.

"Where are you going?" Gigi asked, sitting up.

"Be right back," he told her.

Scooting into the kitchen, he opened the fridge and grabbed the bottle of champagne he'd stuck in there earlier in the day, as well as the two glasses he'd left sitting on the counter. He'd been running his toast through his head all day long, coming up with what felt like a hundred and one things to say. But now that he'd said "I Love You"—and she'd said it back—nothing he had come up with seemed right. Looks like he was just going to have to wing it.

Holding up the items he'd grabbed from the kitchen, he sat back down on the mattress. He handed both glasses for Gigi to hold, as he took on the task of popping the cork.

"We might not be out on the town, but I still wanted us to ring in the new year properly," he told her just before the loud 'pop!' Gigi giggled at the noise, dancing a little in her seat. He filled the glasses and then took one from her before turning to put the bottle on the floor.

"GeorgiaGrace Elyse Shaw Hawthorne, you turned my world inside out in the very best way possible. I can't wait to spend this next year with you."

"You did the exact same to me, Holden Hemingway St. James. And I could not be happier about it. To our best year yet," she replied, raising her glass in a toast.

"To our new year, new life, and new love," he toasted.

The clink of their glasses filled the room as they took a sip. The effervescence tickled Holden's nose as the bubbles danced across his tongue, however he was too busy watching Gigi to care. Her pretty pink lips called his name as she seemed to savor the taste of the champagne. He wondered if he would be able to taste it on her lips, her tongue, and if it would be just as sweet. Pulling her in for a kiss, he had to stop himself from devouring her in search of the answer.

"I love you, Holden," she said in between kisses, the sound of the old wall clock in the dining room signaling that it was midnight.

"And I you, Gigi. And I you…"

25

GIGI

The chime of the doorbell rang through the living room, disrupting Gigi from her perfect dream world. In it, she and Holden were hanging out on a playground, a little boy and girl playing on the swing set. The little boy was the spitting image of his daddy, with those piercing blue eyes and dark hair, while the little girl had matched her own blonde locks, but instead of her gray eyes, she'd been gifted with the same blue as the boy's. Holden alternated pushing their son and daughter, each one laughing, screaming "higher, Daddy!" as he laughed right along with them. It all felt so real, until the doorbell pierced through once again, dragging her back into real life.

Holden wants that too, she thought. *So maybe that could be real life. Just as soon as you explain…*

Ding! Ding! Ding!

It rang out again, in rapid succession, with whomever was at the door obviously growing impatient. Frustrated, Gigi threw off the quilt that they had snuggled under after watching a movie last night and pushed herself up from the mattress.

"It's a little early for guests," Holden muttered, rolling over and looking at his phone. "Who the fuck is awake at eight thirty on New Year's Day?"

"Guess we'll find out," Gigi said, opening the door.

Standing on the other side, dressed in his police uniform, was Officer Nelligan, accompanied by another man Gigi had never seen. His companion was older, late forties maybe, and wearing a tan trench coat over his suit, making him look like something out of an old detective movie.

"Officer Nelligan," Gigi said, suddenly feeling very awake. "What are you doing here so early?"

"Hi, Miss Gigi. May we come in?"

"Of course. Where are my manners?"

The two gentlemen stepped inside, shaking the snow from their feet, their faces serious. They only came in far enough for her to close the door, which made Gigi nervous, but she tried to shake it off. She was sure there was a perfectly good reason for them being here so early on a holiday.

"Miss Gigi, this is Detective Ball from the Vermont State Police. We've come to talk to you about your role in the death of your husband, Bradley Preston Hawthorne."

"My role?" she asked. *Wait…did he say…* "Hold on, his death?"

"Yes, ma'am," Detective Ball said, taking a step forward. "We received a call from the Georgia State Police yesterday informing us that they've been searching for you."

"Me? Why me?"

"Seems your husband's body was found under some…suspicious circumstances."

"Suspicious circumstances?" she repeated, not fully comprehending what she was hearing. Bradley was dead? There was no way. He was alive and well when she left. He was getting ready to walk down the aisle, expecting to find her there to renew their vows. Now he was dead? No, they must have the wrong person.

"Yes, ma'am," Detective Ball confirmed, his face still like stone. "He was found floating in Lake Lanier."

Bradley was dead. Actually dead. Not fake dead like she'd

been saying all this time. She was really, actually free of him. The room started to spin a little as she took in the news. She couldn't believe it. He was gone. She had no idea what he'd been doing up at Lake Lanier, but it didn't matter now. What mattered was that the new life she wanted with Holden could truly be a reality.

"Mrs. Hawthorne, you seem to have disappeared from Atlanta on the tenth of October. Leaving behind everything. You left no note, told no one where you were going. Just up and left. Why is that?"

"I…I…" she stumbled, not sure how to answer that. Did they really think she had something to do with this?

"What's going on here?" Holden asked, startling her as he stumbled over, rubbing the sleep from his face. She'd been so focused on what the detective was trying to tell her that she'd forgotten he'd still been in bed.

"Who are you?" Detective Ball asked in return, looking Holden up and down.

"I'm Holden St. James. This is my house. Who are you?"

"Detective Ball, Vermont State Police. I believe you know Officer Nelligan," he answered, nodding at the semi-guilty looking Colebury cop standing next to him. Holden nodded. "We're here to inform Mrs. Hawthorne of her husband's death and to find out what her involvement may be."

"His death? He's been dead for months," Holden said.

"You knew about this?"

"He had a heart attack over the summer, right?" Holden asked, turning to Gigi for confirmation. She sucked her lips into her mouth, not sure how to answer him.

"Not exactly," she confessed.

"What do you mean, not exactly?" Holden said. Gigi could see the anger rising in him, even though his voice was tempered. But she knew him well enough now to know that his body language was anything but happy.

"Mrs. Hawthorne, can you account for your actions the first

few weeks of October?" The detective ignored Holden's question, his face turning sour.

"I know I told you he had a heart attack, and that I left to get a fresh start, but that's only partially true," she said, turning to Holden. How did she explain this? She knew she'd been wrong to lie to him for so long, but she hadn't expected it to blow up quite like this. "I did leave to get a fresh start. Just when I left, he was alive."

"Alive..." Holden repeated.

Gigi turned around and paced into the living room, trying to collect her thoughts. She knew she had to come clean. If she and Holden were going to have a future together, he needed to know the whole story. Then there were the two policemen still standing in the entry, waiting for her to explain just how he ended up dead. How was she supposed to know? She'd been long gone by that point. She also had no idea why he would go to the lake in October. He barely tolerated it in the summer, much less once the weather had cooled off.

"I don't understand," she said, turning back to the visitors. "I arrived in Vermont on the thirteenth. Officer Nelligan can tell you. He helped me with a flat tire."

"Autopsy shows that your husband had been dead for some time prior to being found. We suspect foul play."

"Foul play?" Gigi and Holden said in unison.

They think you killed him. They think you killed him and ran away...

"Gigi, what the fuck is going on here? You said he was dead. But he's been alive this whole time?"

"Well, apparently not this *whole* time," she muttered.

"Not fucking funny, Gigi."

"Holden, I can explain!" she exclaimed.

"Any explaining will need to be done with us, ma'am. Killing your husband is a felony."

Gigi turned to the detective, giving him an incredulous look.

He could not be serious. Did he really think she didn't know that? Was there anyone, anywhere who didn't know murder was a felony?

"I didn't kill him!"

"Officers, may we have a moment in private?" Holden asked, his teeth clenched and fists balled at his side. Gigi could see the anger radiating off of him, and she wasn't sure what scared her more, the idea that the cops thought she killed Bradley or that Holden was furious with her.

"We can give you five minutes, max," Officer Nelligan said, finally speaking up, a sad smile resting on his face. "But then we need to take Miss Gi…Mrs. Hawthorne down to the station."

Gigi didn't like the sound of that, but she remained silent as the men stepped outside. She didn't need to aggravate them any more than they already were. She'd seen enough episodes of *Law and Order* to know exactly what they were thinking. It was the wife—it was *always* the wife.

"Holden, I can explain!" she blurted out as soon as the door shut, rushing to him. She threw her arms around him, expecting him to hug her back. Except he didn't.

His body was stiff against hers as he withdrew from her embrace, giving her the exact same look he had on Thanksgiving. The look turned her blood to ice, stealing her breath for a moment.

"You better fucking get to explaining, Gigi."

HOLDEN

Gigi's husband was dead.

That was not something that Holden would have ever thought would anger him. At least that was the case when he thought the bastard had died of a heart attack months ago, rather than under suspicious circumstances just prior to her arriving in Vermont.

"I don't know where to start," she said, her voice already sounding resigned.

"The beginning is usually a pretty fucking good place."

"Everything I told you was true—"

"Except it wasn't, Gigi! Is that even your real name?" he shouted.

He didn't know what to believe. She had lied to him. Just how much was a lie? A story concocted so he would take pity on her? Had she known who he was this whole time? Known that he had money? Who his family was? Had it all been some clever ploy to deceive him?

"Yes, my real name is GeorgiaGrace Elyse Shaw Hawthorne. When I was little, I had a nanny who called me Gigi, and I always liked the nickname, although my parents and Bradley insisted on calling me Georgia. It was less "cutesy," they said. Everything I told you about my childhood and how I met Bradley was true," she explained. "He and I met when I was twenty-two, married when I was twenty-four. About a year into our marriage, he became abusive. None of that was a lie. All the stories about the things he said and did to me were true. Including the story about the night you won your championship."

He could see the tears welling in her eyes, and part of him wanted to run to her. To take her in his arms and tell her it would be okay, that he was here for her. But another part—a bigger part—couldn't believe that she had lied.

"That was the first time I considered leaving him. Except, it wasn't as easy as that. Everyone thought we had the perfect marriage. No one would believe me if I told them he was abusive. I was afraid for my life. I knew that he wouldn't stop until I was dead. So I slowly started to funnel money out of my trust fund and figure out a plan. Bradley was insistent that for our tenth wedding anniversary, we throw a big to-do—vow renewal, reception, the whole shebang. So, we planned the whole thing," she continued. "Bradley was a stickler about tradition, so he insisted we spend the night before the renewal apart. So that's when I made my escape. I bought a secondhand car, with cash, and got a pay-as-you-go phone. I told no one. I just left."

"And came to Vermont?"

"No. I was headed to Canada. Montreal, actually. I thought I could make a new start up there, find myself. Then I got lost and ended up taking the long way through Vermont, and ended up with a flat tire, which landed me in the Busy Bean. I overheard Zara and Audrey talking, and the rest is history."

"You lied to me. You've been lying to me this whole time. How do I know you're not lying to me now?" he shouted. He didn't want to be that guy, the same one he'd been on Thanksgiving. But he couldn't help himself. He was so angry it was almost hard to see at this point.

This wasn't happening. He blinked over and over again, trying to make everything come into focus. Reaching over with his right hand, he pinched himself—hard—just trying to make sure that this was real. That this wasn't some nightmare. That his subconscious wasn't fucking with him. He felt the pain caused by his fingers and knew that he wasn't asleep. This was all really happening. His beautiful, sweet Gigi was a liar.

"I'm not! I promise! I didn't plan for this. I didn't plan for you!" she exclaimed, the tears starting to roll down her cheeks. "When they offered me the job, I thought maybe I could make a small town work, because everyone in small towns has secrets, right? I made up a story about my husband being dead so that no one would ask questions. I was afraid that if he found me, he would kill me. That's why I left everything behind, so he couldn't track me down! I was afraid for my life. I didn't plan on making friends, much less meeting you and falling in love. I meant everything I said last night, Holden. I love you. You have believed in me like no one else. You helped me figure out who I am!"

"And who is that, Gigi? A spoiled, real housewife? A widow? I thought I knew you. But the Gigi I thought I knew wouldn't lie to me. The Gigi I thought I knew poured her heart out to me about her abusive husband and all the hopes and dreams he stole from her. She and I bonded over the loss of our spouses and what it was like to grieve in a way no one else understood." He turned and walked into the living room, unsure of what to do. The betrayal he felt clung to him like a wet blanket, weighing him down to the point he didn't know if he should laugh or cry. Maybe both. He needed to do something with all these emotions before he exploded even more than he already had.

"I'm still that Gigi! Bradley has been dead to me since the second I drove out of Atlanta. I left him and all that behind. I *was* mourning—the loss of my marriage and the life I knew."

"You're a fucking liar! That's what you are."

"I only lied about Bradley being dead. That's it," she pleaded, as if all she had done was tell him they were out of cookies because she was saving the last one for herself.

"That's it?" he scoffed. "That's kind of a big deal, Gigi! Telling people your husband is dead when he's not! Fucking another man along the way." He saw her wince at his accusation, taking in his harsh words.

"I was afraid if he found me, he would kill me," she told him again, her voice shaky even as she tried to steady it. He wanted to believe her, but he just couldn't. How could he have been deceived so easily?

"Did you know who I was when I walked into the Busy Bean that day? Know about my connection to Caulfield or about my wife? Was I just some unsuspecting widower that you thought you could con?"

"How could you think that I could do such a thing? No, I had no idea who you were, who your family was or anything. When Kirk introduced us you were just some grumpy guy who was willing to take pity on me."

Holden didn't know if hearing her say that made him feel better or worse. Would he have felt better if he had been some kind of a mark, rather than someone she just happened to be able to take advantage of? Probably not. Either way, her actions were manipulative, and he was still having a hard time wrapping his head around it all.

"Were you ever going to tell me? Or were you just going to let me make an ass of myself?"

"Yes!" she answered, rushing toward him. He backed away from her again. He couldn't touch her right now. Her touch had always been so calming to him, but now he was pretty sure the only thing it would do was anger him more. "I was going to tell you today. So that we could plan our future."

"Future? You think I want a fucking future with you after that?! After you lied to me? After you took advantage of me all these weeks?"

"Holden, that was never my intention."

Her words fell on deaf ears. He wanted to believe her, wanted to know that he hadn't fallen for someone who would do this kind of thing. But she'd already admitted to the lies. If she was guilty of that, what else had she done?

"I need to know. Did you kill him?" Even as he asked the question, he wasn't sure he really wanted to know. He wasn't sure he could live with himself if he found out he'd fallen for a murderer.

"Bradley? No! I was already here in Vermont! I left him, that was it. I ran away, hoping to disappear. That was all I wanted, to disappear. Holden, you have to believe me. I love you."

"No, stop right there," he said, raising a hand. "You betrayed me and my trust. I don't want to hear any more from you. Get out."

"Holden…" she sobbed.

A knock at the door stole his attention away from her and her tears. He walked over and let the cops back in, standing in silence as they nodded their thanks. He didn't want to say anything else, afraid of what he might do. His heart felt like it had been ripped into a million pieces. It'd been crushed thoroughly when he'd found Hannah, but somehow, this pain might be worse. Hannah was stolen from him, but she'd never betrayed him.

"Mrs. Hawthorne, we need you to please come with us," Detective Ball said, his voice rough and emotionless.

"Am I under arrest?"

"Not yet."

26

GIGI

The little room Gigi had spent the last five hours in smelled musty and was obviously not a room that saw a lot of use, other than some extra storage. The cardboard boxes that had been on the table when they brought her in were now stacked in a corner, making the tight space even more claustrophobic. Glancing up at the clock for what felt like the millionth time, she wondered how much longer she was going to have to sit here. No one had been overly forthcoming with any kind of information since she was escorted out of the house and told to wait in here. Officer Nelligan had poked his head in a couple of times to bring her a bottle of water and a snack and see if she needed the bathroom, but other than that, she hadn't seen a soul.

A shiver ran through her, making her long for the reassurance of Holden's arms. Or at least warmer clothes than the ones she was wearing. To do over again she would have insisted on being able to change before leaving the house, rather than just throwing on the shoes and parka that were by the door. For as warm and comfortable as they were at home, Holden's sweatpants and T-shirt were not cutting it now.

Home.

Gigi sighed, realizing that Montgomery Manor was probably not home anymore. It didn't really matter how much she ached for Holden's touch or simply the sound of his voice. The look in his eyes when she was leaving told her everything—he never wanted to see her again. The thought of losing him made her queasy, more so than the idea of leaving Bradley ever had. Why hadn't she just been honest earlier? Why didn't she confide in him that night when they were baring their souls to each other? *Because you were afraid Bradley would find you,* she told herself. Except she knew now that had she told him, he would have protected her. He would have done whatever was necessary to make sure she was safe. That ship had sailed now.

Forget not leaving Bradley sooner. Gigi's biggest regret now was lying to Holden.

"Mrs. Hawthorne," Detective Ball's voice boomed as he entered the room. He let the door slam shut behind him, and Gigi flinched as the noise echoed through the small room. He sat down across from her, resting a set of file folders on the table.

"Detective," she replied, trying to be polite.

"You said you left Atlanta on the tenth of October. Can you tell me about that?"

"Do I need a lawyer?" she asked, trying to recall just how things went down in all those *Law and Order* episodes.

"Do you want a lawyer?"

"I'm just wondering if I need one."

"You're not under arrest. We're just talking right now," he told her. But wasn't that what cops always told people?

"So I don't need one?"

"You are welcome to one at any time. But like I said, you're not under arrest."

Gigi was silent for a moment, trying to wrap her mind around it all. She had no idea what to do in this situation. Part of her thought she needed a lawyer, but she wouldn't even know where to begin in finding one. And if she wasn't under arrest, she was fine, right?

"So, the tenth of October. That's your wedding anniversary, right?" Detective Ball continued.

"Yes."

"And you and Mr. Hawthorne had a vow renewal planned?"

"Yes."

"But you were never actually planning on attending said renewal, now were you?"

"No, I wasn't."

"Why not?"

Gigi swallowed hard. It shouldn't be hard to admit that she had left her abusive husband, but somehow, she was still ashamed. Maybe it was shame that she hadn't left earlier, or that she'd even gotten herself into that situation to begin with. But either way, it clung to her like a wet blanket.

"Bradley was not always the nicest man. He..." She paused, swallowing again. "He was abusive. Both physically and verbally. So I made a plan to leave."

"Did you ever tell anyone he was abusive?" the older man asked, disbelief in his tone. "I wasn't able to find where you ever reported any kind of incident. So, maybe a friend? Family? A counselor?"

"No. No one would have believed me. So I kept it to myself." Gigi shuddered at the thought, the feeling of isolation returning. To everyone else she and Bradley were the picture-perfect couple. They had everything—the house, the wealth, the connections. Too bad it was all a well-crafted façade.

"And made a plan to leave."

"Yes. I knew I would have a chance the night before the ceremony, since Bradley was all about tradition. So I bought a cheap car, and I left."

"And that was the last time you saw Mr. Hawthorne? The night before the renewal? You've had no contact since?"

"I left him! Why would I be in contact with him?"

He opened the top file and pulled out a piece of paper, sliding it toward her.

"Do you know what this is?"

"It looks like a death certificate," she said, reading the lettering at the top. He nodded at her to continue reading. Glancing back down she skimmed the page, her blood running cold as she processed what she was looking at. "This is...this is *my* death certificate! But I'm not dead!"

"Clearly," he answered, deadpan.

"It's dated October fifteenth. How? Why? I don't understand." Her pulse sped up, and her mind was racing. How could this be? What did this mean?

"This was submitted to your insurance company on October sixteenth. Less than one week after you disappeared. It was submitted with a request to pay out your life insurance to an account in the Cayman Islands."

"The Cayman Islands?"

"Yes, ma'am. The account was in the names of Bradley Preston Hawthorne and Ayla Nancy Hatche."

"Who is Ayla Hatche?"

"You tell me." The look he gave her made her uneasy, like he knew something she didn't and he was just waiting to pull the rug out from under her.

"How am I supposed to know? I've never heard that name in my life."

"So, that's not a new identity for you?"

"New identity?" she exclaimed. Just what did he think she was trying to do here? The thought had never occurred to her to use a fake name when she recreated herself, just an old nickname. If she'd been trying to be discreet, why would she have chosen such an odd name? *Wait one second...*

"Wait...the name on the account. Was it eye-la? Or A-la? Is it spell A-y-l-a?" she asked, suddenly connecting the dots.

"Yes, A-y-l-a. So you admit it's yours?"

"It's not mine," she said softly. "And it's pronounced A-la, like

Kayla without the K. Ayla Hachette is Bradley's secretary." Her stomach sank as she said the words out loud. His secretary? She'd never liked that tall, leggy brunette but had told herself that she was just being insecure. Just because she reminded her of the trampy secretary in *Love Actually* who seduced Alan Rickman didn't mean that was *actually* what was going on. Or maybe it did.

Bradley had sworn up and down to her so many times that he'd never been unfaithful. And all those times he'd turned it back on her, accusing her of only coming up with the idea because she was the one fooling around behind his back. She'd always known her gut was right, yet she'd let him convince her she was seeing things. *I should have left him sooner…*

"Mrs. Hawthorne, how did your husband end up in Lake Lanier?" the detective asked, bringing her back to the moment.

"How am I supposed to know? I was here, in Vermont!"

"And the account that was in only your name? That is now mostly empty?"

"My trust fund? It's always been in just my name. That's Shaw family money. My father set it up as an irrevocable account or something, so that whoever I married couldn't touch it. In the event of my death, the money reverts back to the family trust, I think." She'd never paid a whole lot of attention when investments and money were being discussed—numbers were boring. Although she was starting to regret that choice right about now. But she knew that money was hers and hers alone. Even that death certificate wouldn't have changed that.

"So where's the money?" he asked.

"I cashed it out shortly before I left. It's how I paid for the car and everything since I got here," she told him. She'd been so careful to only pay for things in cash so that she could stay off the grid. She hadn't wanted anyone to be able to find her. Even her Busy Bean paychecks were still sitting in a drawer in her room, uncashed. Opening a bank account would have been too risky, and she hadn't taken the time to try and find some place that might cash them without one. "How did y'all even find me? I've paid in cash for everything since then."

"You used your social security number on your employment paperwork at the uhhh…Busy Bean Café," he said, reading from another piece of paper. "We were able to track you through that."

Oh for heaven's sake! Why didn't I think of that? Nice job, Gigi…

"I didn't kill my husband, Detective." Gigi could hear the warble in her voice and said a little prayer that it showed her honesty, rather than made her seem guilty. Detective Ball wasn't trying to hide the fact that he was wholly convinced that she had murdered Bradley. Gigi just didn't know how to change that.

"Then who did?"

"I don't know." Gigi slumped back in her chair. She was exhausted and feeling more than just a little defeated. The news that Bradley was dead should have made her happy. But the only thing it did was turn her stomach. All this time she'd been living in fear of him, and he was out living it up with his secretary. Just great. Thanks to him, she'd not only left behind everything she knew, but now she was about to lose the whole new life she'd come to love. And more than that, the only man she'd ever really loved.

Even in death Bradley was ruining her life.

"Want to know what I think?" The smug look on his face told Gigi that no, she did not want to know what he thought. But then she reconsidered, wondering if she just played his game, she'd be out of here soon.

"What?" she answered, trying to sound sweet and interested.

"I believe you killed him. I think you planned this whole thing out. Fake your death, collect the insurance money, and then kill him. Maybe not in that order, since I'm sure it's not as simple as just that. The autopsy shows he was poisoned prior to ending up in the lake. I'm thinking you had to put quite a bit of thought and effort into this to know what to give him that wouldn't be obvious. Or maybe that didn't matter since he was going in the lake and you figured it would be months before he was found," he said. Gigi felt the scrutiny of his gaze as he spoke, his eyes searching for any kind of indication from her that he'd struck a nerve. "I think you slipped him something before you left, and then paid someone to dump the body. Am I getting warmer? If we search your belongings, will we find papers with Ayla Hatche on them?"

"I didn't kill him. I promise."

"Then why have you been telling everyone he's dead?"

"Because I didn't want anyone to ask any questions about him and why I left. I figured if I told people he was dead, they would just accept that."

"But why admit to being married at all? Why not just be a single woman?"

Gigi was caught off guard by the question. Why had she told that story? She could have just as easily pretended to not have a husband, as he suggested. The thought had never occurred to Gigi. Lying had never been a skill she'd possessed, and it wasn't something she'd wanted to get into the habit of.

"I don't know," she said softly, looking away from him.

"Because you knew he was dead, or at least would be soon. Didn't you?"

"No! I didn't kill Bradley!"

"Not so sure I believe that, Mrs. Hawthorne."

"No! Why would I use my real name and social security number if I had a fake ID?" she exclaimed.

"Only you can answer that, Mrs. Hawthorne."

"I didn't kill him. I promise."

Detective Ball stood up from the table and walked over to the door, opening it and nodding to someone standing just outside it. Gigi watched as Officer Nelligan stepped into the room, his face long and his eyes conflicted. A sense of dread washed over her. Whatever happened next was not going to be good.

"Miss Gigi, I need you to please stand and place your hands behind your back," Officer Nelligan said quietly.

Doing as she was told, she looked between the two men. She

felt as if she were sliding off the side of the earth with nothing to grab on to and no way to stop it. This was not happening. No. She was not being arrested.

"You said I didn't need a lawyer!" she cried, tears appearing out of nowhere.

"You weren't under arrest then," he informed her, his face still as straight and uncaring as it had been this entire time. "Georgia-Grace Hawthorne, you are under arrest for conspiracy to commit insurance fraud and for the murder of Bradley Preston Hawthorne."

27

HOLDEN

Holden knew he needed to get up off the couch. Sitting there, staring at the mess of blanket and pillows crumpled up on the mattress that was still on the floor was not helping anything. Then again, the run he'd forced himself to go on hadn't helped either.

The hollow feeling that was inside him seemed to grow with every passing moment. This morning had been surreal. His plan had been to lazily wake Gigi up using his tongue and to spend most of the day wrapped up in each other, laughing and cuddling, until neither of them could take it anymore. But that stupid knock on the door had changed everything.

He'd run back the conversation with the cops and then his fight with Gigi over and over in his head. She'd been lying to him this whole time. Everything between them had been based on some fabricated story. It was hard to reconcile, since the Gigi he knew was as bright as sunshine, easygoing, and wouldn't hurt a fly. Except, that was just who she wanted him to see, wasn't it? That wasn't the real her. The real her was apparently a lot more deceiving.

You don't really believe that. You know her. You know she didn't kill anyone. And if she lied about something, she had a reason.

He shook his head, trying to stop his warring thoughts from getting the better of him. He needed a distraction. The only problem was everything seemed to remind him of her.

The buzzing of his phone was just enough to jar him out of his head, at least for the split second it took to reach for it. Looking down at the screen, the name flashing there told him this was not the distraction he needed right now. But he answered anyway.

"Hi," he said, his voice clipped.

"Did we interrupt something?" Caulfield replied.

"No."

"Well, aren't you a sparking ray of delight! Put Gigi on. If you're just going to be grumpy, then I don't want to have to be on the receiving end. I'd rather listen to her sweet southern voice anyway."

"She's not here."

"Where is she?"

"In jail," he ground out, his jaw clenched. Just saying the words out loud sent a whole new stab of pain straight to his heart. The thought of her sitting down at the Colebury police station, in what he was sure was an itty-bitty cell, broke his heart. It was no small part of him that wanted to run down there and pull her out, hold her in his arms, and tell her it would all be okay. But the other part of him knew better—she had lied to him. There was also the part of maybe killing her husband.

"Jail?" his mother's voice cried out from a distance. Holden sighed, realizing he must be on speaker phone with the whole family. Great, just great.

"Son, what happened?" his father asked.

"Cops came knocking on our door this morning to let us know that Gigi's husband is dead. Which was news to her," he said, before launching into the whole story. Explaining everything the cops had told them and the fight he and Gigi had afterwards made it seem like they'd been starring in an episode of some soap opera. But no, this was his real life. "After all that, they hauled her down to the police station for questioning."

"Why aren't you down there with her?" Caulfield asked.

"Which part of the story do I need to go over again, old man? The part where she lied to me about her husband being dead? Or the part where she's a murder suspect?" he bit out. His family didn't deserve his rage, but by this point in the day it'd been boiling up in him for too long, and he needed to let it out.

"Holden, we all know that sweet girl didn't kill anyone," his father said.

"No, Dad, we don't *know* anything. Just because she said she didn't do it means nothing. She's been lying to me from day one, so how can I believe anything? If she lied about that, what else has she been lying about?"

"Do you for one second think she killed him? That the Gigi you know would have done that?" Caulfield countered.

"No," he resigned. "But how do I know that the Gigi I know is the real one?"

"Other than him being dead, or not dead…everything else she told you was true, was it not?"

Holden thought back to everything she'd told him. About her childhood, her parents, college. About the things Bradley had done to her, said to her. Her fear. He thought about how skittish she was when she first arrived. How she had shied away from his touch, even if it was just to help her on the stairs. She'd been so lost and afraid. He'd taken it for face value then, a newly widowed woman trying to get back on her feet. But now that he thought about it, those actions made just as much sense for a woman trying to escape an abusive situation.

"So she claims."

"Holden, I'm going to ask you something, and I need you to be really honest here. With us and yourself," Caulfield said. "What are you really upset about here? That she lied to you? Or that you couldn't protect her?"

"What the fuck is that supposed to mean?" he snapped back,

pushing up off the couch and starting to pace the room. He had no idea what his godfather was getting at, but he could already tell he didn't like it.

"You have let the guilt over not being there for Hannah and the baby eat away at you for years. Like it was somehow your fault for not being there to protect them. It wasn't your fault then, and it's not now either, but I can't help but wonder if what you're really upset about is not the lie, but that once again the woman you love was in danger, and you didn't know."

Holden stopped dead in his tracks. His heart split open even more at the thought of his late wife. How dare Caulfield bring up Hannah. That wasn't what this was about. This was about Gigi lying to him. As if the pain from this morning wasn't enough, now he had that extra layer thrown on.

"She fucking lied to me!" he shouted.

"Of course she did!" Caulfield hollered back. "She was on the run and scared out of her mind. She had no idea whom she could trust, and then she moved in with you, who went all caveman on her. I think even you can admit you were not the best of company when you two first met. And I won't bring up your actions at Thanksgiving."

A wave of guilt hit Holden as he recalled that moment. He had not been on his best behavior, and there would never be a time he didn't hate himself for it. Especially after that night he and Gigi had bared their souls to each other and he'd found out the truth about her past life. Or what she claimed was the truth. Why hadn't she just told him then that she'd left her husband and was hiding from him. Could she really not trust him?

"Tell me you never once wished the bastard was alive so you could kill him yourself," Caulfield said, breaking through his thoughts.

Holden sighed. He'd thought that exact thing so many times he'd lost count. Every time Gigi would tell him about something Bradley had said or done, he'd wanted to pound the guy. How could he be married to someone as amazing as her and do nothing but cut her down? He knew full well that if he'd ever witnessed such a thing, he wouldn't have hesitated to beat the shit out of him.

"I have thought that. Lots," he admitted. "Doesn't change the fact that she lied. She should have told me."

"Yeah, probably," Caulfield acquiesced. "And the lie hurts. I'm not saying it shouldn't. But if that knock on the door this morning had been an alive husband there on the hunt for his wife who was running from him, would your reaction be the same as it is now? Know what? I'll answer that for you. Your reaction would have been to beat the tar out of him and protect that beautiful girl. You would have understood that she did what she did because she was scared of him showing up like that, ready to hurt or even kill her. Then you would have taken her in your arms and held her until she felt safe again!"

Fuck, he's right, Holden thought. *That is exactly what I would have done. But instead, I fucking abandoned her, right when she needed me the most.*

"Shit," Holden muttered. "You're right."

"I am quite often. Drives your father nuts," his godfather boasted. Holden couldn't help but smile and shake his head, knowing that his father was right there, probably giving Caulfield the finger in response.

"I gotta figure out how to fix this," Holden said, more to himself than his family on the other end of the phone.

"First things first, put your pants on, and get down there and inform her that you've removed your head from your ass and that you're sorry. That you love her and support her and you're gonna help her prove she didn't do this. Even if the bastard did have it coming."

"I'm already wearing pants, old man," he quipped, looking down at what he was wearing. Why his godfather would assume he wasn't wearing pants was beyond him, but now was not the moment to question it.

"Then you're one step ahead of the game."

28

GIGI

The creak from the rusty hinges on the jail cell door opening startled Gigi out of her half-asleep state. She had no idea what time it was or how long she'd been resting, but it seemed like forever and no time simultaneously. Sitting up on the little bed, she rubbed her eyes, trying to get her bearings. The small cell looked just like the ones did on TV—the only major difference being that there was a real door with a barred window rather than the stereotypical floor-to-ceiling bars. A single bed was built into the wall, complete with a plastic-covered mattress and lumpy pillow. There wasn't a built-in toilet either, since the cell wasn't built for long-term use, so Officer Nelligan had said she would need to alert one of them if she needed to use the restroom. Just what she needed, to ask permission to pee.

Looking up over at the doorway, she found Officer Nelligan leaning against the doorjamb, a satisfied smile on his face. She hadn't seen him smile all day, which had been rather disconcerting, since every other interaction she'd had with the man he'd always been grinning. He reminded her of so many of the guys she'd gone to college with, laid-back and affable, someone who was always fun to hang out with and never caused too much trouble. *Maybe if you'd married someone more like him, you wouldn't be sitting in this cell right now…*

"Well, Miss Gigi," he said, his slight southern accent sounding more pronounced than normal. "We got some good news for you."

"Is that so?" she asked, disbelieving. This day had been filled with nothing but bad news piled on more bad news. She was highly doubtful that there was anything *good* to be had right about now.

"Detective Ball just got off the phone with someone from the Georgia State Police, who have a Miss Myra Willis in custody."

"Who is she?"

"The woman who confessed to killing your husband," Officer Nelligan told her, a sly smile spreading across his lips.

"The what?" Gigi exclaimed, popping up off the bed. Her sudden movements shifted the plastic mattress enough that it was mostly hanging off the far edge of the bed. There was no way she heard him correctly. *The woman who confessed to killing Bradley? Oh Lord have mercy…*

"Yup. Detective Ball made the detective down in Georgia run through it a couple of times just to make sure, but this lady has confessed to the whole shebang. I missed a bunch of the details, and Detective Ball wasn't exactly in a sharing mood, but from what I heard, Miss Willis was also having some sort of um….relationship…with your husband and found out that he and Miss Hatchette had faked your death to collect the insurance money after you disappeared. They were also planning to fake his death for the same reason."

"So, if he faked his drowning, how did he end up actually dead?" Gigi asked, trying to follow along. She knew that Lake Lanier was considered the "deadliest lake in America" since it had more deaths than any other in the country, so a drowning there would be a plausible story. But Officer Nelligan said they *faked* it. So was he not dead?

"Well, that's where this gets interesting."

Interesting? We're long past "interesting," Gigi thought, though she didn't dare say it out loud.

"Turns out, Miss Willis was under the impression she was the only mistress in his life. When she found out about the plan to fake his death and that they planned to run away together, she flew into a jealous rage and poisoned them both. I didn't catch how she then got them into the lake, but with her confession, you're off the hook for his murder."

Two mistresses? Gigi's head spun as she tried to weave it all together. She sat back down on the bed, the metal platform cold even through the sweats she was still wearing. Slouching back against the wall, she drew her knees up to her chest, curling herself in a ball, and closed her eyes, trying to make it all make sense. But her thoughts were moving too fast with all this new information. *Just what kind of trashy daytime talk show nonsense had been going on in my life?*

How did all this get so out of control? Having her suspicions fully confirmed was one thing, but twice over? He was cheating with two other women? And didn't these women know what kind of man he was? Or did his temper not extend to them the way it had her? Part of her knew she shouldn't be surprised—Bradley had always been the charmer, hiding his true self from people.

Doesn't matter now, you're free of him, she reminded herself. Inhaling deeply, she let out a long sigh, thankful for small miracles. He was really gone, and it had nothing to do with her.

"So I'm free to go?" she asked, not bothering to look at him. She could hear the hope in the question, even though that was still the last thing she was feeling. If he said yes, where would she go? All her stuff was still back at the house, and she was certain she was persona non grata there right about now. Not that she would even have a way to get back to the house to get her stuff, anyway. The thought crossed her mind that she could call Hunnie and hope that the friendship they'd created was ready to weather something like this.

"Not quite. There is still the insurance fraud charge. They are still questioning the timeline of your death certificate, since it was dated so soon after you left. Wondering if faking your death for the money was part of your plan all along, even if you hadn't planned on killing your husband," he told her. Gigi shook her head, unable to believe what she was hearing. Did they really think her this conniving? Today just kept getting better and better. She really just needed it to end. "But you do have someone who wants to see you."

Gigi looked back over to Officer Nelligan in time to watch him step away from the door and be replaced by a tall, dark, bearded figure. His piercing blue eyes caught hers right away, but it was his muscular arms crossed in front of his strong chest that called to her the most. Her entire body cried out as she saw him appear in the doorframe, fighting the urge to run to him and lose herself in his embrace.

Holden.

29

HOLDEN

The sight of Gigi sitting on that metal bench, curled up like a frightened kitten, was like a punch to Holden's gut. His stomach lurched as he watched her swallow hard, taking him in, like she wasn't sure if she should reach for him or cower even more. Gone was the vibrant woman he'd come to know over the past few weeks. In her place was the reserved, apprehensive one who had moved into his carriage house. He hated himself for having a part in her transformation back to this state. This was not who she was, and seeing her like this hurt more than any lie ever could.

"Holden," Gigi said, her voice just above a whisper. The sound of it stole all the air from his lungs. She looked at him nervously, as if she still had no idea why he was here and what he was about to say. She doubted him—and after his reaction this morning, how could he blame her? His actions didn't reflect how he felt about her, and now they were both left facing the consequences.

"Gigi," he said, his own voice coming out rougher than he intended. Clearing his throat, he started again, wanting to make sure he got this right. "Gigi, I'm sorry."

"I didn't kill him," she sobbed, tears springing to her eyes.

"I know, I know," he said, rushing over to her. Kneeling down in front of her, he placed his hands on her hips and slid her toward him, until her feet were at the edge of the bench. The bench was low enough to the ground that with their difference in height they were almost face to face. He wanted nothing more than to wrap himself around her right now, but he had no idea how she'd react, so he settled for keeping his hands firmly on her hips, giving them a light squeeze to let her know he was there. "And not just because I talked to Detective Ball on my way in. I know deep down you didn't kill him. That you didn't do any of this. That there isn't a single part of you that could ever even think of doing this."

"I was going to tell you about Bradley, I promise. I didn't mean to lie, at least not for as long as I did. I…I just needed to get away. And it seemed easier to tell people he was dead. I thought that people wouldn't ask questions that way. But then I met you…" she trailed off, her emotions overtaking her. Her body shook as she continued to cry, those gray eyes holding him captive.

He felt his heart squeeze as another wave of guilt washed over him. Caulfield's words rang through his mind again. *Would your reaction be the same?* Holden knew exactly what he should have done this morning, and now was the time to prove to Gigi that he was the man she deserved.

"Sweetheart, it's okay. I get it. You were trying to protect yourself. You didn't do anything wrong. I was wrong. I shouldn't have reacted the way that I did this morning. I should have defended you, made sure you knew you were safe with me."

"But you were right! I should have told you! It's not that I don't trust you, because I do. I trust you more than anyone else in the world."

"I know you do, sweetheart," he said, pulling her closer so their foreheads touched. As much as he loved hearing her tell him that she trusted him, he needed to find the words to tell her he felt the same and to apologize for not being that man when the moment came. "But I failed you. When the time came to be the man you need, the man you deserve, I wasn't there. At least not in the way I should have been. You've spent so long being told you're not important and that you're not a priority. But none of that is true. You are important, and smart...and you are a priority. You're *my* priority. All of you. Your safety, your happiness, and that wonderful mind of yours that keeps coming up with all these new ideas. I am so sorry that I didn't do what I should have."

"Holden," she choked out.

"I can't tell you how many times I thought to myself that it was a good thing that Bradley was dead, because if he'd been alive, I'd tear him limb from limb for what he did to you. For all those lies he told you. So maybe it was a good thing you didn't tell me, because then I'd be the one in this jail and not the least bit sorry about it."

Gigi let out a small giggle through her tears, and just that little bit made his insides come alive again. Taking that as his cue, he moved up onto the bench and hauled her into his lap. Pulling her as close as he could get her, he drew in a deep breath when she wrapped both her arms and legs around him, holding on tight. He squeezed her hard, not caring who might walk in and see them. Right now he only cared about making sure Gigi felt safe, secure, and most of all, loved.

"Gigi, you pulled me out of a darkness so consuming that I had resigned myself to never ever escaping. You helped inspire me and guide me back to my love of writing. You light up my life in ways I never could have imagined and that a few months ago I would have told you were impossible. You might have been running for your life, but you saved mine in the process."

Kissing her softly, Holden's insides lit up as she wiggled in his lap, returning his kiss. Their lips moved together in sync, tenderly expressing everything they were feeling. She felt so good in his arms, like this is where she belonged. It felt like it had been days since they touched, instead of just hours ago.

"Sweetheart, you waltzed right into my life, turned it upside down in all the best ways, and I don't know what I would do without you."

"Well, you wouldn't have had to renovate your carriage house, for one," she said, trying to make a joke.

"As far as I'm concerned, you setting the place on fire was one of the best things that could have ever happened to me. It was the catalyst I needed. It brought us together and set this whole beautiful story in motion," he told her, wanting to make sure she believed it. "You asked if you could borrow my muse, and I made a joke about not sharing, but that's not the real reason. Gigi, you are my muse."

"I am?" she asked, pulling back, a look of surprise covering her face.

"Yes, sweetheart, you are. You are the one who got the wheels turning in my head again. It started that day with the fire, but it continued every day after that with your smiles and your laughter. Your determination to learn new things and find your own way. Watching you be so hell-bent on figuring out your way around the kitchen was inspiring. Once you got going, you weren't going to give up, and I knew that in order to be worthy of you, I couldn't either."

"I love you, Holden."

"I love you, Gigi."

GIGI

Gigi tightened her arms around Holden's neck, nuzzling her face into his shoulder. She couldn't believe just how amazing his touch felt. Moments ago she'd been so sure that this was something she'd never feel again—that the only words she'd ever hear come from his mouth were words of anger. Now, hearing him tell her he loved her, still after all this, was music to her ears.

"I was going to tell you today. I didn't want it to be a secret any longer," she said, fighting back a new round of tears. "I want us to have a future together. I want to read by the fire together and listen to you laugh because I haven't seen some movie. I want to be the first person to read your books, and to travel with you as you tour the country so I can brag about what an amazing author you are. I want to force you to try all my new cupcake recipes and for you to have to lie to me to tell me they're wonderful even when they aren't. I want snow days and trips to the beach. We can skip Thanksgiving, but Christmases with your family are nonnegotiable."

"Pretty sure they feel the same way," he said with a laugh. "And we can figure out Thanksgiving. I think Hannah would want us to. Besides, we can't have our kids being those weirdos who don't celebrate Thanksgiving."

"You're still open to that?" she said, her heart racing at the thought. When she'd woken up this morning, she'd wanted nothing more than to start a family with him. But that was before everything had fallen down around them. To hear him even bring up the idea made her want to melt into him even more.

"Only if you are, sweetheart," he said, placing a soft kiss on her forehead. "Gigi, you are my world. I don't want you to ever doubt for a single second where I stand. I know that finding yourself and standing on your own two feet is important to you, especially after everything you've been through. But I need you to know that I will be by your side, no matter what. Marriage, kids, your own bakery, whatever crazy idea pops into your head, I'm here for it. We're in this together."

Gigi let out a long breath, trying not to start crying again. Only Holden would have the perfect words ready and waiting for her. He was everything she had always hoped for and so much more.

"As long as I'm with you, then I'll have everything I ever need, Holden."

"I like the sound of that, sweetheart."

They were silent for a moment, letting everything they'd just said soak in. Bradley was dead and gone from her life, and she was free to do whatever she wanted. And what she wanted was a life with Holden, here in Vermont. Colebury had become home these last few months, and she hated the idea of leaving. She loved the idea of opening her own bakery, a space of her own where she could experiment with all sorts of different flavors and ideas. She loved that idea almost as much as she loved the idea of a family with Holden.

"I kinda need to get out of jail first though..." she said, hating to bring back the weight of the situation. "They know I didn't kill him, but I guess whether I faked my death is still questionable."

"I already have the officers working on your bail. It should be posted here shortly."

"Holden, I can't let you do that! I'll pay you back. I have the money from my trust fund."

"Nope. It's not up for discussion. It's the least I could do after I failed you this morning. You're also not touching that money until we prove that you had nothing to do with the insurance fraud."

"We?"

"Yes, we. I told you, we're in this together. I am going to help you fight this and prove your innocence every step of the way. I called Rita Kaplan on my way over and—"

"Who?"

"Rita. The intense brunette who won't let anyone else sit on the peach couch at the Busy Bean. She's a lawyer and business partner with May Shipley, who is Audrey's and Zara's sister-in-law. She agreed to help us with whatever you need. She said she has a huge network, so we can ask her to help find a lawyer who specializes in fraud. I don't want to step on your toes, so if you want to do this on your own, just let me know. It's your battle and I'll respect that. But you don't have to do anything all by yourself ever again, Gigi, if you don't want."

Gigi's insides went to mush all over again, hearing him tell her this. He called her a lawyer. He was prepared to fight this with her, without a second thought. She had no idea what she had done to deserve him, but she wasn't going to argue or take it for granted for another second. He was her future, and she was going to enjoy every last little bit of it.

"I love you so much, Holden."

"I love you too, sweetheart. You have no idea."

He captured her lips in his, his kiss just as tender as before. She moaned softly, letting him know just how much she loved this too. She wasn't sure she would ever get enough of him or his touch.

"Ah-hem," Officer Nelligan cleared his throat. Gigi and Holden parted just enough to turn to look at him, standing back in the door frame. "Sorry to, uh, interrupt. But you're free to go now, Miss Gigi."

"Thank you, Officer Nelligan," she said sweetly, watching as he swiftly dipped away from them. Turning back to Holden, she let a large smile take over as she looked at his piercing blue eyes. *I could gladly get lost in these for the rest of my life…*

"Sweetheart, I think it's time we got you home. Because as sexy as you look in my sweats—"

"Even in jail?"

"Even in jail," he continued. "You look even sexier *out* of them. And after the day you've had, I think you deserve to be shown exactly how much I love you."

EPILOGUE

Five months later

GIGI

Gigi stood inside the old Crumbs bakery, taking it all in. The place was dusty and needed a fresh coat of paint, but that didn't stop the excitement from rushing through her veins. This place was hers.

The last couple of months had been a whirlwind, but standing here now, she felt like she could finally breathe again. Rita Kaplan had hooked her up with a fraud lawyer out of Montpelier that she had graduated law school with. He wasted no time in proving that Gigi had no part in obtaining the false death certificate. Gigi had no idea how he'd done it from a small office in northern Vermont, but he had managed to hunt down the person who had forged the document and gotten their statement that it was Ayla Hatchette who had requested it, as well as additional testimony about her and Bradley's behavior immediately after Gigi had taken off. Within two weeks, the police had dropped the charges against her altogether.

As far as Gigi was concerned, Rita had just earned herself free cupcakes for the rest of her life.

Since Bradley hadn't gotten to updating his will before his second mistress had taken matters into her own hands, everything officially belonged to Gigi. Not that she wanted most of it. Forgetting him and the life they'd had together was much more of a priority than figuring out what to do with his clothes. While her own parents had made it known that they were not happy with her choice to run away and were less happy with her choice to not return to Atlanta, their opinion was greatly overshadowed by the scandal as a whole. Bradley's antics had made the local papers, and Shaw Investments now had some major cleanup on its hands. Bradley's parents, who had been incredibly ashamed when the news came out about his extramarital activities, were a lot more accepting of her choice to distance herself from it all and had told her that they would see to cleaning out the house and getting it on the market.

"Hey, hey!" Hunnie's voice called out as she walked into the empty storefront.

"Welcome to Oh, For Heaven's Cakes!" Gigi exclaimed, opening her arms wide, gushing slightly.

"Your very own cake shop! Who would have thought?"

"Not me, that's for sure. Never in my wildest dreams, but I can't tell you how excited I am to get this place cleaned up and open."

"You're really only going to sell cakes?"

"Yup! Maybe a few other desserts here and there, but I'm not really interested in doing anything more. Roderick tried to show me bread, and well, that's just not as fun. You have to deal with that starter and feed it, and that's just not for me," she said. "I'll still make the Dark Horse Mochaccino cupcakes for the Busy Bean as their exclusive item, plus whatever other flavors Zara and Audrey want. Oh, and I still have to call that guy from GoldBelly back."

"Is that the mail order thingy?"

"Yup. It's an online store that finds specialty items from local shops and then facilitates orders nationally. I'm not really sure how the whole thing works behind the scenes, but the idea of them wanting to ship my cupcakes across the country just baffles me!"

"That is seriously cool! And, that right there is more than enough to keep you busy. Will this place be open before you head back to Atlanta?"

"I think so. Holden doesn't think it'll take more than a week to clean and all that. I leave three weeks from tomorrow to finalize the insurance paperwork and all that there, and then move the few things I want to keep from the house up here," she explained. She left out the part that she hoped the townhouse will have sold by then so that she could take care of it all at once, not wanting to have to think about it. Today was a happy day. "So, my hope is we'll do some kind of soft opening and then hold a big to-do grand opening once I'm back."

"Gotcha. Well, I have to run, but I was asked to deliver this," Hunnie said, with another waggle of her eyebrows. She held out a teal envelope that had her name scrawled across the front. Gigi took it from her friend, who curtsied in response and then snuck out the door.

Opening it, Gigi had to catch her breath as she read the words on the card:

Today you are officially the owner of your very own cake shop, and I could not be more proud. Join me to celebrate where you first told me that this was a dream of yours. I'll be waiting…

I Love You, H

Gigi turned into the clearing off the driveway that led to the gazebo. As it came into view, she thought about that first night they had spent together out here and just how magical it was. She'd had feelings for Holden long before that night, but being curled up with him out here, watching the snow fall, that was when she first really started to *fall* for him. She could still feel the butterflies from the night as if it were yesterday. Some days, it felt like it had been yesterday, and others it felt like they'd lived six lifetimes since then.

She got out of her Jeep, thankful that it had lived this long, slamming the door behind her. As much as she wanted to bring her BMW back with her from Atlanta, she wasn't sure how the little convertible would do in the snow. She might need to start thinking about trading that in.

The gazebo was filled with candles, flames flickering in the spring breeze. She looked around, trying to find Holden, but he didn't seem to be around. *Maybe he had to go grab something,* she thought, until she turned around and saw a folded-up piece of paper, labeled "Read Me Out Loud."

Curious, she picked up the paper and did as instructed.

"Once upon a time, in a land very far north, there was a beautiful princess. Now, this princess was not only beautiful on the outside, but on the inside as well. She was smart, and funny, and always saw the best in everyone. When she arrived in this new land very far north, she knew no one. But that didn't stop her. Then one day, she met a grumpy troll. While this troll lived in a nice Victorian home, rather than under a bridge, he was still very grouchy," she read, letting out a little laugh. She had no idea where Holden was going with this, but she loved it.

"The princess didn't seem to care that he was grouchy, though, and agreed to move into his house. There was a small accident where she almost burned down part of the house, but it has been agreed that that part of the story goes unmentioned. So there they were—he was grumpy, and she was beautiful and full of sunshine. One time, when the princess tried to do something nice for the troll, he lost his shit. But thankfully she forgave him. The two even became friends over time. Then more than friends. Bright and early one morning it was discovered that the beautiful princess was actually running away from a horrible beast, so the troll had to rescue her. He messed up his rescue a bit, but being the amazing woman she is, the princess forgave him for that too." Gigi could feel the tears streaming down her cheeks as she read. He'd turned their story into a fairy tale. Well, sort of. He left out a lot of the details, and he was being a little harsh on himself, but she swooned anyway, thinking of the time this all had taken him. Sucking in a deep breath, she continued to read. "Despite it all, the princess still loved the troll. And the troll loved the princess. So now, he just has one more thing to do."

Following the little arrow at the bottom of the page, Gigi flipped over the page, expecting to find more, but all that was written there was a simple instruction.

Turn around, sweetheart…

HOLDEN

Holden watched as Gigi spun around, a loud gasp escaping as she took him in, down on one knee. Her hand flew to cover her mouth, the tears that had started while she read his story flowing even more freely now.

"I'm not sure that there is anything I can say that I haven't already told you. When you walked into my life, you stopped my world and spun it backwards, Gigi. You have made me feel things I never thought I would feel again. Hell, you made me feel again, period. I'd say that I don't know where I would be without you, but that would be a lie. I'd still be that grumpy troll, grouching his way through life. Instead, I kneel here before you, hoping that you're willing to see the prince deep inside me and do me the honor of being mine forever. GeorgiaGrace Elyse Shaw Hawthorne, will you marry me?"

"Yes!" she screamed, launching herself at him. He managed to catch her just enough so that she didn't knock the two of them to the ground, laughing at her reaction. Once they were both sitting down, he took the sapphire ring out of the box and slipped it on her hand. She looked down at it and then looked back up at him, her gray eyes so full of love Holden thought he might burst right there. "It's beautiful."

"Almost as beautiful as you," he said, still taking in her reaction. "It was my Aunt Viv's. Caulfield picked it out at an antique jeweler in college. He said he wanted to get her something as unique as she was."

"This is…" Gigi trailed off. He could see the thoughts rushing through her head as she took it all in.

"It is. He gave it to me back on Christmas and told me he would be honored to keep it in the family and to have you wear it."

"You've had this since Christmas?"

"I have. And one would think having it that long, I could have written a better story, but alas, it was a last-minute addition."

"I love the story. I'm going to frame it and put it up in Oh, For Heaven's Cakes," she said teasingly. He laughed, pulling her in for a kiss. Her sense of humor was just one of the things he adored about her. Sitting here now, he knew he was the luckiest man on earth. "You keep writing stories like that, and you'll be a best seller in no time."

"The only story that matters is the one where I get to live happily ever after with you, sweetheart. I love you more than words can say, Gigi."

"I love you too, Holden. I thought I knew what love was before, but I was wrong. You prove to me every day what it really is, and I don't know what I would do without you. I can't wait to be Mrs. Holden St. James, and to tackle whatever else life throws at us. Together."

"As long as I have you by my side, Gigi, nothing else matters. We've already proven we can handle pretty much anything, so from here on out, everything else will be a cakewalk."

THE
END

ACKNOWLEDGMENTS

Brad – I always said I'd name a character after you. I'm only *slightly* sorry he was the bad guy...

A&B – for everything. Seriously...everything...

KKSB – how did I author before y'all?

Allie – the "I smell you" story has long been a favorite. Thank you for letting me immortalize N by using it. Maybe someday we'll let him know he's "famous"

Rachel - for not only letting me steal Hunnie, but for your friendship and encouragement as we navigated this project

Raewyn – thank you for going to culinary school and becoming a professional pastry chef, all so you could teach me how to (fictionally) start a kitchen fire

Fire Station 15 – for being really, *really* understanding when I called to ask about lighting things on fire and then extinguishing them

Lisa – the best #bookbestie ever, thank you for believing in me, even when I don't always believe in myself

All the other authors in the World of True North, especially the other Busy Beaners –I have loved getting to know and work with each and every one of you. The love, generosity, and support of this group has been incredible

Jane, Jenn, and Natasha – for putting up with all my neediness

Sarina – for taking a chance on me and letting me get to play in the True North world. It's been an honor

And as always, Drew and Denali, for their unending, unwavering, unequivocal support in *everything*. Thank you for loving my particular brand of crazy. *Ik hou van jou.*